SID SANFORD LIVES!

By Daniel Ford

SEPTEMBER SKY PRESS

50/50 Press, LLC
PO Box 197
1590 Route 146
Rexford, NY 12148

http://www.5050press.com

ISBN-13: 978-1-947048-03-4
ISBN-10: 1-947048-03-1
Library of Congress Control Number
LCCN: 2017944827

Edited by: Stephen Hall III
Cover Design: Jonathan Lee

Printed in the U.S.A.   First Edition, June 2017

Sid Sanford Lives!

For my mother

Daniel Ford

PROLOGUE : GRAND CENTRAL

As always, Sid Sanford was following some plan, just not his own.

He debated whether or not to jump the ticket line in Grand Central like a prick. He finally picked up his duffel bag and darted in front of two male tourists who were already sipping out of tall boys disguised in paper bags.

"What the hell, dude?" One of them asked.

"Take me two seconds," Sid said, already striking the touch screen.

"There's a goddamn line back there," the other said.

"I see it, I was just there. And now I'm here. The less we talk, the more I can focus on getting out of your way."

Sid ignored the other comments from the rest of the pissed off rush hour commuters and eagerly slid his debit card into the black prongs.

Unable to read card, the screen flashed. Please swipe again.

He impatiently obliged and started tapping his foot as if he were trapped in a meeting while in dire need of ridding himself of his morning coffee.

The transaction timed out.

"Son of a bitch," Sid said.

"Serves you right," a woman in an ill-fitting pantsuit said. "Your mother should have taught you better manners."

"Who do you think taught me 'son of a bitch'?" He mumbled.

The machine finally read his card. He grabbed his ticket and bolted toward track twenty-six. He sprinted across the station's opulent waiting area, his worn brown shoes desperately gripping the slick, polished marble floor. He hustled through the gate and could see the train's conductor signaling the final boarding call to the people on the platform. He slowed and power walked the final few feet. The doors snapped shut as soon as he stepped into the train bound for Waterbury.

Sid took a moment to savor the mundane victory and then found an open aisle seat. He tossed his bag onto the narrow rack above his head after pulling out his laptop and headphones. He put his ticket in the slot on the headrest in front of him and settled into the bruised maroon and dull blue plastic seats. He opened up his computer, found a decent playlist to zone out to, and closed his eyes.

His phone vibrated in his pocket.

"Shit," Sid said.

He looked down to find Constance's name scrawling across the screen.

"Son of a—" He stopped himself when he caught a glance of the elderly woman sitting next to the window. "Sorry."

The woman shrugged.

He dug his phone out and took a breath before answering it.

"Make it?" Constance asked.

"Yeah, on the train now."

"Good. Have a safe trip."

"Thanks. And thanks for checking up on me."

"It's what I'm here for," she said. "Listen, I know we've had our differences lately...and well...since we've known each other. But I'm always here if you need anything. I know how you get with things like this. You shut down and won't let people in. That's not what you deserve right now."

"Yeah. Appreciate it. We're pulling out of the station. I'm going to sleep a bit."

"Don't miss your transfer."

"I won't."

"Let me know when you get there. I love you."

"Okay, bye."

Sid leaned his head back and tried his best to suppress a memory of Jocelyn. She had moved into an apartment not long ago and had asked for his help. He had gotten assigned a high school track event and couldn't make it. She assumed he was lying so he could spend time chasing after Constance. She wasn't completely wrong—he could

3

have easily caught a train out of the city after the meet—but he had fought with her all the same.

He ended up coming home after Constance broke up with him weeks later, armed with champagne and his mother's whoopie pies. He had another surprise for her—he couldn't remember what it is now—but instead of just handing it to her and winning back her friendship, he made her negotiate for it.

"Always the asshole," Sid muttered.

"Give me a hint," Jocelyn said.

"No," Sid said.

"Why not?"

"Because any hint I come up with will ruin the surprise."

"Really?"

"Really."

"You're probably right, men suck at giving hints."

"True."

"What if I told you that you couldn't have anymore?"

She covered the last few bits of his whoopie pie. Any other Sanford might have bitten her hand off, but he remained calm and defiant.

"I'd have to give it up."

"Are you serious, Sid?"

"Yep."

"You were just having an intimate moment with that thing a minute ago, and now you'd just let it go because you don't want to give me a little hint about my surprise?"

"Correct."

"Is there anything I can do to change your mind? More food perhaps?"

Yes, actually, he thought. Fall in love with me. Marry me. Tell me not to leave ever again. Just say you love me and I'll give you anything you want for the rest of my life.

"Nope," he said instead.

Sid wished he could tell her how much he loved her, how achingly beautiful she was.

But he didn't.

"I thought I was doing you a favor by procuring you some whoopie pies, and come to find out, you're lobbying my mother for them the whole time," Sid said.

"And she said I could come over anytime I wanted, so there," Jocelyn said. *"I really just need her to teach me how to make them."*

"At that point she'd disown me. I would be useless to her. Then she'd adopt you."

"See! Everybody wins!"

Later, he went to peck her on the cheek, but instead kissed her full on the lips. It lasted a heartbeat, but he poured more passion into it than any other kiss he could remember.

"What was that for?" She asked.

I love you, he didn't say.

"I'm proud of you," Sid actually said.

5

"For what?"

"Just everything. If you ever want company again, just let me know."

"I will."

"I'd walk through fire to get back here to you."

Sid coughed, urging the tears to wait until he landed in the passenger seat of his father's car. The train pulled out of the underground tunnel and the brick and grime of Harlem appeared in the window.

He put his headphones on and turned on Neil Young's "Cowgirl in the Sand." He tapped the keyboard for a moment, unwilling to allow his urge to start Jocelyn's eulogy to overpower him. However, it did in short order so he created a blank document and wrote,

"I met Jocelyn during a backyard Wiffle ball game."

PART ONE

Daniel Ford

Pastime

The man yawned.

He stretched out his arthritic fingers and gripped the steering wheel.

"Almost home," Kenneth Sanford said out loud.

The radio shouted at him. The talk show host was angry and letting his listeners know it.

He could usually put up with the back and forth between the right and left wing, but not today. He changed the setting to play a random CD. It didn't take long to recognize Neil Young's voice.

"Hello cowgirl in the sand," Kenneth sang. "Is this place at your command?"

He turned the car off the main drag and onto a side street. He waved to his elderly neighbors who were pulling up weeds in their yard as he pulled into his driveway. He only had two things on his mind now as he turned off his car: his boys and his wife.

He reached for the mug he had discarded on the floor. He decided he was too lazy to reach into the back seat and collect the tie he tossed there at the end of the day. It could wait until tomorrow morning when he needed it again.

Kenneth had barely walked in the door when he heard his wife yell,

"You're cooking burgers on the grill, get moving!"

"Sounds good, Gail," he said. "I'm just going to change first."

He walked into the kitchen, needing his wife's love no matter how abrupt it might be.

"Have a good day?" She asked, kissing him on the lips while pulling the mayo out of the fridge at the same time.

"Not exactly. But it's over now and that's all that matters."

Kenneth pulled her close and put his head on her shoulder.

"Okay, you can love me later," Gail said. "We need to feed these kids."

"But I want to love you now."

"Hurry up!"

Kenneth plodded upstairs to their bedroom. He gripped the railing to give some extra support to his creaky knees. He unbuttoned his white shirt with his free hand. He reached the top landing and felt the ache of work dissipate.

He parked his ass on the edge of his bed and kicked off his clunky black shoes. He tore off the rest of his monotone uniform and stretched out his aching legs. He stepped out of his falling pants as he headed toward his dresser. He caught himself in the mirror after tossing his wallet and keys into his top drawer.

"Holy shit, Sanford," he said, flattening his middle-aged gut.

An angry customer's voice echoed inside his tired mind.

"This circular clearly states..." the high-strung woman said.

"Ma'am, I know what it says," Kenneth said. "I help write it every week."

"Then you should know..."

"I know that I'm right and you're wrong. Feel free to bring it up with customer service."

"I did..."

"And what? Can't you see that I'm busy?"

"They said to tell you the ad is incorrect."

"Well, let me just put a bullet in my brain lady!" Kenneth yelled, dropping the yogurt containers he had piled on his arm.

"How dare you?!" She said as she walked away. "I hope you teach your kids to act better than this!"

Kenneth didn't hear anything about it from his managers, so she must have just left the store without trying to get him in further trouble. Things had never deteriorated that badly. He usually just rolled with whatever jabs the customers threw at him and did the best job he could. However, management's daily meeting revealed another restructuring, which meant he'd have to learn a whole new job on the fly without a pay raise.

"You're home now," he mumbled. "Let it go."

He rummaged through his dresser and pulled out the navy blue Yankees shirt his boys had given him last Father's Day. He put it on along with a pair of cargo shorts. After pulling on a pair of soft white socks and his sneakers, he felt more human.

Thwack!

A white ball smacked the bedroom window, causing Kenneth to jump. He pushed the curtains back. He watched Sid running around the bases while his youngest raced after the ball.

In the kitchen, Gail paused.

She didn't know where to start.

Focus, she thought.

She first filled her soda cup, which her men teased her about, calling it her "bubba." She was particular about it, yes, preferring to fill it all the way up with ice first and then pour as much Diet Coke as the cup would allow. That way, she had a perfectly chilled drink for hours, especially if she got sucked into a Lifetime movie and didn't feel like trudging back into the kitchen. She wouldn't let her husband or sons refill it for her no matter how many times they offered. They never got the combination right and she was left with either a watered down Diet Coke or a lukewarm one within the hour.

Gail tied her apron and dumped the pile of seasoned meat into her favorite mixing bowl. She squished the right mixture of spices into the pink chow and then formed perfect patties.

Ronnie Milsap's voice honky-tonked out of her radio.

"Woo!" She cheered.

Gail washed her hands and danced over to turn up the volume. Between the music and the Diet Coke, she got everything else done well before her husband returned. She sat at the kitchen table reading her romance paperback as he shuffled into the kitchen.

"Wow!" Kenneth said. "You make it so easy for me."

"Lord knows I have to," she said. "If I didn't, none of you Sanfords would be of any use to society."

"Ouch. Remember who's grilling your hamburgers."

He grabbed the tray with one shaky hand.

"Two hands," she said cringing.

"I've got it."

"No, you don't."

"I do too."

Kenneth tripped over his own feet and the tray slipped out of his hand, crashing back to the counter. Gail leapt up just in time to catch the patty that jumped ship.

"Told you that you didn't have it," Gail said.

"Jesus," he said. "Can't do anything right today."

"I still love you to pieces," she said, kissing his five o'clock shadow.

"Why don't you start up the grill, say hello to Sid and Patrick, and I'll send these out with Tom in a couple of minutes."

Kenneth nodded and opened the door to the back porch.

"Take your Sam with you!" Gail said.

The family's black Lab wormed his way out from under the kitchen table, nearly knocked her over, and bounded happily after his owner.

"Wait, I almost forgot something!" Gail said. "I made my man a drink!"

"Thanks," Kenneth said. "I could really use it."

"What happened that has you all discombobulated?" She asked, handing her husband a gin and tonic.

"Nothing, just one of those days."

"You sure?"

"Yes."

"You'd tell me, right?"

"Yes."

"Promise?"

"Promise."

"Okay, get to work," she said.

Gail didn't mean to worry so much, but she sensed a weariness haunting Kenneth the last few days. She didn't know how he dealt with all those customers every day. She had her own struggles dealing with patients at the doctor's office, but they were lambs compared to the grocery store's clientele.

Her mother had been a worrier, so Gail had vowed early in their marriage that she would never be like that. She tried her best to be as even-keeled as her husband, but it never quite worked out that way. It just didn't fit her personality. She had accepted that, to some degree, but it didn't mean she felt good about it.

Gail had some legitimate reasons for stressing as much as she did. Both her and her husband had suffered through one job after another that might have been fulfilling if it weren't for the people they worked under. Gail had found a doctor that not only realized her value, but also was as useless without her as the Sanford men were, but Kenneth hadn't been so lucky. He was one of the hardest workers she'd ever known, but he could never catch a break. There was always someone else who had all of the flash and got all the promotions, while Kenneth, all substance, got left behind. It wasn't in his nature to fight back, even when she urged him to rip people's heads off. He made her believe that he could withstand anything for their family.

However, that didn't stop Gail from wanting to scream some (okay, most) days. How long could they keep this up? How were they going to move beyond putting food on the table and clothes on their backs to putting their three brilliant kids through college? When was their bad luck finally going to get the best of them?

Before she went to get Tom, she looked out of the window and watched her two younger sons chasing after each other in the backyard. Someone had hit the Wiffle ball in Sam's direction and he gobbled it up. They chased him down and pulled the slimy ball out of his mouth. She smiled, knowing at some point she'd have to break them up after one or the other melted down over a silly argument. But for now, she felt as content as the dog, who collapsed in a happy heap next to her husband.

15

Dirt fell off Tom's baseball cleats.

His mother demanded he take them off before he ran across her clean kitchen floor, but he hadn't listened. He didn't have time to waste. The doublehcader had taken up the morning and afternoon, and he had an hour of school reading to do and an hour of personal reading to finish before the night was over.

He adjusted his glasses and tossed his purple hat with its yellow "J" on the front to the other side of the room. He brought his legs down from where he had them propped up on his desk and stretched them. He finally unlaced his spikes and let them fall to the floor, wiggling his toes as they became free. He decided to keep his baseball pants on because he had played well today and wanted to keep the feeling close to him for as long as possible. He quickly rearranged himself on his chair and found his place in the text.

"You're out!" Sid yelled outside.

"No I'm not!" Patrick yelled right back.

"I tagged you with the ball!"

"No you didn't!"

"Are you kidding me?!"

"No way, José!"

"You cheat!"

"*You* cheat!"

Tom really did want to be out there with his two idiot brothers, but being the oldest came with responsibilities. He had to set the best example. Besides, throwing that light white ball and swinging the thin yellow bat could have a damaging effect on his actual baseball skills. He also knew if he won, which he would, those two would cry about it for hours.

In his mind, Tom didn't have much choice but to stay on top of his work. Even if he hadn't overheard his parent's conversations, he would have been able to figure it out by reading their faces. Things were tight, which meant college or family trips were a distant dream that might as well be impossible. Tom wanted nothing more than to go to a good state university and play baseball, but he knew was going to have to get there himself.

He certainly didn't blame his parents for all the extra effort he was going to have to put into the classroom and on the baseball field to accomplish his goals. He didn't want anything handed to him. He'd see and mold the world on his terms.

Smack!

Tom heard the Wiffle ball bounce off his parent's bedroom window. He felt youth and ambivalence tugging him away from the English textbook in his lap. He shook the feeling off and continued to read.

"Crap," he said. "What kind of a word is that?"

He groaned and looked around for his dictionary. He found it on his bookcase, well out of reach. He bounded out of his chair and pulled the well-worn book off the shelf, finding the word he was looking for in no time.

"You're still in your baseball pants?" Gail asked, knocking on his half-opened door.

Tom shrugged.

"Well, at least get off the comforter I just washed!" She said.

"Sorry," he said.

"I need you to bring out the cheese for the burgers to your father in a couple of minutes," Gail said. "Plus, I think he could use another drink sooner than later."

"Sure," he said.

Tom marked his page and closed the book. Gail wrapped Tom in a big hug before he could escape.

"I'm proud of the way you pitched today. Your father can't wait to hear all about it," she said. "But I'm exhausted. It feels like I'm out there with you on every pitch! While you're out there, make sure those two don't kill each other. At least not before I have the chance to."

A sultry September ensured the midnight thunderstorm barely had time to slick the ground before being burned off by heat and humidity.

Ten-year-old Sid stood near home plate and admired his field preparation. He had raked the bare patches of earth that served as the pitcher's mound and home plate, hosed off all of the white plastic bases, and tucked a brand new Wiffle ball inside his younger brother's glove. All the begging he did throughout the day had yielded an inning and half of play so far. Sid had agreed to do the dishes for a month, but only if they actually finished a game.

He strutted to the plate. Normally reserved, Sid carried himself like a major leaguer on his makeshift diamond. He touched the top and the bottom of home plate with his bat and dug in his back foot. He gripped the thin club tightly in his hands and brought it to his shoulders. He barely felt the weight of his aging Yankee pinstriped t-shirt. It had become more of a second skin rather than a piece of clothing. The same could be said for his grass-stained jean shorts and white tube socks permanently stained brown.

Two ghost runners stood on first and second. He felt sweat dampen the back of his neck. He imagined hitting a homerun that would break the tie score. He tugged his hat right before Patrick delivered his pitch.

"Wait!" His younger brother said. "Time-out! I got to go to the bathroom!"

Patrick dropped the ball and raced into the house. The screen door creaked shut before Sid could react. He slammed his bat down hard, thinking of all the wasted negotiations he went through to get the Pop-Tart-eating, video game addict out here.

Sid knew his brother was going to take forever, so he started playing his own game. He crouched back into his stance, tossed the ball up, and launched it into the humid air. He slowly walked to retrieve the ball. The screen door swung open, but Sid didn't get his hopes up. Sure enough, Tom appeared as Sid walked to retrieve the ball. Sam thumped his long tail to greet the new presence.

"Where's Pop?" Tom asked.

"Went to get the mail," Sid said. "Where's Patrick?"

Tom shrugged, placing the tray of cheese down next to the grill.

"Keep an eye on these burgers until Pop gets back, okay?"

"Sure."

Sid stood alone in the backyard once more after his older brother retreated back into the house.

He hurried back to home plate. He threw the ball up again and smacked it. This hit didn't go nearly as far, but that didn't bother him.

"I can hit the ball farther than you!" A voice said.

Sid stopped short. He made eye contact with Sam who panted happily. Any other dog might have barked or at least nosed around a bit, but not Sam. He cocked his head to the side, more interested in Sid's father's return than a strange voice that had gone back into hiding.

Sid decided to hit a couple more because Patrick likely wasn't coming back before dinner. He leaned his weight back on his back leg, threw the ball in the air, took a step, transferred the weight to his front leg, and swung. The yellow bat cut through the sticky evening air, but missed. The ball fell to the ground unharmed.

"Ha!" The voice said. "You stink!"

"Come on!" Sid said. "Who is that?"

The neighborhood answered with stillness. Kenneth walked backed onto the deck and Sam sprang to life.

"What are you yelling about out here, partner?" Kenneth asked, pushing the Lab away lovingly and navigating his way to the grill.

"Some girl keeps making fun of the way I swing," Sid said. "She keeps hiding and I can't find her."

The elder Sanford adjusted his glasses and laughed.

"You might want to open your eyes the next time you look around, bubble butt," Kenneth said, pointing.

Behind the red fence, Jocelyn gulped fear.

She couldn't help herself. She had grown tired of obsessing over this boy. She had noticed him the first day at her new school. He stood in line with all the other fifth graders before they all filed into the building. She saw him in the cafeteria every day after that.

Jocelyn abhorred girly girls. She enjoyed sports, rough housing, and speaking out against all the boys that thought she couldn't play because she was a girl. All of her jeans were ripped and discolored. She got extra tough when her parents told her they were moving.

"We're leaving Pittsburgh?" Jocelyn asked.

"My company is relocating," her father said.

"Where?"

"Connecticut."

"What?!" Jocelyn asked. "They don't have a football team! Wait a minute, the Whalers just moved! They have squat!"

"I'm sure you'll find plenty of sports," her father said. "You'll also be closer to Fenway Park."

Jocelyn never figured out why he liked the Boston Red Sox over the hometown Pirates, but she didn't question falling in love with the team herself. She used to crawl into her father's lap as he listened to games on a transistor radio he had rewired.

"Are the boys stupid there too?" Jocelyn asked.

"The boys here aren't stupid," her father said. "That's not nice to say."

"Well, are they smelly?"

21

"Boys aren't smelly here either."

"I'm going to beat them up anyway."

"Please try to be nice."

"Only if they are nice to me."

"I'm sure they will be."

"As long as they let me play baseball, we'll get along."

Jocelyn tried to talk to Sid a few times, but always chickened out. She never thought to take a good hard look at the two boys who were always playing outside in the backyard next to hers. She admonished herself for being scared (she wasn't scared of anything!). She didn't have a whole lot of options now that Sid's father had spotted her. She adjusted her Red Sox hat so the brim rested just above her brown eyes. She flicked her blond ponytail to pump herself up and stood.

"We don't bite," Kenneth said. "You can come over!"

Jocelyn didn't hesitate. She leapt the short fence, which prompted Sam to finally investigate the new blood. She laughed and let the Lab jump up and lick her face.

"What's your name?" Sid asked.

The girl wiped her wet face then extended her hand. Sid reluctantly shook it.

"My name is Jocelyn. I'm ten-years-old, I'm going into the fifth grade, I have a dog named Cisgo, and I like to play baseball more than anything in the world," she said.

"Well, I'm Sid and that's my Pop. Can you pitch?" Sid asked.

"You call your dad Pop?"

"Yeah."

"Why?"

"I don't know. He likes it. Can you pitch?"

"I can probably do that better than you too!"

Sid fired the ball at her, trying to get it over her head, but she caught it easily. He tugged his hat, determined not to let this girl get the best of him.

"Wait!" Patrick said. "I want to play!"

The younger Sanford burst through the screen door and ran out into the yard, prompting Sid to roll his eyes.

"What's up little guy?" Jocelyn asked.

She gave the youngest Sanford a high-five. Sid flung his bat in frustration.

"This is my brother Patrick. Patrick, this is Jocelyn," Sid said. "She's a girl and she's from next door."

"Hi, Josh-e-Lyn," Patrick said, murdering the pronunciation of her name.

"You can just call me J," she said.

"Can we play or what?" Sid asked.

"Relax," Jocelyn said. "I'll make you a deal. If you hit the ball farther than me, I won't make fun of you anymore. But if you can't, I can play baseball with you two anytime I want."

"Yeah, sure, whatever," Sid said.

"Can I pitch? Can I pitch?" Patrick asked.

"I guess so," Sid said. "You can hit first, Jocelyn."

23

Patrick retrieved his abandoned glove and Jocelyn chose a bat. She blew a bubble with the gum she had tucked away in the corner of her mouth. Patrick wound up, just like Tom had taught him, and heaved the ball toward the plate. With no effort at all, she took a step forward and mashed the ball onto the roof of the porch.

"Wow! Nice hit," Kenneth said.

Even Sam lifted his snout to see where the ball had landed.

"All right Sanford, the potato salad is done, so we're waiting on you," she said poking her head out the door. She motioned for her boys and then went inside with Sam on her heels.

"Hurry up guys," Kenneth said. "Jocelyn, you're more than welcome to join us if you're hungry."

He went inside with the grab with Patrick close behind. Jocelyn tapped her foot on the mound and waited for Sid to get ready again.

"Let's get this over with so I can chow down," she said. "Winning makes me hungry."

Sid took his time. This was serious business. He focused all his attention on the ball in Jocelyn's hand. She reared back and threw. Sid rifled the bat through the strike zone. He made contact, but the ball dribbled only a few feet in front of him.

"Ugh!" he yelled, stomping his foot.

Jocelyn didn't laugh, but instead ran over and threw her arm around his shoulders.

"Can I ask you something?"

"As long as it's not another bet," Sid said.

"I just moved here and everything and I don't really know anyone. I was wondering if you wanted to be my best friend. I know you probably have like a million best friends at school, but what do you say?"

"Sure," he said.

Sid raised his hand to give her a high-five, but she pulled her hand away at the last minute and he fell forward. Jocelyn laughed as she raced into the house.

Sid didn't follow right away.

He had taken only a handful of swings that night and none of them had turned out the way he had expected. Sid strode back to the plate with renewed confidence. All of his failures up to this point were forgotten. He owned the game again.

He dug in his back foot. He waved his bat toward the pitcher's mound. He adjusted his cap one last time.

He tossed the ball into the air, waited a heartbeat, and swung.

GIRLS

Sid hopped on his car's hood and propped himself up against the windshield.

The park he had chosen to wallow in used to be a real gem. It had been a privilege to play on the baseball field's velvet green grass and players almost didn't want to step in the batter's box for fear of disturbing the well-manicured infield dirt.

However, the parks department grew more lackadaisical and underfunded as time passed. While the city pumped money into building new wings for the two high schools, this park became a haven for beer league softball players and mediocre club teams.

Sid had played for one of those club leagues while in middle school. He wasn't very good, of course, since he hadn't played Little League. Jocelyn hadn't beaten the shyness out of him in time for him to sign up. Sid regretted the confidence she finally drilled into him after nearly breaking his kneecap during Pony League tryouts. He completely missed a ball at first base (why he decided to

26

play an infield position is a mystery to all) and embarrassed his older brother by crumpling to the ground in tears. Tom was obligated to draft him anyway and both suffered through the embarrassment of Sid's short-lived baseball career.

Sid smirked, remembering his one and only stolen base.

Are you kidding me? He thought.

Sid sprinted toward second base. He could feel the dirt kicking up under his cleats and hitting the back of his legs. He heard the ball hit the catcher's mitt.

"Run, you slow bastard!" Jocelyn yelled from the stands.

The umpire barked a call he couldn't hear. Out of the corner of his eye, he saw the catcher heave the ball to the shortstop covering the bag. He accelerated again the best he could and then pushed his legs out from under him. His outstretched foot hit the white bag before the fielder swiped his glove across it.

"Safe!" The umpire bellowed.

He raised his hand up to call timeout. He stood and shook the brown earth off his gray baseball pants. He took his helmet off and wiped the sweat from his forehead. While the pitcher readied for his next pitch, Sid glared at Tom, who was cracking up along the first base line.

"The pitcher was in his windup, I had to send you," Tom said. "Your wheels still made it a close play."

He ran back to the bench when the inning was over and grabbed his glove without saying anything. Tom patted him on the back.

"Might want to grab the heart you left on the base paths on the way back to the outfield," Tom said. "Pretty sure we're going to need to call the paramedics for Mom and Dad."

"Thanks, Coach," Sid said. "Real inspiring."

Sid dropped a ball in the outfield during the next half inning and the season, and his career, ended a day later.

A few large raindrops splattered forcibly against the windshield. Sid did his best to protect the damp, unlit cigarette he had stuck on his lower lip.

"Uh oh. All aboard the trite, self-loathing train. Woo! Woo!" A baseball hat with blond hair said, walking up next to his car.

"I like the wrong girls, Jocelyn," Sid said. "And the wrong girls like me."

"Women," she said.

"What?"

"Women. You said girls."

"Would you consider anyone I've been romantically involved with a woman?"

Jocelyn waved her hand across her body like she was a letter on "Wheel of Fortune."

"Fine," Sid said. "Women."

"Continue brooding," Jocelyn said.

"I mean, run down the list..."

"I don't need to hear the menu of disaster. I've lived it right along side you."

"Humor me."

"Do we have to do this in the rain?"

"Yes."

"Ugh. Are you going to start with Sarah?"

"Sure, why not! Let's begin with my first kiss."

"More of scheme than a kiss," Jocelyn said. "I could have stopped it. My bad."

"Yeah, a heads up would have been nice. One minute you're an eleven-year-old kid in a dark basement, being kissed by the neighborhood girl you've followed around since birth, and the next she's running up the stairs screaming."

"Your cousin swore me to secrecy. Girl's have a code too."

"Jesus, she said she was hypnotized and that's why she did it," Sid said. "Some kids would need therapy after that."

"Don't be so dramatic," Jocelyn said. "You loved every minute of it. Would you rather have not kissed her at all?"

"That's not the point," he said, rubbing the back of his head.

"It's a little bit the point."

"The beginning of a long line of 'women' I couldn't be with."

"Please, don't bring up..."

29

"Julie!" Sid said. "Ms. Popular! Friendly, fashionable, athletic. Dark olive everything: hair, eyes, skin."

"You're not going to start reciting couplets, are you?" Jocelyn asked.

"You never know. But she's the envy of every girl in high school, always has a boyfriend, and yet flirted with me all last year when I sat behind her in math class. She even wrote me notes!"

"Yeah, did you ever ask her out?"

"Come on."

"Then you don't actually know if she would have dated you or not."

"I guess not, but..."

"I would have gone for it. You had nothing to lose."

"Except dignity. Remember when I asked Tina to be my girlfriend in elementary school. She screamed in my face on the playground and ran away. Hmm, this screaming thing seems to be a trend."

"Why are you bringing all this up?" Jocelyn asked, hoping to avoid the rest of Sid's sad list.

"Rachel broke up with me."

"Really?"

Sid handed her the folded piece of paper in his pocket.

"Who writes a note?" Jocelyn asked.

"Better than nothing."

"Still, this is a tad impersonal."

"What does she care? She ended it."

"*I need time,*" Jocelyn read. "Time to do what? Peruse our yearbook over the summer for better options?"

"Go to Texas to visit her aunt for a week."

"Well, let's hope she gets abducted in a Golden Corral and is never found," Jocelyn said, handing Sid back his note.

"I drove with her mother to the airport yesterday morning," he said, shielding the damp notebook paper from the rain and folding it back along its worn creases.

"Are you shitting me, Sanford?"

Sid shrugged. Jocelyn tapped on the car's hood, signaling she wanted more details.

"Yup, quite the scene," Sid said. "I cried, her mother consoled me, Rachel was indifferent as she walked on the plane. I don't think she told her mother about the break up either, so I looked even stupider. Oh, and Rachel wants me to come pick her up when her flight gets in next week."

"You do that and we are no longer friends," Jocelyn said.

"We'll see."

"I was wrong."

"About what?"

"You might be a lost cause."

"Thanks."

"Why didn't you tell me about any of this?"

"You've been busy with Harry lately. I didn't want to bother you with this weepy shit."

"It's Brian, and you're more important. You're family."

31

"You sure it's not Harry?"

"I made out with Harry at a school dance years ago, which made you really jealous. Remember, you sat in the corner of the bleachers and sulked all night?"

"I just realized these are the kinds of conversations people have right before they kill themselves."

"Sid!"

"I'm just saying…when do we get to the uplifting part?"

"I'm afraid to ask what you did instead of reaching out to me yesterday."

"Drank."

"What?!"

"Couple of shots of gin. Few warm wine coolers. Stuff my parents had in their liquor cabinet."

"Alone?"

"Yep."

"Your parents didn't notice you were doing shooters and pounding Seagram's Escapes like a hillbilly housewife?"

"Jocelyn, my parents go to bed at 9:30. Doesn't take much to outlast them."

"Your father might figure it out the next time he makes a gin and tonic," Jocelyn said. "You're a freakin' idiot when you're heartbroken."

"Yeah, who isn't?"

"Sid, we're seventeen years old and in a month we'll be seniors in high school. This crap isn't going to mean a damn thing in a few years."

"Well, as much as I'd like to be future Sid right now, I'm not. So it still matters to me. And it hurts like hell."

"That's because you open up your heart to every girl that shows interest in you, and you make up things you have in common to justify your decision. You know they are wrong for you every time. Rachel was a bitch."

"How do you explain the girls that didn't want anything to—?"

"Stop," Jocelyn interrupted. "All the fighting you did for those girls was just as bad. What do you think would have happened if you had landed one of the 'loves of your life?' Do you really think it would have been any different?"

Sid knew she was right in some way, but just wanted to be still. He glared at her with hurt eyes.

"I only say these things because I love you," she said. "Don't ever do something stupid because of these girls. I'd be lost without my best friend."

"You know I was just thinking about my stolen base," he said, trying to change the subject.

"Oh yeah? I'd bet you money that was the slowest sprint in recorded history."

"Yeah, yeah," Sid said. "One more than you ever had."

"Not my fault the league wouldn't let girls play. I'm still pissed about that. You get to strikeout fifteen times in seventeen at-bats, and I don't even get to try."

"Thank you for remembering that stat. Would you like to recite my lifetime average for shits and giggles?"

"Now that you mention it..."

"Nope," Sid said holding up his hand. "I don't think my broken heart could handle it."

33

"Wuss," Jocelyn said. "You know what memory I associate with this park?"

"No, but I have a feeling you're going to tell me."

Jocelyn found Sid sitting at the end of the aluminum bench.

"Could you at least take the Red Sox hat off before you say whatever you're going to say?" He asked.

"Not a chance," she said. "You okay?"

"What do you think?"

He shrugged off the hand she had placed on his shoulder. He grabbed his glove and packed up his bat bag. Sid walked toward his parent's car without looking back.

However, only Jocelyn's car remained in the parking lot.

"Shit," he muttered.

"Yeah, I told your parents I'd give you a lift," Jocelyn said, knocking his hat off his head.

Sid crossed his arms.

"Sorry," he said.

"Are you done being an ass?"

"For the moment."

"Good."

She forced his arms open and hugged him. Sid buried his face in her shoulder. She put her hand on his head and rocked him back and forth for a minute.

"Come on, silly," Jocelyn said. "I think it's my turn to treat you to diner food."

Sid pulled away and took her hand.

"Would it have killed you to swing, by the way?" She asked.

"Shut up, Jocelyn."

Sid tossed the ruined cigarette away after Jocelyn finished talking.

"So what happens now?" He asked.

"Let's go fill you up with some bacon and eggs at Riverside Diner," she said.

"I'm game. You realize food solves most of our problems? That's going to catch up with us some day."

"Pft, speak for yourself. I'm a hell of an athlete. Judging by your father's belly, you're screwed."

Sid laughed, but stopped suddenly.

"Wait, you don't come here alone do you?" He asked.

"What do you mean?"

"You were headed here before you knew where I was, right? I don't like the idea of you being by yourself in a slummy, abandoned park."

"This town is pretty white bread, buddy. But you are here. I'm sure that you'd protect me if some deranged hobo barged out of the woods and held a knife to my throat."

"Not after you just told me I'm going to get fat."

"Your heart wouldn't let anything happen to me," Jocelyn said. "You've got a good one, Sid. You just have to figure out how to use it better."

Sid watched her walk away. He slid off his car and opened his door dramatically, knowing Jocelyn was watching. He plopped into his seat and shoved the key into the ignition. Jocelyn drove past, allowing him to take a breath and find a decent radio station. He ended up turning the sound off, listening to the leftover rain. He felt for Rachel's soggy note in his front pocket and mentally re-read it. He grimaced as he rolled down the window and tossed it out.

Sid put the car into drive and hit the gas.

PHOTO ALBUM

Sporting a gut eighteen years less inflated, Kenneth paced his mother-in-law's small living room. He wiped his glasses with the bottom of his shirt and put the frames back on again. He watched the basketball game on television while pacing and stroking his moustache.

"Please Kenny, sit down and have some of this before you put a rut in my living room floor," Cecile Blanchette said.

Her French accent reassured him, but only to a point.

"I stood by her when Tom was born. I held her hand. I helped her with her breathing. She was scared," he said. "If I'm not with her tonight, I'll never forgive myself."

Snow fell in white clumps outside. He got the call that Gail was going into labor at work and raced out into the biggest blizzard to hit Connecticut in twenty-five years. He imagined Tom safe and sound at his Mémère's house, excited to welcome his brother to the family. Kenneth decided that if he was going to see his new son being born, so was Tom. Now they were both stuck.

37

"Daddy, am I really going to see him tonight?" Tom asked. "I have his stuffed animal all ready."

Tom stood in the doorway dressed in his winter parka and holding his gift that was ensconced in a plastic bag. His winter hat was pulled down past his eyebrows and his face wore a serious expression.

"Of course you are," Kenneth said. "Daddy is just waiting for Uncle Skip to come pick us up with his big truck."

"Is he coming soon?" Tom asked. "All I hear you say is 'soon,' I want 'now!'"

"He's on his way to save the day right 'now.' Take your jacket off. It's warm in here and I don't want you to get sick."

Tom held his head down and dragged the plastic bag on the floor behind him as he trudged back to his playroom.

A truck thundered up the steep driveway moments later. Its big headlights cut through the falling snow and illuminated the house. A heavy knock on the door raised the snowbound family's mood.

"Need a lift?" Skip asked, shaking off his wool hat.

"I do! I do!" Tom said, sprinting for the front door.

Cecile stopped him and wrestled his jacket back on. He allowed it, grunting as he pushed his arms through his sleeves.

"Mom, the weather's bad out there," Kenneth said. "Skip can come back and get you when it clears up."

"Kenny, I lived most of my life in upstate Maine, had eleven children, and helped a stubborn Frenchman run a potato farm," Cecile said. "When those words dropped out of your head, did you really think I would listen to them?"

"No."

"Good. Now get your head out of your ass and put on your coat. Make sure you button it all the way. It's freezing out there."

He had never heard his mother-in-law curse so he quickly did as he was told. He helped Cecile up into the truck and hopped in himself. Skip put the truck in gear and they started out into the snowy night.

At the hospital, a nurse fluffed Gail's pillow every so often, her doctor had nothing but kind words, and the staff allowed her to eat as many ice chips as she wanted.

She didn't give a shit. Two things remained out of her control at the moment: giving birth and killing her husband. Sure, the storm shut down most of the state, but she managed to get here without a whole lot of extra effort. Gail couldn't be too annoyed at the newest Sanford male until she held him in her arms, so she resolved to forgive him for lollygagging out of her uterus.

"Speaking of," she said, wincing.

"Did you say something?" The little pixie nurse asked, appearing out of nowhere.

"Talking to myself," Gail said. "You know a good divorce lawyer?"

"We get that a lot," the nurse said. "Are you comfortable?"

"No, but if you rearrange my pillows or feed me any more ice there's going to be a homicide," Gail said. "Would you mind checking to see if my husband is lost somewhere in these hallways?"

"Of course. The doctor will be back in a minute."

Gail's pain subsided. She vowed she would take it easy on Kenneth if he walked through the door right now.

"Hi, love," Kenneth said.

The little shit, Gail thought.

Kenneth stood at the edge of her bed looking tired, but with a twinkle in his brown eyes and an apologetic smile on his face.

"Where the hell have you been?" Gail asked. "Do you know how many hours I've been in labor? Did you get lost on the way here? Do you know I've been alone all this time? You better have a good reason for nearly missing the birth of your child! Speak!"

Kenneth tossed his jacket on a chair and kissed the top of his wife's head.

"You wouldn't believe the snow. Your brother-in-law rescued us from your mother's house. I should have came right here, but I didn't want Tom to miss it."

He grabbed her hand and held it tight.

"Okay, that's a good enough reason for now. I don't have time to properly admonish you anyway; I'm having another child. How is Tom?"

"Worried my parents will miss his little brother. I told him that everyone would be here as soon as they could."

"Good job."

"How are you feeling?"

"Do I really need to answer that?"

40

"I saw your doctor in the hallway. He said he'd be in soon."

As if on cue, the doctor walked through the door.

"How are you feeling?" He asked.

Kenneth sensed his wife was about to attack, so started talking before she did.

"It's a sore subject with her at the moment."

"Somebody is going to be sore by the end of this and it's sure as hell not going to be you two idiots," Gail said, visibly in pain.

The doctor peered under the bed sheet.

"I think your little man is ready to come out," he said. "He just wanted to wait for Dad."

Kenneth felt his wife's grip tighten. The doctor commanded her to start pushing.

After fifteen minutes, still no baby.

"Honey, can we switch hands?" Kenneth asked.

"Are you fucking kidding?" She started pushing again. Kenneth winced.

"I'm serious darling," he said. "My hand really hurts."

"It's not as bad as your head is going to hurt after this is over, so suck it up!"

Kenneth braced himself. Gail crushed his fingers together as she made her final push.

"Gail!"

"Shut up!"

"You're breaking my hand!"

41

"I told you to shut up!"

"Ahhhhhhh!"

In the waiting area, Tom swung his legs.

He felt like he had been waiting forever. He wanted his little brother now!

Tom stood up straight when he saw his father running in his direction with an ice pack on his right hand.

"You want to come see your new baby brother Sid?" Kenneth asked.

Tom pumped his fist in the air.

"So what do you want to do?" Sid asked in the present.

"Look at more pictures and hear more stories," Jocelyn said.

"Come on, seriously, you want to go see a movie?"

"Nah."

"Play a board game?"

"Nah."

"You want a hit in the head?"

"Sure," she said, balling up her fist.

Jocelyn jabbed Sid's shoulder.

"I have more questions," she said.

"Really?" Sid asked. "So unlike you."

"I'd take some notes on my interrogation techniques instead of mocking them," she said. "You're going to need them when you become a reporter in New York City. I can't believe I'm letting you go to that city alone. They might eat you alive, but it won't be my problem. Anyway, what is a Mémère?"

"Mémère is French for grandmother," He said, pointing to the picture on the next page. "That's her holding me."

Jocelyn absorbed every detail. Sid's Mémère had the biggest grin on her face even though Sid appeared to be screaming. She wore a white sweater over a pink dress and had pride leaking out of her patient eyes.

"She is your mother's mother?"

"Correct."

"And your mother's maiden name is Blanchette?"

"Correct."

Jocelyn turned the pages slowly. She couldn't help noticing that Sid was crying in just about every picture.

"Someone break your heart in the womb?" She asked.

"I ate my twin, I was in mourning."

"You are disgusting. I am ashamed I wasted these jeans on you."

"You're aware that I cried every day until I was...well...you know."

"Five minutes ago?"

"Right," Sid said.

"With all those tears, did you live up to all of Tom's expectations?" Jocelyn asked.

"I don't know. Ask him."

"Tom hasn't said three words to me since I've known him."

"Well, that's because he only knows one."

"He reads more than the editors of *The New York Times Review of Books*," Jocelyn said. "I'm pretty sure he knows all the words."

"What was your question?" Sid asked.

"Did Tom like you as much after the initial excitement wore off?"

"I think I annoyed him more than anything else once I started crawling around and stealing his toys. I used to dump out my entire toy box to get one at the bottom and leave Tom to clean up the mess. As soon as he'd finish and leave the room, I'd do it again. There's a picture of it somewhere in there."

Sure enough, Jocelyn found Sid's butt sticking out of his empty toy box. In the next photo, he smiled for the camera as Tom visibly sulked in the background.

"I can see where you developed your charm with the ladies" Jocelyn said, pointing to a picture of Sid on the floor in his diaper kissing a Cabbage Patch doll.

"Yeah, she was hot. Never called me back though. One night thing."

Jocelyn rolled her eyes and continued to scrutinize the pictures pasted in his baby album. Sid sighed right next to her ear, so she dumped the binder in his crotch and walked over to the living room shelf filled photos of his ancestors. She liked the picture of Sid's French uncles drunkenly playing poker the best. The men wore sloppy smiles and all their cards faced the wrong direction. His Mémère Cecil did not look as happy.

Sid pretended not to notice how well his best friend's figure filled out her new pair of jeans. There wasn't a trendy tear or Metallic patch to be seen. She bent over to retrieve one of the larger albums and Sid stopped pretending. He averted his his eyes as she made her way back to him.

"Show me more," she said.

Jocelyn had seen every picture and had heard every story twice over.

"No," Sid said, contorting his face.

"Come on, please?" Jocelyn asked. "It'll put you in the right frame of mind for your speech tomorrow."

"How exactly?"

"I don't know, it just will. We're not going to figure out anything better to do, and I'd rather do this than sit and stare at each other."

"Good point."

"I want to hear all about what your life was like before me."

"Again..."

"Yes, again," she said. "Maybe I'll learn something new. You say you're a storyteller, so impress me with your words."

"Can I impress you with other things?"

"Not a chance."

"Fair enough."

"I appreciate you checking me out though."

"I didn't check you out."

"Yes, you did."

45

"No, I didn't."

"I wrangled my curves into these damn jeans so you could adore my figure in them, so don't hurt my feelings," Jocelyn said. "Say you did."

"Fine, I did."

"Yeah you did! Good, commence memories."

Sid opened the next album. He ran his fingers over the fading stickers pressed to the back of the front cover, which documented his height and weight, his date of birth, and the name of the hospital.

"So cute!" Jocelyn said. She wrapped her arm around Sid's shoulders and inched in closer. "Look at that hair!"

In the picture, Sid was wrapped securely in a blue blanket with his hand balled into fists. He had a full head of dark hair that had been combed and parted perfectly.

"My mother likes to tease me by saying I came out fully prepared to hit on all the nurses," Sid said. "After crying my head off for two straight days, she didn't have anything to worry about."

"Trying to hit above your weight class even out of the womb. Classic," Jocelyn said. "What happened to your face in this one?"

A one-year-old Sid had a bandage over his left eyebrow and a cut on his right cheek.

"I had a little accident over my Mémère's house," he said, pushing one of Jocelyn's index fingers up against a tiny white scar on his forehead. "She used to cry whenever she saw these pictures."

"Story, please."

Young Sid found trouble as easily as he formed tears.

Cecile tried turning him around and at her clean living room's threshold, but her efforts failed each and every time. Before Sid, toys were forbidden, no one dared sit down before being directed to the proper seat, and food was certainly not allowed. Tom followed the rules and played with his "Masters of the Universe" and "Star Wars" action figures in the playroom down the hall.

Sid giggled his way past the rules, dropping toys in every room just in case he wandered in at some point. Much to everyone's surprise, Cecile let him get away with all of it. She told everyone that she was too old to walk down the hallway every five minutes to corral her grandson, but they all knew she just wanted to see what he'd do next. Cecile finally told Tom that he could play anywhere in the house now, but he had a routine that superseded his brother's evisceration of the old rules.

Cecile's valuables fell as often, and as hard, as Sid. His balance wasn't great yet, so he hung on to everything as he penguin-walked from room to room. When he drop to the floor, he'd cry until his Mémère came over to see what was wrong, and then he'd laugh and pull himself back up. Within a few weeks, Cecile's breakables had either been stored away or thrown in the garbage can.

Sid clung to her dress every day while she made lunch for her boys. He hadn't tripped her yet, but Gail warned her the day was coming. Cecile waved that off as nonsense and continued to spoil him.

On the day in question, Cecile formed chocolate lumps on a cookie sheet at the counter with Sid attached to her hip. She craned her neck to catch a few minutes of her favorite daytime soap opera while Sid babbled. He eventually got bored and wobbled across the room. He lost

47

his balance, grabbed onto the small television cart, which happened to be on wheels, and fell right on his diapered butt.

Cecile didn't have time to react. She heard Sid cry out before everything came crashing down on his head.

At the hospital, she couldn't stop crying, even after doctors assured her Sid would be fine.

She wiped her eyes again with her frayed tissue. She had forgotten her glasses atop her head, so the lobby appeared blurred and gray. She looked toward the emergency room doors, unable to erase the sound of Sid screaming.

Cecile hadn't been able to stop the bleeding at first. She tried to call her daughter, but her bloody hands shook while she dialed. Sid didn't stop crying in the emergency room until Gail walked in with Tom. The pout remained on his lips, but the sight of his older brother calmed him down.

The doors leading into the emergency room finally pushed open. Gail held Sid. Tom relieved his younger brother was okay, followed close behind. Cecile closed her eyes for a moment, said a quick prayer, and then quickly hurried to find out how much she had damaged her baby.

"He just needed a few stitches, Momma," Gail said. "He's going to be fine, really."

"I'll never forgive myself for this," Cecile said. "He just wondered off. I'm so sorry."

"Let's get out of here before we have to admit Mémère," Gail said. "Sid still loves his Mémère, right baby?"

Sid reached out for Cecile. He started getting cranky and squirmy. Cecile hesitated and then scooped him up in her arms. Sid laughed and bumped his head into her shoulder. Cecile angled him so he didn't hurt his cuts and bruises.

Sid grabbed her face and planted a wet open-mouthed kiss on her cheek.

"Are you crying?" Jocelyn asked.

"No," Sid said, wiping his cheek. "Leave me alone."

"Aw, you are! That is so sweet."

"Yeah, yeah. Can we do something else?"

"No way! Not when we're finally getting you in touch with your feelings."

"I don't know if you've noticed, but that's all I seem to do."

"Yeah, but at least it's about something real and not little pixies you shouldn't have been with in the first place."

"I also have a speech to practice…" Sid said, reaching for a sheaf of papers on the coffee table.

"You still won't let me read it?" Jocelyn asked, batting her long eyelashes.

"Nope. You'll be in the audience. I want you to react to it like you're hearing for the first time. And don't just say you like it because you're my best friend. I want you to be unmerciful in your criticism."

"Think I'll have a problem doing that?"

"Probably not."

"Right," Jocelyn said. "Okay, who is this?"

49

In the picture, a tall woman stood behind Sid in front of a brick school.

"Nursery school teacher. She loved me. I don't know why, I cried. A lot."

Sid didn't do well on first days of school. A true momma's boy, he had trouble letting go after spending a long summer with her. He wailed the first day of kindergarten, first grade, fifth grade, and so on. He had chased his mother's car in the school parking lot on a day he didn't want to go to school. He spent hours in the nurse's office feigning sickness.

"How come you never had any problems when we went to school together?" Jocelyn asked.

"It's because I had you to look forward to," Sid said.

"Smooth, Sanford," Jocelyn said, moving in to kiss him.

"Hey guys!" Patrick asked, bounding into the room. "Whatcha doing?"

He plopped down on the other couch next to Jocelyn, tore open a sleeve of crackers, and wasted no time stuffing his face. Sid wished he could have been mad at his younger brother, but he had gotten used to these missed opportunities.

"Ugh, Sid's pictures are so boring," Patrick said. "Why don't you come over here and look at a real man."

Patrick retrieved his album from the shelf. He returned to his seat and draped his arm around Jocelyn. He opened his album with care; most of the pages had been ripped out because of his constant need to admire himself. As a toddler, Patrick hounded Sid to look through it with him and make up stories and characters for each photograph.

Gail would find Patrick laughing hours later because he was still thinking about all the funny voices Sid acted out when telling his tall tales.

"You're right, you're way cuter than your brother was as a baby," Jocelyn said. "I think Sid knows it too judging by the look on his face."

In the legendary photo, Sid held Patrick for the first time with a huge scowl on his face. Everyone assumed he thought he was being replaced.

Sid cleared his throat. He loved trying to set the record straight.

"Are you feeling okay, Momma?" Five-year-old Sid asked.

His eyes peered over the edge of the bed. He felt relieved when she reached out and touched his cheek.

"I'm fine, love," Gail said. "Go meet who Pop is holding."

Sid's father held what appeared to be a pile of blue blankets.

"Come here, you two," Kenneth said. "Say hello to your new brother Patrick."

Tom gave Sid an encouraging nudge.

"Give him the stuffed animal you brought him," Tom said. "It's just like the one I gave you when you were born."

Sid nodded and walked toward his father. Kenneth stood up with Patrick and motioned Tom to sit down. Once the newborn was in his arms, Tom made all kinds of faces.

"Are you ready?" Kenneth asked.

Sid gulped, but signaled an affirmative.

51

Kenneth carefully placed Patrick on Sid's lap. He taught Sid just how to hold his brother so he didn't hurt the baby's neck. Sid's heart thumped while Kenneth reached for his camera.

"Wait, don't!" Gail said. "Look at the scowl that's on his face!"

Kenneth snapped a picture anyway.

Patrick made a noise, yawned, and opened his eyes. He stretched out his little arm toward Sid.

His father missed the smile that had replaced the scowl.

Gail's footsteps barely elicited a squeak out of the creaky steps. She held her Diet Pepsi can in one hand and videotape in the other. She had listened closely as Sid talked glowingly of his past. Her heart swelled every time he talked about his brothers and his Mémère. The memories had inspired her to unearth one of the last home movies the family had left. Kenneth had unknowingly used the rest to record "Live with Regis and Kathy Lee" for her.

"Jocelyn, do you want to see some of these memories in action?" Gail asked when she reached the living room.

"I sure do!" Jocelyn said, climbing over Sid.

He knew whatever was on that tape would be embarrassing. He was twice the ham on camera that he was off it. Sid and Patrick grimly followed the two into the study. Everyone got comfortable on the couch and Gail pressed play.

Snow appeared on the screen before snapping into focus. Kenneth, Patrick, and Sid waved to the camera.

"Good lord," Sid said. "This is worse than I thought."

"What...are you wearing?" Jocelyn asked.

Sid wore a purple Colorado Rockies t-shirt with the matching shorts, while Patrick had on a teal Florida Marlins outfit. Both brothers' shorts went up well above the knee and their tube socks were hiked up as far as they could go.

"I don't think I was dressing myself at that point," Sid said. "I'm pretty sure Momma Sanford is to blame for this."

"You were ten years old!" Gail said. "You threw a fit when I said I wasn't going to buy it for you and then you threw a fit when I wouldn't let you wear it two days in a row. That's all you!"

Sid hung his head.

The family had been visiting Gail's hometown of Frenchville, Maine. Tom hadn't gone because he was coaching a youth baseball tournament. It took all of Kenneth's will power not to cancel the trip so he could watch his son's team. Tom had tried to convince his father that it was okay without sounding too excited that he was going to have the house all to himself for a week.

Currently in the video, Gail was manning the camera, zooming in on her two sons throwing rocks into Long Lake, which was across the street from their hotel in St. Agatha's.

"Are you sure you can see me, Momma?" the young Patrick asked. He posed for her before he flung the rock in his hands. "I sure throw far!"

"Full of yourself even then," Sid said.

"With good reason, Purple People Eater," Patrick said. "That's easily a fifty-foot throw."

He beamed with pride and stuffed another Ritz cracker in his mouth.

The scene shifted. Gail could be seen at the far end of someone's kitchen. Pots gurgled on the stove. A woman stirred one while tying her apron.

"Tante Valeda," Gail said. "I didn't realize we had caught her on tape."

"I don't think she knows yet either," Sid said. "Hope Pop's not the director because she's going to be pissed."

Jocelyn watched the older woman navigate the small country kitchen. Her curly hair was perfect and her oversized glasses matched Sid's Mémère's pair. French sayings were stitched all over her green apron. Jocelyn couldn't understand anything the woman was saying to someone off camera, but she liked the way it sounded.

Finally, Valeda realized she was being filmed.

"Eh!" She said. She ran out of the shot. Gail stepped in the frame and motioned for her to come back.

"What did she say?" Sid asked. "Didn't sound friendly."

"'I'm not going over there until your husband shuts off that damn camera,'" his mother said. "She also mentions she recently sharpened her butcher's knife."

The screen went blank.

When the tape started again, Route 1, the town's main artery, appeared. A motorcycle drove closer and closer to the camera. Gail's cousin Ivan pulled into the driving as Kenneth squealed behind him.

"Do I have any hair left?" Kenneth asked.

"There's nothing wrong with your husband's lungs," Ivan said. "I had him screaming pretty good down the hill."

Everyone nearly fell off the couch they were laughing so hard. Kenneth shuffled into the room, looking confused.

"What's the matter?" Gail asked.

"I thought you were going to get us some ice cream," he said.

"I told you I was going to show Jocelyn this home movie and then I was going to get you a snack."

"Right." He adjusted his glasses. "I really wanted to know what I was missing. You're laughing at my expense aren't you?"

Jocelyn was the first one to lose it. Sid and Patrick's laughter followed close behind. Gail made room next to her and motioned her husband to sit down. She rewound the tape and pushed play. Kenneth's face reddened.

"That was a really steep hill!" He said. "I did look pretty good with that moustache though."

"Don't worry Pop," Sid said. "The next scene shows you walking up the road to retrieve it."

Kenneth ignored the remark and stroked his bare upper lip. Gail planted a kiss on his cheek.

"Honestly Kenneth, you are quite the trip," she said.

For the next half hour, most of the laughs were directed at Sid. There was footage of him in his Superman cape, playing the clarinet on Thanksgiving, and the Christmas morning Sid and Patrick received roller blades. It hadn't snowed that Christmas, so the two were able to try them out right away. Tom narrated as his two brothers played roller hockey. The game didn't last long. Patrick couldn't convince Sid to play in the street. Sid said it was against the rules. He fell flat on his ass moments later. Tom caught Sid pouting on his trip back into the house.

The last bit of film featured a family picnic. Kenneth was behind the camera this time and put everyone on the spot with random questions. At one point, he focused on Sam, the family's black Lab. His skin allergies had flared up and his fur was falling off in places.

"Sam, you look terrible," Kenneth said. "Who's a good boy? Are you a good boy? Are you a good Christmas dog? Who loves you?"

"You didn't know what Momma got us for Christmas, but you spent five minutes showering the dog with love and affection," Sid said. "Real nice. Feelin' the love, Pop."

Sam looked up at the camera, panting and wagging his tail.

"Poor Sam." Kenneth said. Sam had broken his leg on the back deck about a year ago and had to be put to sleep. There were still nights that Sid had trouble sleeping because his shedding, ninety-pound friend wasn't there.

The movie ended.

"Well, I'm going to feed the motorcycle man here and then go to bed," Gail said. "Sid, You should take Jocelyn home and call it a night."

Sid held out his hand to Jocelyn, but Patrick swooped and walked her to the front door.

"You remember that Robert Frost poem you used to read to me all the time?" Sid asked, now standing in Jocelyn's driveway. He leaned on his passenger side door while she kicked the gravel in front of her. "Something about a couple of roads in the woods?"

"Don't play dumb, you know the poem," she said. "You're the one who read it to me in an attempt to get in my pants."

"It would have worked too if I had landed the metaphor," Sid said. "Think I should use it tomorrow? Maybe I can embed it in my speech as a little acknowledgement of our friendship."

"I want that to stay between us. Some of your words need to be for my own personal use."

"Are there other things—?"

"Easy killer," she said. "We can flirt without your blunt, sexual invitations. A lady needs wooing occasionally."

"If I find a lady nearby, I'll be sure to woo the dress right off her."

"Your mother is right. You Sanford men are hopeless."

"She says that a lot, but she willingly married one," Sid said. "Got to make you wonder how reliable her information is."

"Seriously, do you think this will ever actually happen?"

"It won't if you stay all the way over there."

Sid took a step forward. Jocelyn met him halfway.

"You remember that night we sneaked out of our houses and drove to the beach?" Sid asked.

"We had just gotten our licenses," Jocelyn said. "We were grounded for weeks when our siblings sold us out."

57

"Right. Do you remember the sky? How it made love to the water as if there was nothing between the waves and the clouds?"

"Much better metaphor," Jocelyn said. "I wanted to tell you I loved you that night."

"Why didn't you?"

"You were dating a friend of mine."

"Minor detail."

"Sid."

"I know, I'm just kidding."

"What made you think of that?"

"Before when I was checking you out, I thought about you walking on the beach," he said. "Maybe we can relive that moment someday."

"You know what?"

"What?"

"There's going to come a time when I am going to want to forget all about you," Jocelyn said. "When I bury all of my feelings for you down so deep they'll vanish completely."

"But?" Sid asked.

"I don't think that's going to happen any time soon," she said. "Goodnight, Sid. I can't wait to hear your speech tomorrow."

Jocelyn stood in her front lawn long after Sid had driven away. Like always, she convinced herself there would be other opportunities. She finally hugged herself and walked inside.

"Ladies and gentlemen, good evening," Sid said the next night. "Baseball fans remember two things about a great baseball game; the beginning and the end. If you ask a fan who the starting pitcher was or who ended the game with a walk off homerun, you'll probably get an answer. Few fans remember the third baseman that came in the seventh for defense or the relief pitcher that laboriously tries to clean up the starter's mess. Beginnings and endings hold a very special place in our mind's eye and that is why we are here tonight. This class is here to end something. We are here to begin again."

Sid stood in front of more than 2,000 people, but appeared as calm and as confident as he'd ever been. The boy who always loved the spotlight had finally found a big one.

Jocelyn saw the fathers in attendance sit up straighter. Unlike most graduation speakers, Sid had everyone's attention.

"In 'Field of Dreams,' Kevin Costner's character mentions a moment when the universe opens itself up to new possibilities. This class has arrived at that moment. Tonight marks the turning of the page; tonight marks the end of an era. In this end, however, we find new beginnings. Some of us are off to the workplace, where we will strive hard to supply our families with a safe and happy life. Some of us are off to college, where we will continue to challenge ourselves and discover the pleasures of education.

"Whatever the case may be, this class is playing in a very different ball game. The world has become a darker place that has left all of us uncertain of ourselves and uncertain of what tomorrow might bring. However, in the ashes of tragedy and despair, the world is uniting to create new beginnings. This class is a part of that. We are the next answer to evil. We are now all citizens of Planet Earth, something bigger than any of us has ever known, and great change is on the horizon. My peers and I have to be ready to face this tremendous challenge. We begin our quest to make the world a better place for those who will come after us. We have the chore of reversing the decisions of negligent politicians who have been afraid of change. We are left to restore hope to a world now afraid of its own shadow.

Sid paused. He neared the end, but felt like he could talk to the crowd all night.

"Tonight, high school gets left behind," he said." There will be no study halls that last forever or endless excuses for forgotten homework. We are left with only the memories of first loves and horrible break-ups. We leave behind a piece of ourselves tonight. We leave behind the rebellious teenager to embrace the responsibilities of adulthood. Tonight, this class walks off the playing field, eager for the next season, the next at-bat. I realize now there are no endings. There are only beginnings. Endings are merely a place where we stop to catch our breath. My advice to my classmates is, take a breath. We have a long game ahead of us. Thank you."

Sid felt Jocelyn tugging at his arm.

They stood in the middle of the huge mass of humanity exiting the school. She pulled him in the opposite direction. Sid did his best to wade against the current. He found himself in a deserted hallway moments later.

"You're choosing now for this to happen?" He asked.

"Stop being you for a minute," Jocelyn said. "I wanted to tell you that I loved your speech. Each and every word. You certainly have a way with them."

"Thanks, but why..."

"I got you a graduation gift. It's not much, but I wanted to give it to you before you got any of your other gifts. Don't open it in front of me. You know I get embarrassed. Great job tonight, buddy. I'm proud of you."

Before Sid could respond, Jocelyn ran away. He opened the brightly colored package. He turned over the small blue photo album in his hands a few times before finding out what was inside.

The album contained pictures of Wiffle ball games, school trips, prom pictures, birthdays, Halloween costumes, and plenty of silly faces. Just Sid and Jocelyn.

Sid examined the crowd, but she was long gone. He tucked the album under his arm and walked back into the scrum.

NEW MORNING

A Metro North train lurched across the tracks headed toward Connecticut. Sid's stomach flip-flopped to mark the inches.

"Fuuuuck," he muttered as the train screeched around a turn.

His hangover didn't hit him full force until he boarded the train at Grand Central Station. He tried sitting in every position imaginable, but hadn't found a way to make the hard plastic seats bearable. Every one of his pores excreted last night's dive bar, cheap American beer, and 1980s music.

His stomach rumbled. He wasn't sure how well his system could digest a breakfast sandwich, but he was more than willing to find out. All of the Sanford men were meeting at a local restaurant later in the morning to kick off the weekend festivities, so all Sid had to do was survive the rest of the train ride.

His cell phone vibrated in his pocket.

If it hadn't been for Jocelyn's numerous text messages he might have forgotten to come home. He looked down and saw a flurry of emojis.

"Wonderful," he grimaced. "She's perky."

Jocelyn fiddled with the sticky tuning button on her car's radio.

She struggled with it for a few minutes and then settled for listening to Guns N' Roses' "Sweet Child of Mine" through the static. Her head bopped along to the music and she mouthed the lyrics. The song always reminded her of Sid. They had gone to a middle school dance together and he had made a complete fool of himself. She had to admit, he did shred a mean air guitar.

Most days, she didn't regret saying no to him before he left for school. She knew once he landed in New York City, he would be incapable of managing a relationship, especially a long distance one. He kept regaling her with watered down stories of his new life in the city thinking she was other people, but she knew his lifestyle would continue to rage until Sid decided he had to grow up. Jocelyn had faith despite the possibility this was as grown up as he was going to get. Sid usually found a way to tighten his head to his shoulders in his own time.

That was when she'd be in real trouble. Sid could take no for an answer, but not for long. If his heart got involved and he wanted it badly enough, he'd fight day and night. Jocelyn wouldn't be able to say no to him then. She couldn't imagine what that would be like.

She checked her face in the rearview mirror after hearing the dull, distant train whistle. She wasn't quite sure what she was looking for since she rarely cared about her appearance. She questioned her outfit and took off her Red Sox hat. She tossed it in the backseat, but then remembered Sid said he found her most attractive when she wore her ponytail hanging out of the back of a baseball cap. Jocelyn groaned as she stretched her arm around her seat to retrieve it. She crisscrossed the elastic she stored on her wrist around her tight ponytail and slid the lid back on just like he liked it. She felt ridiculous and special at the same time.

The train whistled again, closer this time.

Jocelyn turned up the radio and sang louder. She hadn't seen much of Sid in the flesh since he left for college. Jocelyn stayed up nights talking on the phone with him; reassuring both of them that whatever holes had been blown through their friendship were patched as if nothing had happened. She believed they were back on solid ground, but it wouldn't take her long to figure out if she was deluding herself.

She felt the excitement bubble back up through her system as the train pulled into the station. Jocelyn left all the doubt and indecision behind as she leapt out of the car.

"Jocelyn, I'd be careful," Sid said. "I drank a lot of Budweiser last night and washed it down with McDonald's."

She had him wrapped in a bear hug. Sid dropped his bag and did his best to hug back, but Jocelyn was using all her strength and he had left all his at the bar. He couldn't deny it felt great, like home.

"Sorry. It's just good to see you in one piece, rock star," Jocelyn said.

"The amount of trouble I get into is limited."

"Doesn't sound like Sid Sanford to me. Especially if he's thinking with his dick."

"I'd have a brassy response to that if I wasn't being forced to look at the top of your Red Sox hat. Let me go before I upchuck."

"Sounded like you drank more than a few Buds last night."

"Is it that obvious?"

"Well, yeah, but you also drunk-texted me all night."

"Esh."

"With pictures."

"Sorry."

"Don't be, it was the highlight of my night. I got a bunch of upvotes on Reddit."

"Yeah, yeah. Where's the Sanford male meet up."

"Riverside Diner," Jocelyn said.

"A classic haunt, nice," Sid said. "What are the hens doing to stay occupied?"

"If you're chauvinistically referring to your mother and I, then we're picking up our dresses. I don't know why we bother looking good for you when all you do is make fun of us."

"You better bring you're A-game because I don't want people to think a good looking specimen like myself picked up his date at the honky tonk."

"This from the guy on the wrong side of the freshman fifteen?"

Sid finally pulled himself out of Jocelyn's vice grip and dragged his heavy duffel bag to the car. He was searching for a better music station when Jocelyn settled back into the driver's seat.

"Did I mention it's always good to see you?" She asked.

Sid turned up the radio's volume as high as it could go.

"What did you say?" He asked.

"Jerk."

He returned the rock 'n' roll to a tolerable level.

"It's great to see you too," Sid said. "I missed you."

At the diner, Kenneth jotted an answer in his crossword puzzle.

He brought the newspaper back up to his eye level and then held it at arm's length. He tapped his pen up against his head as he murmured to himself with his mouth wide open.

"Pop, we're in public," Patrick said. He blew his straw wrapper at his father. "People are trying to eat."

"Quiet, bubble butt," Kenneth said. "Are you the one that likes that singer named Sam Something?"

"Smith?"

"Yeah, that's the one."

"No, I don't know this stuff."

"Really? I hear him on the radio a lot."

"That's great, Pop. I've still never heard his music."

"I forgot, you don't like anyone not named Bob Dylan. But you really don't know a Sam Smith song with...hang on...one, two, three...ten letters?"

"No."

"Are you sure?"

"Pop, how would I know the name of a song I've never listened to?"

"I don't know," Kenneth said. "Hey, lighten up, will ya?"

"You know what I'd like to know?" Patrick asked.

"What?"

"Where the hell my brothers are. I'm going to need muscle to dump your body."

Tom unplugged his iPod from his car lighter adaptor.

He placed it gently into the glove compartment and locked it. He checked to make sure he had put his cell phone into his pocket and then shut off the car. He put his car keys in his right jacket pocket and reopened the glove compartment to double-check he had turned off his iPod. Satisfied, he tossed it back in and finally got out of the car.

"Keys, wallet, cell phone..." he mumbled, tapping his pants.

Tom gave the inside of the car another once over and shut his door. He hit the lock button on his key chain a few times. He moved to the front of the car and tapped the button again. When the front lights flashed, he nodded happily and walked toward the restaurant.

He stopped suddenly and ran back to the car and made sure the doors had locked correctly. They had. He looked inside the car one more time, took a deep breath, and released the driver's side door handle.

"That was quite the display," Sid said. "Even for an abnormally anal bastard."

Tom jumped.

"Real funny." Tom gave his brother a playful shove. "I'm just making sure I didn't forget anything."

"Three times?"

"Yep."

The two brothers shook hands and slapped each other on the back.

"How's Kristen?" Sid asked.

"Good," Tom said.

"How's work?"

"Good."

"You're teaching fourth grade now right?"

"Yes."

"Do you like teaching the fourth grade?"

"Yes."

"Jesus, I didn't think my hangover could get any worse," Sid said. "Can we go inside without any more of this stimulating conversation? Patrick's probably close to killing Dad, so we should hurry."

Tom followed his brother after surveying his car's interior one more time.

"So after sitting in traffic for a solid three hours taking me back to UNH, we're finally coming up on the toll booth," Tom said later over a half-finished omelet. "Now, remember, Sid and I are crammed into the back seat because my crap is piled roof high in Pop's little shit box of a car."

"Hey, I loved that Chevy Lumina," Sid said. "And you're not telling it right cracking up like that. I should tell the story."

"You don't tell it right," Tom said. "We finally start making progress when...this ancient looking woman...cuts Pop off driving this huge Cadillac...And then...Pop...ha, ha..."

"Pop starts going nuts," Sid said. "He's honking the horn and waving his middle finger right up against the windshield. He's saying, 'God damn it, you old lady! Come fucking cut me off again, you old bitch!'"

"The best part was that the car was quiet for a few minutes because the two of us were in shock," Tom said. "Out of nowhere, Pop goes nuts again and growls, 'I hope you see my finger! I hope you fucking see me!'"

Kenneth turned an even darker shade of red.

"It was the dead of night and I was trying to get to the New Hampshire border before I pissed myself," he said. "I feel bad now, but she deserved it."

"Remember when Pop picked Kristen up on the side of the highway when her car died?" Patrick asked. "He nearly ran Kristen over he hit the shoulder doing at least sixty miles per hour. As if that wasn't bad enough, we ride on the rumble strip for a mile with Pop yelling, 'Jesus fucking Christ, what's wrong with this car!'"

69

"Okay, okay," Kenneth said. "I'm certainly not the only Sanford male at this table who's done some dopey things."

Sid raised his hand.

"Does the groom sweeping his car for illegal wiretaps earlier count?" He asked.

"Too easy," Patrick said. "Although it's worse when he parks somewhere like Yankee Stadium."

"I can't choose," Sid said. "It's either the Dylan concert in Boston when he covered his ears for The Raconteurs opener or the Dylan concert at Mohegan Sun when we missed half the concert because Tom wanted to drink one more beer in an empty bar."

"Tom: 'This warm up act sounds a lot like Dylan,'" Patrick said. "Me: 'That's because it is Dylan!'"

"I'm surprised you guys would pick those two over the Springsteen concert at Gillette Stadium when my back went out and I got sick after drinking two expired beers I found in my trunk before the show," Tom said.

"Hey, we felt bad for you that night," Sid said. "We're not soulless animals."

"Am I the only normal Sanford?" Patrick asked.

"Sure, if you don't consider all the times you punched Pop in the balls when he wasn't looking," Tom said. "What was worse is that when he crumpled to the ground screaming, you'd cry and blame the whole thing on Sid."

"Yeah, Jesus, what an asshole," Sid said. "We could have had another brother or sister. Or at the very least, Pop would have felt like a man all these years."

"Guys, I'm right here," Kenneth said.

"Oh hey, Pop," Tom said. "I forgot about you because I was thinking about Patrick strumming a tennis racquet guitar in the living room pretending to be Billy Ray Cyrus."

"In my defense, Sid was using a couch cushion as a keyboard. And we owned keyboards!" Patrick said. "But fine, I admit I'm as dimwitted as the rest of you. Do we even need to waste time talking about Sid?"

"I'd say my favorite has to be..." Tom said.

"The $300 cell phone bill," Kenneth said.

"Whoa, too soon," Sid said.

"'But Tom, I didn't know text messages cost money,'" Tom said. "'I don't know whose number that is.'"

"Didn't Momma end up calling it?" Patrick asked.

"You bet she did," Kenneth said. "Which ex-girlfriend was it?"

"Doesn't matter," Sid said. "It wasn't the first time Tom threw me under the bus, but this one stung because he missed every signal I gave him to stop harping about the bill."

"Yeah, that's the real injustice," Tom said. "Not the guy with the woman of his dreams right in front of his face and choosing to be hung up on losers. Do you ever plan on making a move on Jocelyn?"

"I'm working on it. Ask me that again in a couple weeks."

"Is that how long you'll be in the hospital after she denies you and then beats the crap out of you for taking so long?" Patrick asked.

"It very well could be," Sid said. "Girl has a helluva left."

71

Kenneth put the money for the bill down on the table and got up.

"Okay, we've had enough fun for one morning," he said. "Besides, I've got to fire out everything I just ate and finish my puzzle."

"Yup, that officially about does it for me too," Patrick said. "Sid, you going with Tom?"

"Yep."

"Good," Tom said.

"Please, your excitement, it's too much," Sid said. "Dial it down."

The four men shook hands and walked out together. Sid waited until Tom put his seat belt on to get out of the car and started examining the roof.

"Get in the car, Sid! I'm wasting gas here!"

"Sorry. I thought you'd want me to tell you that you have a huge scratch up there, big guy."

"Are you kidding me?"

He leapt out of the car and scanned the roof.

"You're an easy mark, brother," Sid said. "Drive me to a warm bed before my head explodes."

Jocelyn smoothed her silver dress and adjusted her shoulder straps as she sat back down in her chair. She giggled watching Gail try to get her husband to move his hips on the dance floor. Jocelyn knew it was a lost cause because the Sanford men weren't blessed with any kind of rhythm.

"Come show him how it's done, hun," Gail said.

Jocelyn shook her head and mouthed, "No way."

She noticed Sid had disappeared. She felt color creep into her cheeks as she thought about catching him staring at her midway through the wedding ceremony. He would usually make a face or do something silly in those situations, but this time was different. His eyes were so intent and entrancing. He motioned his head toward Tom and Kristen at the altar. She had nodded; wanting to believe that he was imagining the two of them standing there. He mouthed the words "I love you." He held her eyes until he walked out of the church behind the bride and groom.

The current song faded out.

"This is an oldie but a goodie on request, folks," the DJ said. "Get close to the one you love."

All-4-One's "I Swear" prompted a few chuckles, but a bunch of guests made a beeline for the dance floor.

"You're going to dance with me, right?" Sid asked.

He had sneaked up on Jocelyn and stood right by her side.

"I hate dancing," she said.

"You don't hate dancing with me."

"I hate all kinds of dancing."

"We were in middle school and the guy was a jerk," Sid said. "It's time to let it go."

"Is this the song?" Jocelyn asked.

"You mean the song I played on my car radio so we could dance in the parking lot while I consoled you? Yes, this is the one."

"You're good."

"I know," Sid said. "Why don't you get off your ass so I can feel it up."

"This is a family event," Jocelyn said.

Sid stepped out of her line of sight and pointed his thumb in the direction of his parents.

Kenneth had one paw planted firmly on his wife's backside.

"Gross," Jocelyn said.

"I know," Sid said. "Let me make it up to you by twirling you around the hardwood for a bit."

"We need to wait for a more up-tempo number."

"I planned for that."

"Shut up," Jocelyn said. "You did not."

Sid nodded to the DJ.

A brassy orchestra replaced 1990s harmonies.

"'A String of Pearls.' Nice touch," Jocelyn said. "Your grandmother would have liked that."

"I thought 'In the Mood' would have been too on the nose."

"Constantly battling clichés. My hero."

"Can we dance now? I ran out of cash to grease the DJ."

"I suppose," Jocelyn said. "I'm going to shoot down my virgin Diet Coke like a cowboy about to rescue his dame."

"Dramatic," Sid said. "Should I wait over there in my bonnet so we set the scene right?"

"Shut up and lead."

"Yes, ma'am.

Sid pressed his cheek up against Jocelyn's once he had pulled her close.

"You're the most beautiful woman here," he said.

"Not burying the lead today, are we?" She said.

"I learned a few things at school."

"You have to say that though, I'm your date. And besides, it's Kristen's wedding, she is the most beautiful today."

"Fine, but you are easily in second place."

"What about your mother?"

"You're never going to just accept a compliment are you?"

"Nope."

"Good to know."

"You do look pretty sharp in your tuxedo." Jocelyn gripped his jacket. "You should dress up more often. You'd have more luck with the girls in the city."

"I told the tailor that I needed to impress this beautiful woman that keeps telling me no," Sid said. "And she lives in Connecticut. My Pop still groping my mother?"

"Yep."

"Old man still has it."

"A family of horny Don Juans. Twirl me, please."

Sid extended his arm and Jocelyn waltzed away from him. She raised her eyebrows seductively and then curled back under his arm.

"Was it Bob Dylan who said something about not being able to be wise and in love at the same time?" Jocelyn asked.

"Possibly," Sid said.

"I can't be a lot of things and in love at the same time."

"That's how you make me feel. Unwise and..."

"In love?"

"I don't think that's what tonight is about," Jocelyn said.

"It's what all nights are about. Wait, what about tonight?"

"I have this crazy idea. I've been thinking about it since the church, which is probably one of the many reasons I'm going to hell..."

"You think we should get a room?"

"Hey!" Jocelyn said. "You get to be suave arranging my favorite songs and dishing out tired pickup lines, and I can't even sweetly ask a question that could change our relationship."

"Sorry," Sid said. "You're absolutely right. Continue."

"Apology accepted. Now go book us a room as soon as this song is over."

"What the hell? That's your idea of romance?"

"I'm a fickle muse Sid, what can I tell you. I'll make it up to you in bed."

"What are we going to tell our parents?" He asked.

"We've been sneaking out together all our lives," she said. "I think we can come up with something."

"So you kind of love me, huh?" Sid asked.

Jocelyn lifted her head and kissed him strongly.

"Maybe," she said.

Jocelyn woke up to cheering on the television.

Sid was undressed from the waist up and had an extra pillow propped up behind him. His eyes were half-closed. She snuggled into him, feeling that he was still warm. She ran her hand over his chest and felt it rise and fall with each breath.

Her body tingled all over because there wasn't an inch of her that Sid hadn't electrified. They had taken their time. When two people took this long to come together, it shouldn't be rushed, it shouldn't be dirty, and it shouldn't be merely physical. There had been tears and breathless discussions about how badly they had wanted this. The lovemaking stopped out of exhaustion, not desire.

Jocelyn kissed Sid on the lips, which jumped him into consciousness.

"I didn't realize you were awake. You want me to turn this off?" He asked.

"No, it's okay. I don't mind."

"I'm just checking the scores. I'll be passing out soon. You really tuckered me out."

"Didn't the Red Sox play the Yankees this afternoon?"

"Yeah, Tom actually had tickets for it. They were part of his weekend season ticket package. Missed a good one. Only my brother would think it was a good idea to have his wedding during baseball season. This is why we're getting married in the winter."

"Oh, one night together and we're getting married now, huh?"

"You know what I mean."

"Sid?"

"Yes, Jocelyn."

"I have to go to sleep now."

"You have my permission." He turned off the television and tossed the remote off the bed. "I'm right behind you. Can I spoon you?"

"What a stupid question."

"Hush," Sid said. "Go to sleep and leave me alone."

"Sid?"

"Yes, Jocelyn?"

"Can we do it again in the morning?"

Jocelyn hugged him at the train station the following morning.

She didn't want to let go. Sid didn't want to leave because he knew he couldn't do this from so far away.

"Promise me you won't hurt me too badly," Jocelyn said.

"Promise."

He didn't know whether or not he was lying. He felt awful.

She kissed him on the lips and he kissed back. He turned away and walked up the steps to the train platform.

He didn't want to look back. He couldn't hear or say anything else. He'd think on the train.

"I need you to come back to me," she said. "I was wrong, it's our time."

"I'll be home for the summer," he said.

He walked away.

The first scotch wasn't Sid's mistake a couple of nights later. It was the hubris and stupidity of the third that did him in.

Sid had no idea whose couch he'd passed out on. His mind had erased any memories related to why he was lying here and not up against a curb on Queens Boulevard.

"I see you're awake."

The person standing in front of him was tall—six-foot if Sid had to guess. He was wearing a dark blue short-sleeved shirt depicting a wolf howling at the moon that was jammed haphazardly into a pair of khakis. He pushed his glasses back up the bridge of his nose with one hand and held out his other in Sid's direction.

"Damon Lord," he said. "I'm the welcoming committee."

Sid shook Damon's hand tentatively.

"Sid Sanford. This isn't hell, is it?"

"Some women have called it that."

Damon handed Sid a glass of water.

"Are you some sort of Boy Scout?" Sid asked.

"Eagle Scout. That's another way of saying I had no life when I was a kid and like nature more than the average

79

person should. This is for you." Damon pulled a piece of paper from his pocket. "This girl you were with last night wanted me to give it to you. You were too far gone at that point to manage your own affairs, so I stepped in."

Sid didn't remember who Lydia was or why he knew possessed her number.

"Hungry?" Damon asked.

Sid nodded. Damon put a big plate of bacon and eggs in front of him.

"Hey, who is Jocelyn?"

"Huh?"

"You were muttering Jocelyn in your sleep. I figured she was a girlfriend or something like that."

"Yeah, something like that."

Jocelyn had left him several voice and text messages. He could tell she was worried he was dead, or worse, had found someone else.

Sid's headache intensified.

He scrolled down to Jocelyn's number. His thumb hovered over the "call" icon under her picture. His eyes darted over to the small piece of paper on the table.

He rubbed the back of his neck.

"Hey, Damon?"

"What's up? You need anything?"

"Do you have hot sauce?"

"Coming right up!"

Damon had a bright red bottle in front of Sid in no time. Sid dumped some hot sauce on his eggs and took a huge mouthful.

"Damon, one more thing."

"What's up?"

"You looking for a roommate?" Sid asked with a mouthful of eggs.

"Heh, why, eager to move off campus?"

"I am if you're going to make eggs like this regularly."

"We'll talk after breakfast," Damon said, laughing. "My screening process is a little more vigorous than picking up drunk strays off the street."

Sid saluted and gulped water. He let his eyes burn for a moment and decided the two women could wait too.

CONSTANCE

Sid's arm was trapped under something…someone.

He ignored the momentary panic that flooded his brain and removed his numb appendage out from underneath the figure lying next to him. He rolled over and tried to massage some feeling into his muscles. It didn't take long for a burning, tingling sensation to reverberate up and down his arm. He put his head back down on his pillow once he was able to move all of his fingers without thinking about it. He knew a headache would arrive as soon as the rest of his body realized it was awake. A burp bubbled up in his throat and he let it out. He followed that with a yawn. He glanced at his alarm clock, which read 3:30 p.m.

His blinds glowed orange, trying their best to keep the sun out. He pushed away the covers and dangled his legs off the side of the bed. He put his head in his hands and left it there. The ache didn't come all at once; it crept into his brain slowly. He forced his eyes open. His room was small, so he had no trouble opening the blinds just enough so he could see outside.

Beads of water stuck to the window's outer screen from last night's downpour. The rain had come out of nowhere, just as everyone was walking home from the bar. He vaguely remembered saying something stupid standing in an ankle-deep puddle.

A scrap of paper leapt from the nightstand and landed on the carpeted floor. He felt the alcohol boomerang in his stomach as he bent down to pick it up. He focused drunkenly on the numbers scrawled in blue pen.

"Son of a bitch," Sid muttered.

He remembered he had a date today. He was staring at the girl's number. He stumbled around his room, piecing together a respectable outfit. He couldn't remember the last time he had done laundry. At least he knew the shirt he picked out was clean; it was the last one hanging up in his closet. The jeans had been worn several days in a row, but smelled okay.

Once he made it to the bathroom, he scrubbed his face with body wash and ran water over his shaved head. He sprayed on half a bottle of cologne. He almost felt human by the time he walked into the kitchen where Damon sat at the table.

"You look like shit," he said.

Sid shrugged and grabbed a bowl from the cabinet. He opened the small pantry and took out a box of Honey Nut Cheerios. He slowly poured the cereal. He made sure the milk he pulled out of the refrigerator wasn't expired and poured it into the bowl. He plucked a spoon from the drying rack, brought his breakfast over to the table, and started crunching away.

"I see you and Lydia have mended fences," Damon said.

"Huh?" Sid asked.

Damon motioned to the figure making its way toward the bathroom. It didn't look like she was wearing much more than the small blanket Sid kept at the end of his bed.

"I have a date," he said.

He watched his roommate brush pencil shavings from his shirt and returned to scrutinizing the numbers on his spreadsheet. Sid envied the qualities Damon exhibited on a daily basis: dependability, honesty, and meticulousness. Damon knew everything about him, but never judged him too harshly. The rent check cleared every month and morning coffee was always made, which is all that really mattered.

"What's her name?" Damon asked. "Where did you meet her?"

Sid swallowed a last bite of his cereal. He knew a lot about this one; she had blue eyes and a smile that he could sketch blindly. He just couldn't remember her name.

"I guess I'll find out," Sid said.

"What time are you leaving?" Damon asked.

"What time is it now?"

"I think it's just after 4:30 p.m."

"I'm pretty sure I'm late."

Sid tossed his bowl into the sink. It clanged noisily against the other dishes he had neglected. He ran back into his room, grabbed a jacket, and bounded back out into the kitchen.

"I'll be back!" Sid said.

"Have fun!"

Constance had no trouble waking up that morning.

In fact, she never had an issue getting out of bed. Her grandmother never allowed her to linger under the covers, even on the weekends. The older woman she shared a name with would quietly open her door, shuffle over to the bed, and plant a kiss on her forehead. Then, she'd loudly tell her that the coffee was ready and she should get her ass up and moving. Most mornings, Constance was already awake, eagerly anticipating the daily exchange. She'd arrive at the kitchen table, holding a steaming cup of coffee in her cold hands, before the older woman had made her way back. The routine was no different on the day Constance was going to finally spend a few hours alone with Sid outside of school.

"Can you believe the Mets?" The elder Constance threw down the sports section of the newsletter in disgust. "I don't know why they even bother playing in September."

"They'll be better next year, Grandma," the younger Constance said.

She dumped cream and sugar into her cup and swirled her spoon to mix everything up. She watched as the inky liquid turned a pale shade of brown. She took her first sip when she noticed her grandmother standing in the middle of the kitchen giving her a confused look.

"What?" The younger Constance asked.

"Better next year? How many years do you think I got left?"

"Hush. You have plenty left."

"Probably not enough to see the Mets be competitive."

85

"Have some faith!"

"I pray for them, but I might give it up. Who needs 'em?"

Constance knew her grandmother would continue to pray for her favorite team, as well as yell passionately at the television no matter how well or terrible they were playing. Complaining about them was just part of her shtick.

Out of nowhere, a homemade baked good landed in front of the young woman.

"What's this?" She asked.

"Just eat it. It's delicious. Trust me, I made it. Enough chit-chat, I've got to get to work."

"You know how upset Mom gets when you overdo it, so watch out!" The younger Constance said.

Her grandmother walked over to her and lightly slapped her granddaughter's cheek.

"What else am I going to do? Wait to die? Hey, isn't today the day you're hanging out with that Simon kid?"

"His name is Sid, Grandma. And yes it is! I'm excited."

"Well, he better be cute is all I have to say. If he's not, don't bother introducing me."

Constance quickly finished the rest of her coffee, not allowing herself to daydream. She was going to make shit happen today. She rinsed her coffee cup, stretched her arms out, and yawned loudly to the empty kitchen.

She wondered what it was going to be like to talk to him for hours on end. What kind of life had he had? What would his eyes look like staring back at just her? What would it be like to hold his hand or kiss him? Was he thinking about her like this at this exact moment? Why was she losing it so badly over this boy she hardly knew? She put all her questions and desires on hold as she walked back to her bedroom. Before she found out the answers to any of them, she had work to do.

Constance pulled off her hoodie after she closed her bedroom door. Her sweatpants came off next. She stood in the middle of the floor wearing only her black bra and underwear. She caught a glimpse of herself in the three mirrors above her dresser. She patted her flat stomach, and flexed her arm muscle. Her body looked good, so she felt good. She was about to make it feel even better.

She pulled a sport bra and a pair of baby blue shorts out of her bottom drawer. It was her favorite workout combination. She had washed the pair so many times, the colors were fading and any logos or writing had disappeared. She clipped her iPod on her waistband. She put the earbuds of her headphones in her ears, but didn't turn the music on right away. She wanted her tunes to blast through her head the exact moment her fist first made contact with the punching bag.

Constance ran full speed down her basement steps. She raced past the trophies from her father's numerous hunting trips hanging on the walls and finally made it to her sacred space; just a naked light bulb and her punching bag. She searched for the music she wanted, and then pulled on her pink boxing gloves her mother had bought for her. Constance may have outgrown her punk rock phase, but black was still her favorite color. Pink anything would never have been her first choice, but she had learned the hard way what happened when she criticized her mother's choices.

A Metallica album rumbled into her ears as she made her first punch.

87

"God, that felt good," she shouted, already throwing her second.

She always liked to be in an angry mood while she did this, but today she felt too good to care. She got into the rhythm of the music and the sound of her fist hitting the bag. She started dancing around it. Her footstep and movements never felt so light and precise. Instead of a determined snarl, her face wore a broad smile. It got even wider as sweat streamed down her arms.

The first time she saw Sid, he sat cross-legged on the floor, devouring a book. He wore a baseball cap pulled close to his eyes. She could hear the music coming from his headphones from across the hall. He didn't notice she was staring at him. They walked into the same writing class, but not together. She walked in behind him, too nervous to say anything to him just yet. She needed to observe him more. Plus, the more she stared, the more likely he would notice her and then he would make the first move.

Needless to say, it didn't happen during that first class. His eyes were focused on the professor and his notebook the whole time. She knew because her eyes never left him. It didn't happen at the second class even though she wore her favorite outfit and was brave enough to sit closer to him. She made sure she was smiling the whole time. By the third class, she resorted to putting on makeup.

A few days later, the professor finished reading an assignment this boy wrote. Everyone clapped. He got embarrassed, but also looked proud. She imagined he spent hours crafting each word perfectly like she did. She knew it was silly and something a high school teenager would say, but she just couldn't shake the belief that she would like this boy for a long time if he managed to open up his damn eyes.

She watched as he glanced around the room seeking...something. She wanted him to find her so bad. His eyes landed on her after what seemed like an eon. She smiled and he smiled back. After class he ran away like a scared child.

He had lingered sheepishly outside class one day while she walked away looking back obsessively to make sure he was still there watching her walk away. A classmate she had befriended took pity on the both of them and introduced them.

"I've been trying to find a way to talk to you for weeks now," he said.

"I've been trying to get your attention, so you're in good company," she said. "I like the way you write."

"You're not so bad yourself. And you're really cute. Do you want to go out with me? On a date? Soon?"

Surprisingly, she hadn't scared him away again. He said yes and they set a date and time. He gave her his number. She gave him hers. He started walking off to his next class without a word. But he looked back at her and his eyes reflected the afternoon sun. She smiled intensely and gave a cute wave.

Constance was hooked.

Her iPod died. She had lost all track of time. Her arms ached. She was out of breath and her voice was a little horse from screaming along with the music. She realized her knuckles were as pink as the boxing gloves she pried off her hands. She was soaked in sweat. She wasn't

89

nervous about what they would do, talk about, or if they'd kiss. She wasn't worried he wouldn't like her once he got to know her better.

Constance crouched and gave the punching bag one last sharp hit with her bare hand.

Sid tried to turn his brain on as he walked down Union Turnpike. The cool breeze, cloudless, sun-filled sky, and nervous anticipation were doing nothing to combat his worsening hangover. He recited the alphabet through his haze to try to remember what her name was. All he could clearly remember was her constant smile. He liked that, but he couldn't help thinking that smile was leading him into another situation he didn't want or couldn't handle. He already had two of those, one passed out in his bed, and the other in Connecticut.

Sid resolved to cancel the date. All facets of his life were a mess and he didn't have the will to face any of it, never mind adding to it. He knew he'd feel even worse if this girl turned out to be nice. It was his duty to protect her from all his crap, which is why he had his phone out, fully prepared to march back inside and lie with all of his bad decisions. He just couldn't find the slip of paper with her name and number on it. There was no way he could go back into his apartment to look for it.

His cell phone vibrated in his pocket. He willed the text to be a cancelation on her part. Maybe she had food poisoning, remembered she had a boyfriend, or had simply come to her senses and wanted nothing to do with him. No such luck.

"You got pretty drunk last night, huh?" Jocelyn wrote.

"Not that bad," Sid wrote back.

"You remember anything you said to me?"

"Sure."

"Liar."

"Give me a break."

"Why? Do you have a hangover?"

"No, just be nice."

"Did you sleep with Lydia again?"

"No."

"Good."

"I'm on my way to that date."

"Oh boy. You're still going?"

"Why wouldn't I?"

"You have a hangover and had sex with Lydia last night."

"Yeah, yeah."

"Don't fall in love with her right away."

"I don't think that will be a problem."

"Good luck...but not too much. Talk later."

"Bye."

Constance said she'd meet him at their school's main entrance and that's where he found her. She had one leg up against the brick wall, glancing at passersby nonchalantly. She wore a pair of skinny jeans that complimented her slim figure and a black tank top with a thin blue sweater over it.

Sid stopped walking. He swallowed, trying his best to control the burp that threatened to bellow out of his throat.

He didn't want to throw up all over himself steps away from this girl whose name he couldn't remember. He suddenly felt self-conscious about the polo shirt he was wearing, the condition of his tired eyes, and his worn out sneakers. He walked another few steps. Her eyes found him easily. He smirked and then had an epiphany.

"Hello, Constance," he said. "Sorry I'm late."

Constance's question made Sid drop the diner's oversized menu in his lap.

"What?" He asked.

"So do you have a girlfriend?" She asked again.

Sid rubbed the back of his head, took a breath, and looked her right in the eyes.

"Sort of," he said.

"You're going to need to explain that one."

Constance tried not to sound prosecutorial, however, the guy sitting across from her smelled like a distillery and had whined about the long bus ride to Astoria.

Sid opened his mouth and shut it again. He let out a short, nervous laugh. He rubbed the back of his head again. Constance saw sweat beading up along his hairline.

"Do you know what you want, sweetie?" The waitress asked.

"Well, I know one of us does," she said.

They both ordered a coffee and got back to staring each other down. The waitress had given him a moment to regroup and Constance could see he had taken full advantage of it. His eyes were as clear as they had been all night, his hands were folded calmly on the table in front of him, and he appeared like he was ready to talk honestly.

"I'm single," he said. "I have a good friend in Connecticut, she's family really, and we have a relationship that defies explanation. We've never really been on the same page at the same time, and probably never will be. And you know what, I think both of us have made some kind of peace with that and our friendship has been better for it recently. 'Sort of' was a poor choice of words. If I had a girlfriend, I wouldn't be here tonight. I'm not that kind of person. I'm a good guy."

"Do you love her?"

"I'm not in love with her."

"But you do love her."

"Of course I do."

"And you don't think that would be a problem when you start dating someone else?"

"You don't think someone can love a person without being in love with them?"

"I do, but you didn't answer the question."

"I'm content with the expectations for that relationship, and know that it won't affect any relationship that comes along."

"Are you running for office?"

"I've heard that before."

"I bet you have."

The waitress brought their coffees. Constance reached over to grab the sugar and cream, but Sid brushed her hand away and held the cream container over her cup.

"Tell me when," he said.

"That's your plan to get back into my good graces? Has this ever worked for you before?"

He laughed, causing his hand to shake. Cream spilled down the side of the white cup and puddled into the saucer.

"I figured what better way to impress an over-caffeinated New Yorker than to find out how she takes her coffee," Sid said.

"I didn't tell you to stop," Constance said.

"Seriously?"

"Yes."

"Should we get you a bigger cup so you can have a little coffee with your cream?"

"Funny. Keep pouring."

"You got it."

Constance watched as he continued his mission. She nodded when she was satisfied. She handed him two sugar packets. He dumped them in and clanged the spoon up against the sides of the cup as he stirred everything together. He slid the saucer closer to her and bowed. She applauded.

"So, what do you want to know about me?" Sid asked.

"I'll decide whether I want to know anything more about you after I determine how good of a job you did on my coffee," Constance said, blowing across the surface of her drink.

"Of course, take your time. Don't hold back your judgment."

"I think you know by now that's not my style."

"This is true."

Constance finally touched her lips to the cup and took a small sip.

"Okay, you pass."

"That's it?"

"Yup."

"No other observations, comments, concerns? I just pass?"

"Don't push it."

"You got it."

Sid rubbed the back of his head. Constance couldn't help being fascinated by the boy in front of her. She really believed he was being genuine at this point.

"How do you know I love coffee?" Constance asked.

"You always have one in class."

"It's my first class of the day, I could just need the energy."

"Yeah, there's more to it than that."

"Such as..."

"It's just how you drink it."

"And how do I drink it exactly?"

"I don't know."

"You've been creepily watching me drink coffee for weeks and don't know exactly how I drink it?"

"It's hard for me to take my eyes off of you."

95

Constance put her head down and tried to hide the smile that had burst onto her face like a child's soap bubble on a summer day.

"That is sweet," she said. "Thank you."

"You're welcome."

"You certainly have a way with words, Sid Sanford."

"God, I hope so, I want to be a writer when I'm all growed up."

"Me too."

"Well, why do you want to be a writer?"

Constance thought of all the notebooks she had stacked up in her closet. Notebooks she had written in since she was a little girl, notebooks that were yellowed and faded in spots, notebooks that she had never shown anyone outside of her immediate family. Some contained scribbles and rambling thoughts, while others contained fully formed story ideas in various stages of completion. She often looked to them when she needed a spark of creative inspiration. She wanted to be a writer because that's all she'd ever done and all she ever wanted to do. She was good at it and wanted to improve on a daily basis.

"That's a great answer," he said.

She hadn't realized she'd been talking out loud.

"Too much information for a first date?" She asked.

"Not at all. Exactly the answer I was hoping for. I'm the same way. I wasn't an athlete, I wasn't the smartest kid in the class, and I didn't have the sense of humor to be the class clown. Writing has been the only thing I've ever been good at, so I figured majoring in journalism in New York City was a no brainer."

She loved that he was tripping over his words telling her this. It was as if his mouth couldn't keep up with the passionate thoughts.

"I was going to ask you about that. How does a Connecticut boy like you end up in the big city?" She asked. "You didn't want to stay close to home?"

"I've been in love with the city since my mother took me to the Radio City Christmas Spectacular when I was nine years old," he answered. "My life's goal from that point on was to live here. Besides, practically my entire high school went to UCONN. If I had stayed, I would have never left home."

"Did part of you leave because of your complicated relationship with your best friend?"

Sid shrugged.

"That's a yes," Constance said.

"That's an 'I don't know, I've never thought of it that way before.' Maybe, but my love for New York City outweighed every other consideration."

"Fair enough. Do you miss your family?"

Sid pursed his lips tightly. He looked down, seemingly looking deep into the coffee that was no longer in his cup.

"It's okay, you don't have to answer," Constance said. "I didn't mean to make you sad."

"I miss them all terribly. I love my family," he said. "I don't know why they put up with me, but they do."

"Do you consider yourself a good man?"

"I like to think so. I do try. I can't say I've made a lot of smart decisions since I've been here or before that, but my parents hammered a good soul into me. I guess it's just

97

about being young right now and accepting that fact rather than rebelling against it."

"Aren't you going to ask me if I think I'm a good person?" Constance asked.

"I don't need to," Sid said. "What's after dinner?"

Not long after, the Robert F. Kennedy Bridge towered over Sid and Constance and every light on it stood in sparkling contrast to the darkening September sky. The bridge produced so much light that Sid felt the beams illuminating Astoria Park's running track were utterly redundant.

"Whoa..." He said.

"Yeah, I thought you might like this. And thank you for not complaining about the walk here."

"Worth it. Well, this and getting to know you better of course. Sorry I was cranky earlier, I had a much longer night than I intended."

"You're forgiven. Otherwise, I would have left you stranded in that diner after you said 'sort of.'"

"Probably not going to live that one down, am I?"

"Nope."

"Excellent."

The two stood silent for a handful of moments. Sid didn't want to disturb the perfect New York tableau of runners laboriously circling the red field turf of the track, couples in various states of conversation or argument, kids stoking the final embers of a hot summer, and his newfound companion holding his hand.

"Why don't we pop a squat on that park bench under the trees," Constance said.

"What the hell does 'pop a squat' mean?" Sid asked.

"Sit down."

"Why don't you just say sit down?"

"Do you really care?"

"No."

"That's what I thought. Get moving."

Sid stumbled to the bench, unwilling to take his eyes off the scene in front of him. Constance continued to talk, but Sid only replied with a smile or nod every few minutes. He felt strangely at home for the first time during his short tenure in the city.

"I've lost you completely, haven't I?" Constance asked.

"Huh?"

She put her arm around him.

"It's okay. I want you to enjoy the moment. I know you said you missed seeing stars, and this is the best I could come up with."

"Pretty perfect in my opinion."

Constance smiled sweetly as he finally turned his attention back to her eyes.

"Tell me something," she said.

"Like what?"

"Anything. Something you haven't told anyone. Not even Jocelyn."

"Hmm, let me think," Sid said.

He momentarily tuned out the traffic driving over the bridge and the din of a city park.

"I didn't cry at my Mémère's funeral," he said.

"What's a Mémère?"

"Grandmother in French."

"Ah, continue."

"I always felt guilty because I loved her so much. She let me get away with everything as a kid, and, trust me, Cecile Blanchette was not one to let anyone get away with anything. Just ask my uncles. I used to really beat myself up whenever I'd ball my eyes out after breaking up with someone. A lot of the girls I dated didn't deserve it. Some of them did, but any tears just seemed less important and unnecessary."

"Tears don't necessarily define how sad you are, Sid. I'm sure she knows you love her and you miss her. She doesn't need your tears to tell her that. Besides, I'm assuming you were younger when it happened. You didn't understand how to mourn at that point. I'm positive she was okay with you being a stoic little boy."

"I've never thought about it that way. Makes sense."

"Damn straight it does. I'm a smart young woman."

"I can tell. Thanks for the insight."

"I know you don't completely buy it," Constance said. "That's fine. Give it time to sink in."

Sid couldn't remember all that much about the funeral. It was warm for a spring day in upstate Maine. He remembered how loud the logging trucks had been as they thundered through the center of town with their weighty cargo and sitting on his Uncle Bobby's lap on his Tante

Valeda's front porch blowing soap bubbles toward Canada. That was about it. Except for the fact that everyone had been really sad the day of the funeral and tears flowed freely from his emotional family. No matter how hard he tried, he couldn't figure out what was wrong, and why he couldn't feel the same sadness as everyone else.

"Hey," Constance said, poking Sid in the side.

"I'm here," he said.

"You aren't, but that's okay too."

"Thanks. Your turn. You tell me something."

"I want to kiss you."

"I think I can be persuaded to let you."

"Oh really?"

"Pretty sure."

"How long have you been thinking about kissing me? When you stepped foot in the park perhaps?"

"Long before."

"Good."

Constance put her hand on his cheek and led Sid's face closer to hers.

Sid felt his resolve weakening.

He had effectively, and politely, managed to decline every advance that had been made. However, each offer was more and more tantalizing and he could now envision himself giving in completely to temptation and not being sorry about it. Sid could sense this was all leading to an end game that he had lost the moment he walked through the door. He wasn't quite ready to give up the illusion he still had some free will left to control the situation, but he was close.

"Well, how about I heat up this last piece of apple pie," Constance's mother asked. "I'm just going to throw it out if you say no, which would be a waste of my delicious food."

She glared at Sid over the top of her glasses with an expression mixed with maternal concern and menace.

"Leave him alone, mother," Constance said. "If he was hungry, he'd have said yes to one of the other hundred things you offered. When he wants something, he'll let you know I'm sure."

"Well, maybe he's too shy to tell me right now," she said.

"Are you hungry?" Constance asked.

"Well, I mean..." Sid stammered.

"Are you kidding me? You're caving, aren't you?"

"I haven't had apple pie since the last time I was home, which was a couple weeks ago. It's my favorite."

"Ugh, fine. Pie it is, mother."

"Yes!" Constance's mother raised her arms in triumph. "Apple pie for the win!"

"This was a bad idea," Constance said.

She pulled out a chair at the kitchen table. She gestured for Sid to sit down wearing the sweetest, most sarcastic face she could muster.

"Your table is ready sir!"

"Thanks."

Sid doffed an imaginary hat. He slid into the seat quickly, not wanting to cause any more trouble or give Constance any more ammunition to pick on him. Constance brought him a cup of coffee he hadn't asked for and patted the top of his head as she sat down next to him.

"I think you're beautiful." Sid said.

"You're just saying that because I kissed you in the park, aren't you?"

"That might have something to do with it, yeah."

The microwave loudly announced it was done nuking his piece of pie, and Constance's mother rushed back into the kitchen.

"Do you need anything else, Sid?"

"No, ma'am."

"Ma'am! I like this one."

"How many of them have there been?" Sid asked.

"And he's funny!"

Constance rolled her eyes.

"I think you're really cute too," She whispered. "Hurry up and eat that pie so I can kiss you some more."

A wrinkled face appeared in the doorway.

Sid looked up as he put the last piece of the pie in his mouth. He watched as the older woman shuffled into the kitchen and patted her granddaughter's head.

"This is my granddaughter, who I'm assuming you've met at this point," the elder Constance said. "She stole my name, you know."

"I didn't steal it! My parents gave it to me. Take your complaints to them."

"They don't listen to me."

"That's not true."

"Are you calling me a liar in front of your new friend?"

"Nope."

"That's what I thought." The older woman said, sitting down next to Sid.

"Sid Sanford." He extended his hand. "It's a pleasure to meet you, ma'am."

"I'm sure it is." She accepted his handshake. "Okay, you can stick around Simon, you're cute."

"My name is Sid."

"What team do you root for?"

"Yankees."

"In that case then you'll be Simon from now on. I'm out of here kids, don't stay up too late necking like I used to do."

"Grandma!"

"It's not like he wasn't thinking about it. But he should think differently if he knows what's good for him."

"Yes, ma'am."

"Good boy. We'll get along just fine. Night!"

Sid looked to Constance for some kind of affirmation that he hadn't made a fool of himself. She winked, putting him at ease.

"Hey Constance, can your friend play video games with me?!" A young voice said. Sid craned his neck to get a glance at her younger brother.

"Absolutely not," Constance told him.

"Boooo!" He yelled back.

"I'm willing to bet, you'd enjoy that for hours, wouldn't you?" Constance whispered.

"Yup," Sid said.

"Typical," she said, pushing him toward her room.

Constance's room not only had a huge bookcase full of books, but also stacks covering nearly every surface. He wasn't surprised to find similar titles that he loved. There was a small pile of notebooks on both of her nightstands, as well as the small desk she had up against the tall window at the far side of her room.

"Those are just in case I have an idea come out of nowhere," Constance said. "I'm prepared to write anywhere in this room. Feel free to keep looking around."

Sid walked over to her dresser. There were pictures of her and her family on every available space and tucked into the wood framing the large trio of mirrors. He could follow Constance's progression from a tomboy toddler to an attractive, dark-haired beauty from one end of the dresser to the other. He noticed a book on her desk that had no cover and looked well worn. He picked it up so he could to read the title page.

"This is an awfully loved copy of *To Kill a Mockingbird*," Sid said.

He held the book up in the air for her to see as if she didn't know exactly what it was.

"It's my favorite book," she said.

"Mine too."

Sid smirked and put the treasured book back in its place.

"What?" She asked.

"Nothing..."

"Spill it."

"You just assume I'm going to just tell you everything you want exactly when you want to hear it from now on?"

"I do."

"Well, at least you're honest about it."

"Only way I know how to be."

"I can appreciate that."

"Well..."

"I was just thinking this looks a lot like my room back in Connecticut. All that's missing is my younger brother hitting on you and leaving a trail of Pop-Tarts across the room."

"That's a wonderful image."

"Don't make fun of me, I was being serious."

"I know, I wasn't ribbing you."

She wrapped her arms around him and kissed him passionately. He hugged her just as tightly as he was hugging him and lifted her off the ground. Her feet found the ground gently as he lowered her down out of the air.

"Kind of feels like I was meant to be here," Sid said. "Like I was meant to meet you at this moment in time."

"So now we're soulmates?"

"You have a problem with that?"

"I'm not opposed to the idea."

"You're just saying that because you want to keep kissing me, right?"

"That might have something to do with it, yeah."

"Constance, your father is home!" Her mother yelled from the kitchen. "Why don't you ask him nicely if he'll give young Sid a ride back to campus?"

Sid tried his best to regain some kind of composure as Constance led him by the hand to meet her father. Standing in the kitchen was a tall, dark-haired Italian man speaking with the thickest New York accent Sid had ever heard.

"Daddy, this is Sid, my new friend from school," Constance said.

"Hey, nice to meet you. Have anything to eat?"

"Your wife kindly gave me the last piece of apple pie, sir."

"Wait, you ate the piece of pie I've been fantasizing about all day?"

"It would appear so."

"Well, I'm just glad you didn't go hungry while you were here," Constance's father said. "Not that anyone could considering my wife force feeds everyone the minute they walk in the door."

He took a moment to listen for his wife's reply, and was somewhat relieved when none came.

"You mind giving Sid a lift home?" Constance asked.

"Sure! We'll take the Lexus."

"Lexus?"

"That okay with you?"

"Yeah, sure," Sid said. "By the way, is that a real coyote in your living room?"

There was complete silence in the car on the way home.

Constance hadn't said a word and neither had her father. He drummed his fingers on the steering wheel even though she was sure he had never heard of any of these artists. She knew he was dying to say something, but wouldn't unless she made the first move. She thought she was home free when her father pulled the car into the driveway. Constance reached for the door handle and grimaced at the sound of her father triggering the child safety locks.

"Just answer me one question," he said.

"Sure, Daddy," she said.

"Can I invite this one hunting?"

"I didn't see that coming."

"Well..."

"Yes, but don't put him on the wall."

"Ah ha! You really do like this one then!"

"I didn't say never put him on the wall," Constance said. "Just don't do it any time soon."

Sid stared at his front door.

He pulled his keys out of his pocket, but looked back toward the street. He meandered to the edge of the sidewalk. His eyes followed the route her father had taken from his place. He didn't move a muscle for several minutes. The coffee he drank at Constance's house had him jittery. Sleep would be impossible tonight, but he didn't care.

Sid walked back to the front door. He pulled out the CD she demanded he listen to. He had no idea who this band was or why she liked them so much. She said something about a punching bag. He nervously smacked the case against his other hand. He wasn't sure what was stopping him from walking into his apartment. He wanted to tell Damon everything. He wanted to tell everyone everything.

"Maybe not everyone," he muttered.

Since Sid stepped foot in New York City, he'd been at war with the man he was acting like, and the boy he had started out as. He questioned if he really was a good guy at heart, or if the mistakes he kept committing were indicators of a darker nature he'd never be able to outgrow. Tonight, all his fears were quiet. By no means did he think that he had things figured out completely, or that whatever this was would lead to something lasting and uncomplicated. He knew youth prevented him from knowing what came next, so that meant he couldn't say for sure which Sid Sanford he'd face in the mirror in the morning. All he knew in this moment was that he felt a little happy and ready for more.

His cell phone vibrated in his pocket.

He dropped the CD and cursed. He pulled out his phone so fast it slipped out of his hand. He swore again. The phone landed in the bushes. He reached his hands into the branches, but felt nothing but plant life. He got

109

down on his knees and scooted as far under brush as he could. Sid could now see his phone a few feet away. He could feel its buzz the closer his hand got to it. He grabbed it with his arm extended has far as it could go. He ended up throwing dirt in his own face as he rushed to scc who had sent him the message that started this chain reaction.

"Are you in love yet?" Jocelyn wrote.

Sid brushed off the dirt still camped out on his jacket and glanced at the CD case on the welcome mat.

"Maybe," he wrote back.

He hit send, shut his phone off, and walked through his front door.

Sid shut off the television. Damon's snores stopped immediately. He struggled to come back to reality.

Sid waited. His roommate tensed up when he realized someone was standing over it.

"I didn't expect to see you back here tonight," Damon said. "I figured you'd be dining out on someone else's eggs tomorrow morning."

"Tell me that wasn't your attempt at a double entendre."

"It wasn't."

"Good."

Sid sat down and pulled off his sneakers and tossed them back toward the door. He started tapping the CD case against his palm again.

"Is that my signal that you want to talk about what happened tonight?" Damon retrieved his glasses from on top of the book he had been thumbing through hours ago.

"You know, this question kept running through my head all night. 'What would Damon say?' Now, here I am with the opportunity to find out and I got no words. Nada."

"Sid, tell me you aren't in love with her already."

Sid shrugged. Damon's eyes moved down the hall leading to Sid's room.

"What?" Sid asked.

"You know what."

"Do I look like someone in the know right now?"

"You left quite a mess that you might need to clean up sooner than you thought."

"No way."

"Yep."

"She's been here all day?"

"All day."

"Have you talked to her?"

"Nope."

"Did she leave my room?"

"Went to the bathroom a couple of hours ago. No sound or visual since."

"Well, fuck."

"Seems appropriate."

"Shuddap."

111

Sid marched past Damon and headed toward another closed door, one he was much less inclined to enter than the first one. Unlike Jocelyn, he couldn't push this particular problem away for a couple more hours. He paused before gripping the doorknob.

"What are you going to do?" Damon asked.

Sid felt a broad, goofy smile break out on his face.

"Go to bed before the fireworks, Lordy."

He walked into the room and shut the door.

FRONT LINES

Constance's back ached.

She had worked the Queens bookstore's register all morning without a break. Her stomach grumbled, but she ignored it. Her feet hurt; she ignored them too. She was focused on her upcoming finals, the last she would ever take.

"Have a good day sir," she said. "That's a great book, you won't be disappointed. Thanks for shopping. Please come back soon."

The man muttered and left.

She had worked at this mom and pop bookstore since high school. Her mother would bring her here as a kid, and soon she spent so much time browsing books after school and reading on one of the overstuffed, burnt orange armchairs wedged between the narrow stacks throughout the shop that they finally offered her a job. Constance accepted without thinking twice and spent most of her days off happily directing customers to her favorite titles.

Speaking of, her cell phone vibrated in her pocket again. That was twenty texts so far.

"What am I going to do with that boy?" She mumbled.

Constance patiently explained to Sid over and over why they couldn't be together. She had found someone else and she wanted to give the relationship every chance to succeed. She told him to deal with his feelings for Jocelyn and get his other priorities in order. Constance knew Jocelyn was like family to him, but no other girl liked playing second best. She loved Sid, she really did. More than a little part of her wanted to give into everything he had talked so passionately about. But it just wasn't their time, so she had to play the bitch most days.

"Excuse me, Constance?" A female customer asked. "I think that young man outside with the roses is trying to get your attention."

Constance didn't want to look up. Her boyfriend was away with his parents for a few days.

"Is that your boyfriend, hun?"

"No," Constance said. "That's my Sid."

Constance slammed the store's back door "You can't keep doing this shit," she said.

"How much do you want to bet I can?" Sid asked, holding out the roses.

"I have a boyfriend who can buy me flowers for no reason. I'm going to have to tell him where these came from, and I'll get shit for it. Do you understand?"

"I understand that you shouldn't be with this guy in the first place and that you should break up with him and come back to me where you belong."

"So you've said many times. However, that is my decision and I want to be with him right now. End of discussion."

Sid held out the roses again, more confidently this time. Constance smiled tersely.

"Do you like them?" He asked.

"Yes, but that doesn't mean I like you spending your time and money trying to make me go back out with you."

The line she drew never moved, and he always walked away alone and disappointed. She knew there was something in his heart that wouldn't let him stop.

"Thank you, Sid, they are lovely." She said, putting her face close to the roses and inhaling. "Now go home."

"Okay."

Constance followed him to the front of the store and opened the door for him. He lingered a moment longer to see if she was going to say anything he wanted to hear. She didn't.

"Goodbye, Sid."

"Goodbye, Constance."

Sid walked out the door and she went back to work.

"How'd it go?" Damon asked.

Sid tapped his cell phone to his ear, not waiting to admit the truth just yet.

115

"I'm going to walk around for a while and clear my mind. You want to grab a drink at Gantry's later?"

"That bad?"

"Yeah."

"Maybe surrounding yourself with alcohol isn't a great idea."

"One drink. I can't stay out late either; I've got a paper due at the end of the week. All I need is one."

"I guess. I'll meet you there."

"Perfect."

Damon hung up the phone.

The next night, Sid quietly pushed through Gantry's front door. He saw Damon awkwardly straddling a stool, nursing a can of light beer. His friend looked no worse for wear after being stood up yesterday. Damon's brow was as furrowed as always, so Sid couldn't know for sure until he sat down.

"Miss me?" He asked.

"That seat is taken," Damon said.

"Oh yeah? By who?"

"Anyone else."

"You're that upset?"

"Did I not make that clear? Waited here an hour. Killed my schedule."

"I was…"

"I don't want to know her hair color, her name, or her cup size. I just want to finish this beer and go home."

"You could have had a beer at the apartment," Sid said. "You didn't have to agree to meet me."

Damon tapped his finger on the bar.

"What can I get ya?" The bartender asked Sid.

Sid craned his neck to see around the mountainous New Yorker's neck. Not surprisingly, the dark alcohol offerings hadn't improved since the last time he had slummed it here.

"Ya want me to come back, Nancy?"

"Shot and a beer."

"What kind?"

"Surprise me."

"Ain't that kind of place."

"Jameson and a Bud."

Sid put his money down. The bartender poured out the whisky into a greasy shot glass and slid it over. Half of it puddled on the faux mahogany. Sid downed it and eagerly drank a quarter of his beer.

Damon cleared his throat.

"She had..." Sid said.

"I didn't ask..."

"Sure looks like you want to ask something."

"Do you even know her name?"

"I do," Sid lied.

"Good. No further questions."

Sid watched sports highlights on the television above the bar. He took another swallow of the metallic, watered down beer.

"Would it help if I apologized?" Sid asked.

"You've been doing that all day," Damon said.

"I'm persistent when I'm sincere."

"Judging by the parade of dumpster fires raging behind your bedroom door the last couple of years, it would seem you're persistent even when you're full of shit."

"Ouch."

"Sorry."

"Don't be. I deserve it."

"True," Damon said. "How many drinks am I going to need to listen to the smut I know is coming."

"Depends. How many have you had?"

"Just this one," Damon said. He shook his can, which was still full enough that suds escaped the wide-mouthed opening.

"Probably more than that."

"What color was her hair?"

"Red."

"Hang on," Damon said, gulping his beer. "Order me the Sid special."

Sid signaled for the barkeep. The guy held up the whisky bottle and another beer. Sid held up two fingers. By the time the shot glasses slammed back down on the bar, the pair had fresh beers on their coasters.

"Why do red heads give you so much trouble?"

"Well, to be fair, I really haven't found any other type that doesn't give me trouble."

"I'm married to a ginge," the bartender said.

"Crazy, right?" Sid asked.

"The worst."

"Jesus fucking Christ," a silver-haired woman at the end of the bar said. "Do I need to flash my tits to get service in this shithole?"

"Shut the fack up, Aunt Francis," the bartender said. "I've got your peach schnapps right here."

The guy grabbed his crotch and sauntered away.

"Imagine their Thanksgiving dinner," Sid said. "A couple of family members probably end up on the menu."

"Can you get on with the story before I catch something from this place?" Damon asked.

"Good idea," Sid said. "She had a strut."

"Excuse me?"

"She had a strut."

"In that case, I forgive you."

"Really?"

"No."

"Fine, but believe it or not, I showed up early last night. I grabbed a hold of that front door, fully prepared to hang out with my best friend Damon. However, a woman wearing fuck-me heels marched right over to me."

"You got a good look at the strut then."

"I did," Sid said.

119

"What else did you get a good look at?"

"You know, you play the straight-laced Boy Scout well, but it's nice to find out you're just a heathen like the rest of us sometimes."

"I'm going home," Damon said.

He knocked over his beer as he got up from his stool.

"Jesus, sit down," Sid said. "She was an angry, leggy red head wearing a skintight green dress. That about do it for you?"

Damon nodded after giving the bartender an apologetic smirk.

"Suck my dick, fuck-face," Sid said. "That's the first thing she said to me."

"Keeper."

"My thoughts exactly."

"So you took her home based on these sweet musings?"

"Not right away," Sid said. "I had to drop some money for a few drinks to calm her down. And then quite a few more dollars after taking the subway to Manhattan."

"You going to make rent in a couple weeks?"

"Provided she doesn't show up again, yes. I'm surprised you didn't hear us come in. She had half her clothes off before I opened the front door."

"Fell asleep at the computer lab."

"Second time this week, huh?"

"Means I wasn't late for class two days this week, so it balances out."

"Plus, you cut down on laundry. One outfit for two days. Might catch on."

"I'm a trendsetter," Damon said. "So, are you going to see her again?"

Sid shrugged.

"Probably not in my best interest," he said. "I have two women I'm trying to get to love me; I don't need a third one for fun."

"New mission statement?"

"Testing it out. Hold the fort, I need to piss."

Sid quickly walked past Aunt Francis, who was exploring the bottom of her drink with her dirty pinky finger. He reached for the bathroom doorknob, but found an empty hole. The toilet was positioned close enough, so Sid was able to hold the door closed with one hand and pry his sore dick out of his pants with the other.

He found the bar had gained a patron after washing his hands in cold water and wiping them on brown toilet paper. A woman dressed in black was engaging Damon in conversation and swinging her bare white legs.

"Atta boy," Sid said.

The woman leaned back in her seat and laughed so hard she had to catch the edge of the bar to prevent falling. Sid cringed. He had heard that laugh reverberate in his head all day while trying to push aside his sex-over. He foolishly ignored the impulse to flee—he didn't feel right about abandoning Damon two nights in a row—and walked calmly over to reclaim his stool. He avoided eye contact while the woman motioned to the bartender.

"Do you know who that is?" Sid asked.

"You don't have to whisper," Damon said. "She knows who she is too."

"Can we go?"

"That would be rude."

"This won't end well."

"And, oddly, I don't care."

"Take it out on me in some other way."

"Sup, slut?" The bartender said.

Sid and Damon watched as she spread her fingers wide and slapped them across the guy's second chin.

"Nice shot," Sid said. "Now can we go?"

"Yep," Damon said.

"Gawd, I facking love you when you talk to your skanky princess like that," she said. "I'm going to be extra bad for you tonight."

The bartender ducked his head under the wine glasses hanging above his head and shoved his tongue into her ear.

"I love you too, Lacey," the guy said.

Sid's eyes widened as recognition fully set in.

"Lacey," he said. "That's it."

Aunt Francis cackled into her newspaper, momentarily distracting the bartender from Sid and Damon's retreat. A slight pause was all the surprisingly athletic barkeep needed to roll over the bar, crushing the friends' abandoned beer cans, and position his girth in front of the front door.

A fist collided with Sid's face soon after.

The next day, Sid wrote his answers to the test down slowly.

He reread each question carefully, stopping frequently to take a breath and look around the auditorium-style classroom. Constance furrowed eyebrows admonished him, making him darken the Scan Tron bubbles forcefully, angrily.

He put his head back down and started to record his answers faster. The test was easy, so he finished everything swiftly. Sid felt his black eye and bruised cheek gingerly. He didn't remember much after the first punch, but he had a vague recollection of Damon weakly pushing the lumpy bartender out of the way so they could escape. Sid woke up that morning with a slimy bag of peas on his face.

Constance poked him with her pen and smiled worriedly. He didn't appreciate her trying to feel sorry for him. He was certain it was an act designed to make herself feel better. Her boyfriend Derek had indeed been pissed off about the flowers. Constance promised Derek that he could talk to Sid in exchange for not beating the shit out of him. She had told Sid right before the test started. Derek waited outside. That was the only reason Sid had been taking his time. He already had one black eye, so he was in no hurry to get a pair.

He eyed the exit behind him.

"Don't do it, you scared fuck," Sid told himself. "You can't tell Constance you would do anything for her love and then start making concessions."

He stood up, picking up his blue test booklet and putting on his jacket. Without making eye contact with her, he hopped over Constance's outstretched legs and walked down the aisle. The urge to use the back door was strong, but he ignored it.

"Are there no average-sized asshole's left in the world?" Sid muttered.

Predictably dressed in a black t-shirt tucked into black jeans, Derek appeared double Sid's height even while leaning against the building's brick exterior.

"I thought ya'd be taller," Derek said.

"You're as advertised," Sid said.

"Heard ya had a rough night."

"Yup."

"I don't plan on hitting ya."

"Good to know."

"Well, Constance told me not to. Ya know why I'm here, right?"

"I suppose."

"I'm her boyfriend. I buy her flowers."

"Okay."

"Do you understand?"

"I do."

"That's it?"

"You're right, I'm wrong," Sid said. "Is there anything else?"

Derek's composure loosened.

"Nah, we're straight."

"Good, take it easy."

"See ya," Derek said.

Sid walked down the sidewalk, knowing the man behind him judged every step he took. He was thankful his landlord's mother wasn't outside sweeping cat shit off the driveway when he got to his apartment. He held his breath and avoided the six cats that were congregating on the linoleum stairs leading up to his apartment. He picked up a plate of food his landlord had lazily wrapped in tinfoil and left on the top step. Sid smelled weed and heard "Hotel California" playing below him. They only listened to The Eagles while conducting feline funeral services.

Sid dropped his pants before doing anything else. He wearily examined his laundry pile and pulled out a pair of extra-large sweat pants from the top. Its matching gray hoodie conveniently hung in the bathroom. It was far from a cool day, but Sid needed the comfort of familiar clothing.

He settled on the futon in the living room and channel surfed for hours without landing on anything. His finger pushed the remote's buttons robotically. He watched a PBS documentary one moment and a reality show the next. The sun had set by the time Damon returned home. Sid braced himself for unwanted human contact.

"You look like a retired track star from the 1980s," Damon said.

"My day was good, how was yours?" Sid asked.

"I think I can brighten yours up a little."

"Please. Don't."

Damon stood in front of the television with his hands behind his back.

"What's your favorite animal?"

125

"Not now…"

"Come on."

"Lion."

"Well, this isn't a lion, but it should help."

Damon placed a stuffed elephant holding cloth flowers on the coffee table.

"This is from you?" Sid asked.

"Nope."

"Is it from my mother?"

"Nope."

"Is it from your mother?"

"There's a note," Damon said.

"I might have led with that," Sid said. "Can I have it?"

"What?"

"The note."

"Oh, here."

Sid held the envelope wrapped with a red ribbon in his hands for a moment. He got up and walked into the kitchen. He pulled out the envelope opener and sliced through the heavy paper. His eyebrows rose as he read.

"I hope you are smiling, because I am (despite the scene my boyfriend caused)," Sid read. "Here's a little something for you to snuggle with if you get lonely without me. Love, Lacey."

"Holy shit!" Damon said.

"Told you she was a keeper," Sid said. "We have to move."

"Tell me something I didn't know before."

Sid heard his phone chirp on the couch.

"Bunch of us going out. No Derek," Constance texted. "Buy me a drink so we can go back to normal."

Sid glanced at Damon, who was holding the bear and making kissy faces at him.

"I'm going out," Sid said.

Sid didn't know many people at the bar, so he quietly got trashed alone. One Constance's former friends-with-benefits bankrolled everyone, so Sid made sure the guy regretted it. It wasn't top shelf, but it was aged enough to set the guy back some. For the eighth time that night, Sid wandered into the kitchen instead of the bathroom. Several short, dark-skinned short-order cooks shouted in multiple languages for him to get the hell out. He calmly obliged and walked out the front door.

He stared at the cemetery across the street.

"Only a Queens city planner would think this was a good idea," Sid slurred to himself.

He tapped his pockets for a pack of cigarettes, but came up empty. Lacey had probably smoked his last one. He was pretty sure she had lit up during one of their fuck sessions.

He knew he was officially past his drinking limit because he started weeping. He kneeled down on the concrete and put his head up against the chain link fence.

"You okay?" Someone asked behind him.

"I need to find a way home," Sid said. "But I fucking hate the Q74!"

The stranger left in a hurry.

He started hitting the fence. Shaking it uncontrollably, he let out a guttural scream.

"Sid, you have to stop, you're going to get arrested."

Constance's sister had her hand on his arm.

"I can't fucking go back in there!" Sid said. "Everyone is fucking laughing at me! Everyone thinks I'm a joke!"

"No one in there knows you well enough to make fun of you," she said. "Stop being a dick. Let me help you inside."

"No! I'm going to stand here, right here. I can breathe here. I can't breathe in there. Someone is hording all the air in there. The air out here is all mine. Do you get that?"

More people filed out of the bar. Sid crawled out of the streetlamp's spotlight to hide.

"I'm just trying to help," Constance's sister said. "Constance is crying inside and she's worried about you."

"Yeah, she's real worried seeing how it's you out here and not her," Sid shouted.

Sid cried harder, but stood up. The dirty sidewalk had soiled his jeans pretty well. He put both hands to his face and breathed in the remnant weathered steel smell. He could feel sobs reverberating in his chest.

"I can't do this anymore," Sid said. "I can't do this anymore."

Constance's sister tried to wrap her arm around him, but he shrugged it off quickly. He controlled his sobs momentarily, and ran.

Sid woke up hours later to a cup being pushed up against his lips. He felt water in his mouth. He swallowed reflexively. The cup disappeared, replaced by Constance's glare.

"Why are you here?" He asked.

"If I wasn't here, you wouldn't be here either. It took me a while to find you."

Sid recalled fluorescent lights and blurry, multi-covered awnings on his run down Francis Lewis Boulevard. He made it all the way to Cunningham Park before slowing to a walk. He had taken the long way around campus, up Utopia Parkway past the baseball field. He had leaned against the black iron bars of the university's perimeter fence. He tried texting Jocelyn, but was too intoxicated to manage anything other than an incoherent run of auto-correct nonsense.

"Why do you keep doing this to yourself?" Constance asked.

She had tears at the corners of her eyes. He knew she wasn't faking this time.

"Because I'm in love with you," Sid said.

"This ain't love, buddy," she said. "You have to stop before you hurt yourself or someone else. Can't you just be my friend?"

Sid felt sleep tugging at his consciousness. He licked his lips and coughed. He tried to return Constance's tired smile.

"No," he said.

FRONT PAGE

The man in the baseball cap nursed his lukewarm coffee.

His leather jacket squeaked as he put the mug back down on the diner's counter. He coughed loudly into his fist, causing the matronly waitress to jump.

"Sorry," he said.

"S'okay," she said. "Lost in my thoughts. You want a warm up?"

He shook his head, glancing toward the kitchen door.

"Hold your horses, it'll be out in a minute," she said. "We were pretty much closed."

The man shrugged. The wad of bills in his front pocket had done all the negotiations necessary to keep the dive open.

"Where you coming from?" She asked.

"West."

"Brings you out here?"

"Heard upstate New York is God's country."

"And?"

"You could make a case."

"Tough audience."

He smirked and hoped the woman would recognize it as a signal to stop talking. She did.

"I'll go check on your meal, sir," she hissed as she pushed angrily through the swinging door.

The man showed no emotion as he picked up his white mug and brought it to his lips. He eyed the ancient brown stains lining the inside of the porcelain mug. Grimacing, he set it back down and examined his silverware.

Dirty. Unwashed. Impure.

His mother's voice cut through his ears. He had been all of those things to her. He spent hours in the bathroom scrubbing his skin, never enough to satisfy her. His parents hadn't taken photographs, but if they had, those images would have revealed an anxious pink mouse clothed in homely rags.

"Fried chicken dinner," the waitress said, returning with a beige plate. "Condiments are right in front of your face."

The man nodded, unfurling his napkin and placing it on his lap. His stomach growled, eagerly awaiting its first meal in some time.

"Hmm," he said, freezing.

The food's colors—a burnt orange brush stroke of chicken, dull green smudges of peas, and a muddled lump of white potatoes—transported him to the last night he saw his parents alive.

His mother dropped a TV dinner on the tray table. He was too engrossed in "Leave it to Beaver" to notice.

"Ungrateful bastard," she said. "A thank you wouldn't kill you."

His father's snoring halted as the tin container housing his meal landed in front of him.

"Kid, eat," he grunted.

The boy complied meekly, but he kept his eyes glued to the screen. Beaver was in quite the fix. He had lied to his parents about buying a model car with his birthday money.

The boy had known Beaver would be fine in the end, he always was. Ward and June were tough, but fair.

"You know what you'd get if you pulled that, right?" His father asked.

"Yes sir."

The boy eyed his father's jet black belt. He was less afraid of that than the pistol lodged somewhere in the man's waistline. He had swallowed more peas and watched Beaver's parents take mercy on their son, a lesson always to be learned honestly and free of violence.

In the present, the man remained motionless. He felt a familiar memory indent the back of his neck. He didn't remember the chill of his father's gun so much as its dense urgency.

One of his father's associates interrupted dessert. His mother cursed and waved her cigarette at him. A raised backhand was all it took to silence her.

The boy ignored the brief meeting. His ice cream dissolved into lumpy paste. He scooped it up eagerly, careful not to touch the stickiness invading his spoon.

"Kid, take this to the safe," his father said, holding out a fan of bills.

Shocked, the boy quickly abandoned his treat and rushed to his father's side. The old man actually needed him for once, wanted him to perform some duty outside his normal chores.

"Move it."

They stood in front of the family safe, the boy expecting his father to reach over him to turn the dial.

"Left, twenty-six, right, fifteen, left eight."

Random numbers. The boy was sure his father didn't remember birthdays or anniversaries.

The door opened easily. That's when the father pushed the gun against his son's neck.

"Get in."

The boy sat in the darkness, taking shallow breaths, not yet aware of the oxygen tank his father kept hidden for just such an occasion. He imagined himself being carried somewhere, a place his parents could rid themselves of his impurity for good. He longed to twist the hot water handle to its full power and run his hands underneath the boiling stream of water. He intertwined his fingers viciously, unable to hear the bullets spray through the apartment's

133

thin walls. The temperature in his newly fashioned prison cell escalated after the fire started. The flames consumed the building and the heat nearly microwaved the safe's inhabitant. Firefighters would ax their way through his steel walls, hearing his weak tapping long after the ashes surrounding him had cooled. They pulled him out, naked but unfeeling, newly christened something "other."

"That's what you ordered, ain't it?" "

Huh?" He asked, startled.

"Your food. You still hungry?"

"Oh, yes."

"Well eat it and git going. We're tired."

"I will. I'm late for an appointment."

"You know, a thank you wouldn't kill you."

"It really would."

She snatched his plate away before he could stab his fork into the fried meat. "I'm wrapping this to go," she said, rushing back to the kitchen.

The man wiped his hands on his napkin and walked out.

Hours later, transformed into a killer again, he knelt over a body.

He could feel flesh cooling. He had befriended this townie at a strip joint a couple of days ago. He was impressed with the cad's stamina tonight, making it through Jay Leno's monologue before passing out on the couch. He had picked up his target's bloated arm, which hung off the couch onto the tan and sea green shag carpeting, and snapped it at the elbow. His hands had gripped around the guy's nose and mouth before he could shout. There hadn't been much of a fight.

Now, the killer heard a gasp behind him. He grimaced and pulled a silenced Kel-Tec .380 out of his inside jacket pocket. He turned quickly, aimed, and shot the battered wife through her right eye. She slumped against the brown recliner before landing on the carpet. Stepping around her, he walked briskly down the hallway.

He paused before a door covered in Superman stickers. The killer opened the door slowly.

Empty. The bed was made.

He turned the light on and listened for movement or heavy breathing. Nothing.

The killer checked his watch. He had plenty of time for a thorough search. He crouched down, finding only "Star Wars" action figures and coloring books under the bed. He rolled open the closet door, but only found a row of clothing interrupted by empty hangers.

Sleepover? He thought. Hiding in the basement? Escaped to a neighbor?

He spent the next half hour investigating the premises but discovered no sign of the couple's son. On his second pass through the home he noticed a "Challenge" motivational poster depicting a snowy mountain range had come loose from the pushpins holding it to the wall. He could see a small safe behind it. He felt the impulse to tear the rest down so he could rap on the steel door, but he knew the man he had just snuffed out wouldn't have been as smart as his father. He used the pistol to scratch at his two-day stubble and then retreated back to the living room.

He struggled to prop the man's dead weight up on the couch. The guy's sleeveless undershirt ripped underneath yellowed pit stains. He swore, but managed to arrange his victim in a satisfactory position. He placed his gun in the man's hand, looked away, and pulled the trigger. A bullet ripped through the guy's temple and lodged itself in the ceiling.

The killer lit a Rocky Patel Royale Toro cigar and admired the scene. He pitied the local police officers because they wouldn't be able to enjoy this tableau he had created for his own amusement. Budget cuts nationwide had blessedly allowed him to fashion clean-cut cases detectives could add to their bogus crime statistics. Here lay just another deadbeat father who had gone too far after binging and whoring at a house of ill repute. He inhaled deeply and then tossed the stogie toward the man's crotch. It wouldn't take long for the carpet to ignite.

He went unnoticed by the pedestrians strolling downtown. There was no blood on his tailored suit or leather jacket, his hands were clean enough to perform surgery on those he had just slaughtered, and the car he had stolen the night before waited in the parking garage. Any evidence of his presence had been wiped away and sent to the hell that surely awaited him.

He paid his ticket and placidly drove away.

"I told you I'd get you to the top of the Empire State Building," Sid said. "Took a little longer than expected."

"One promise kept in all the years I've known you," Jocelyn said. "Not exactly a win."

Her blond hair unraveled in the wind. Sid reached to push strands away from her face.

"Get away from me," she said.

Jocelyn quickly transformed her mane into a manageable ponytail. Sid couldn't help looking through the opening in her jacket to ogle the red dress underneath. She caught him. He coughed, adjusted his tie, and turned his attention to the glass and concrete city.

"I don't care how you treat me," Jocelyn said. "But you better start calling your mother or I'm going to kick your ass."

"It's been crazy at the paper. She knows that."

"Still covering high school track meets or have they bumped you up to college intramural softball?"

"I guess you're right," Sid said. "It's not as hard hitting as filling prescriptions all night for unruly senior citizens and drug addicts."

Jocelyn hugged herself inside her jacket without replying. Her bare legs shivered.

"Sorry," he said.

"No, you're not," she said. "We can't do..."

"This again?"

"No, this forever."

"You really want to have this conversation now?" Sid asked.

"Considering it's the last one I plan on having with you, yes."

"I don't owe you any explanations."

"How about an apology?"

"For what exactly?"

"Sleeping with me and then immediately banging a slut you met a few days later," Jocelyn said. "And then you fall in love with…"

"Don't," Sid said.

"I have swallowed so much of your bullshit over the years."

"Are you sure you weren't swallowing something else from that Kurt Cobain wannabe you dated for a couple years?"

"You are such an asshole."

"I've never pretended to be anything else."

"Yes, you have. That's what makes you such a sinister dog."

"I didn't ask you to tag along," Sid said. "You chose to remain friends."

"So our friendship meant nothing to you? You would have just walked away?"

"I like fighters, Jocelyn. You never fought hard enough for it."

"You resent me because I didn't worship at the altar of Sid Sanford like all your New York sluts? While you were being a closed off douche who couldn't communicate honestly outside of a notebook?"

"Didn't seem to mind when you were the one I was screwing," Sid said.

"You're really just going to be a dick about this, aren't you?"

"Yes."

"I have done nothing but…"

"But what? Love me? Take care of me? I need an equal, not a cheerleader or a mother."

"You need easy," Jocelyn said. "And that's something that I refuse to be."

"That's not what I hear from people back home," Sid said.

Jocelyn slapped him hard. Sid took a step back, but made no move to rub the growing pink stain across his cheek.

"You can take your wit and shove it up your ass," Jocelyn said.

"Is there anything else?" Sid asked.

"What, are you just going to leave me here?"

"Yep."

"I don't know how to get back to our hotel!"

"I don't care," Sid said. "Money well spent on my part. Ditto for the dinner reservation I had to put my credit card down for."

"I didn't ask for it."

"No woman ever asks, she just expects," he said.

"We're both angry, we just..."

"Need to walk away? I couldn't agree more."

Sid didn't turn around as he made his way toward the elevator.

Jocelyn numbly watched the elevator doors close. She slumped against the fence and pressed her face to the cold aluminum. The city beneath her appeared foreign, suspect.

She mentally kicked herself for thinking that Sid was capable of having a mature, adult conversation. His world had become as ordered and linear as New York's gridded streets and subways lines, but what was left of the small-town boy still controlled his emotions, which were as fiery and unpredictable as the first day she had met him.

Tears formed and Jocelyn did nothing to prevent them from falling. She watched one slide off her chin, clutch the fence's gray metal momentarily, and then get swept away by a violent gust.

Steps away, the killer finished his cigarette.

He flicked the butt off the tower to the ire of the security guard nearby. The killer shrugged and coughed into his fist. He adjusted his wool hat and blew hot air into his gloved hand.

The blonde cried, but he was the only one who noticed. Her legs, propped up by tall, nude heels, hid her visible pain effectively. He was admittedly attracted to her voluptuousness, but her curves didn't distract him from mentally carving circles into her flesh.

He smirked, thinking about how easy it was to find victims in his hometown. He had just exited the Broadway–Lafayette subway stop when he spotted a young man screaming at a woman in a red dress. He had stopped at the McDonald's on the corner and bought a coffee. The couple had continued to fight as if they were in their own bedroom. He had stepped back onto the sidewalk, flung his coffee cup lid toward the trash can, and observed the fallout. The young man had grabbed the blonde's hand impatiently and led her down the subway station's steps. The killer had followed.

At the peak of the city, he now followed her again as she swayed distraughtly through the tourist crowd. He allowed a group of inebriated naval officers to fill the space between them. He pulled his cap over his eyebrows and pushed his way into the elevator. The uniformed men were too busy high-fiving and taking pictures to notice the blonde in the corner wiping away her smudged makeup.

The doors closed and the elevator descended.

Hours later, Jocelyn stumbled into her hotel room.

She opened her cell phone and used its light to find the bathroom door. She crawled to the toilet. It didn't take her long to vomit everything in her stomach. She hugged the bowl tightly. She wiped her mouth and struggled to stand. Her reapplied makeup was now in full retreat down both sides of her face. She belched.

Jocelyn said yes to every free drink she was offered at the bar. Each man had a sob story to unload; she had wanted to ignore her own. The vodka sodas that had accumulated rapidly had gone to her head immediately. There had been nothing in her system besides heartache and stomach acid.

Jocelyn moved out of the bathroom and threw herself down on the king-size bed. Sid had spared no expense. He always went overboard, but she couldn't process the lavish hotel she currently inhabited, which included high ceilings, a flat screen television that filled an entire wall, and a bed populated with bright, fluffy designer pillows. The flowers and bottle of wine he had presented her with at the train station rested forlornly on the nightstand. The extravagant scene spun out of control in front of her drunken eyes.

141

"Fuck," Jocelyn said.

She scrambled to retrieve her cell phone from the bathroom. She sent Sid a text message taking all blame for their fight. She told him she loved him and that he should get his ass over to this hotel room so they could have multiple rounds of makeup sex. Jocelyn knew that he wouldn't be able to resist that. He'd come back, even if it was just for her body. She'd find the words to make it right in the meantime. She swallowed two Advil and drank half a bottle of water. She stood in front of the mirror and grimaced. Jocelyn unzipped the back of her dress and let it drop to the beige carpet. She grabbed a towel from the closest and headed into the bathroom to shower and get sober.

The killer waited patiently at the end of the hall.

He had walked by her room moments ago and heard water running. He envisioned her washing herself thoroughly, her soapy hands traveling over every curve. Even in the dim light of the bar downstairs, he could tell her skin was well taken care of. Her red dress made her a beacon to city-dwellers numbed by a black and gray pallet. Men had abandoned less radiant females sporting drab colors in order to approach a crimson ray of sexuality. She had exuded sassiness despite uttering only a handful of polite rejections.

He knew, judging by her sloppy exit, that it would take more than a long shower to bring her back to dry land. He picked up the tool bag next to him and strapped it around his waist. He had dispatched the maintenance worker smoking in back of the hotel easily. No one would find him until morning, and by that time he would be halfway across the country. Or out of it.

He buttoned the top three buttons of the dead man's shirt. He looked like any other hotel employee making a call to an irate guest. He bent over and calmly picked up a used steak knife from a room service tray that had been left outside, feeling the serrated bladed against his forearm as he pushed his weapon up his sleeve. He stood by her door, listening to the stream of water.

Jocelyn turned the shower knobs tightly, stopping the water flow instantly.

She stood still for a moment, reveling in her wet nakedness. Sid loved the smell of her body wash. She couldn't have scrubbed more into her skin if she tried. He always said wonderful things about her body, but she never accepted them as facts. She certainly didn't hate her figure, but she didn't love it like he did. For the moment, she was content that she was clean and that his hands would be the next ones to touch her.

Jocelyn drip-dried while standing in front of the mirror. She fantasized about all the places he was going to kiss and touch. She felt beautiful for a moment, thinking he'd be here soon so they could put everything back in order. She'd go back to loving him as an absent friend and his ambition would continue to outpace reality. But at least Sid would be in her life. At least he wouldn't have abandoned her. She really did love him and no one wanted him to find the man he was supposed to be more than her. Jocelyn would play the game his way tonight and see where they were in the morning.

She walked out of the bathroom holding a white robe. She picked up her phone. No response yet. Jocelyn wasn't worried; Sid liked to make his entrances dramatically. She knew he was already on his way. The flowers were already here, so that was one less thing he had to stop for. She pictured him running through red walk signs, swiping his MetroCard at the closest subway turnstile, and hoping the next train waited expectantly with its doors open. She pulled a black pair of underwear up her pale legs and curled into the robe. Jocelyn sprayed herself with a small amount of perfume and plopped down in the uncomfortable artistic chair in the corner of the room.

On cue, she heard a knock at the door.

"Who is it?" Jocelyn asked.

"Maintenance," a voice said.

"You called us."

"Sorry, there must be some mistake."

"I got the order right in my hand."

A smile broke out on her face. Sid's fake New York accent was horrific.

"I think you have the wrong room," Jocelyn said.

She heard a heavy sigh on the other side of the door. He wouldn't be able to keep this going for long.

"Listen, sweetheart, it's late," he said. "You want to let me in or what?"

Jocelyn opened the door ready to jump him. She recoiled and tightened the sash on her robe when she saw an unfamiliar face.

"Oh!" Jocelyn said.

The man elbowed past her and headed for the heater.

"Hey, I really didn't call maintenance. It must be some mistake."

She shut the door and nervously crossed her arms in front of her. The killer turned around.

"I know you didn't, love," he said. "And it's no mistake."

In Forest Hills, Sid's headboard threatened to bulldoze its way into the next room. Sid's anger intensified with each thrust.

"Um, Sid?" The woman underneath him asked. He felt her tighten up, a good indication she was uncomfortable.

"Sorry," he said.

"It's hot, just take it down a notch," she said. "Fucking give it to me."

Sid had already forgotten her name. After storming away from Jocelyn, Sid had stopped into Dirty Pierre's, a hamburger joint near the Forest Hills Long Island Rail Road station, and drained a regular Budweiser. Burly bikers in ill-fitting leather vests had postured around him, giving him more reason to down four more beers in short order. He had slurred his words asking for the check and stumbled down Continental Avenue toward the two-bedroom apartment he shared with Damon on 112th Street.

He had decided he wasn't done. He poured himself into Irish Cottage, but left abruptly after discovering the average age of the crowd to be somewhere in the mid-sixties. He had found the young, sloppy crowd at 5 Burro Cafe much more to his liking. Sid had procured a seat at the cramped bar and waited for his next conquest to approach him, all while hammering Dos Equis. He had struck out more than once owing to his impaired speech and alcohol-infused body odor. He didn't remember how he had sparked a conversation with a woman wearing a black flowered dress, but it wasn't long before she was spreading her legs open suggestively. He had crudely rubbed his hand up her thigh and loudly announced they should leave and fuck. She had eagerly agreed and was now on her back moaning louder than anyone Sid had ever heard.

"Come on, daddy," she said. "Fuck your bad girl to next week."

Sid winced as she scratched her nails into his back.

The two of them had charged through his front door, startling Damon who had fallen asleep in the recliner. Sid had pointed out his bedroom and gone to take a piss. He remembered he had reached behind him to turn off the light because he could see his reflection in the mirror. His shirt was torn, his five o'clock shadow had darkened into a beard, and his eyes were stained red. His urine smelled like a distillery. He had made the switch to bourbon just before talking to whomever he had brought home. Sid had walked out of the bathroom and directly into his confused roommate. Damon's narrow eyes had said, "really?" Sid had shrugged and slammed his bedroom door behind him. Her dress had been hung on the back of his desk chair. She had been waiting, naked, in his bed.

"Stuff me, daddy," she said.

"Stuff your little girl with that hard..."

Sid laughed.

"What the fuck?" She asked.

"Sorry, I laugh when I'm about to cum," he said.

Sid felt himself start to go limp as she ground into him harder, faster. The alcohol, horrid pillow talk, and her obvious daddy issues had switch off the power. He willed himself to stay erect as she convulsed and screamed. "You better cum for your little girl, daddy," she said.

"Called it" Sid mumbled.

"What?"

"I said 'I did.'"

Sid didn't move for a moment.

"Oh. Well, good."

She pushed him off her and headed for her dress. She wriggled into it and tiptoed into her black heels.

"I'm sure your underwear is around here somewhere," Sid said.

"I don't wear any," she said.

"Ah. Are you really just leaving?"

"Uh, yeah. You didn't want to fucking cuddle, did you?"

"No, but..."

"I met you in a bar and fucked you an hour later. You could be a serial killer or something."

Sid cocked his head in disbelief.

"Get home safe, I guess," he said.

"Thanks!"

Sid pulled his condom off with the underwear he had discarded on the floor and found a pair of shorts. The next moment, the front door slammed.

"That was easy," he said out loud.

Sid rummaged through his nightstand drawer, trying to find a pack of cigarettes. He came up empty and settled back onto the bed, which was soaked with leftover regret. He thought about checking his phone to see if Jocelyn had called or texted him, but he wasn't completely sure where he had left it. He said a quick prayer to the drunk people gods that it hadn't been hijacked at the bar or dropped in a sewer drain.

Damon knocked on his door.

"Please tell me this can wait until morning," Sid said.

"Your phone was on the floor by the door..."

"Oh, thank god! You can just throw it on my desk."

"Sid..."

"I know, buddy, we can talk about this shit storm tomorrow. I didn't mean to wake you."

"It's not that..."

"Then, don't take this the wrong way, but for fuck sake, get out. I need to wallow in peace."

"Jocelyn kept calling your phone..."

"Tell me you didn't answer."

"It wouldn't stop, one after another. Twenty-five times at least..."

"Well, she's pretty pissed."

"Sid..."

"What the fuck Damon?"

Sid finally sat up. His roommate held his phone out. Damon's face looked ashen.

"What the fuck?" Sid asked again.

"A detective..."

"Give me the fucking phone!"

"Hello?" Sid asked, grabbing the phone out of Damon's shaking hand.

"Is this Sid Sanford?" A deep male voice asked.

"Yes."

Sid listened as the solemn detective told him Jocelyn had been murdered.

Sid's mother held his hand as they walked to Jocelyn's gravesite. Rain pelted his dark suit, and he pushed his wet hair back above his forehead. Kenneth walked next to them, sniffling and shuffling his feet, and Tom and Patrick were close behind. She was theirs as much as his, so he felt comforted having them nearby.

A priest spoke. The rain intensified as Bible verses drifted further and further into empty clichés. Gail's grip on his arm strengthened each time she swallowed a sob. Patrick put his large hand on his shoulder and squeezed.

His attention drifted to the green felt covering the dirt surrounding the six-foot hole in the ground reserved for his best friend. The priest's words jumbled with the instructions for a card game. He remembered laughter, and suddenly his mind was somewhere else entirely.

Sid drummed his fingers on the green felt draped across the kitchen table. He couldn't decide if he wanted to be an asshole and raise the pot.

Everyone else had made bets. He took his time, slowly lifting his two cards one at a time. He calculated his chip stack, and then checked his cards again.

"You seriously need to make a decision," Patrick said. "Even Momma made a call faster than this and she barely knows how to play."

Sid watched his mother smack his younger brother across the back of the head. She had gotten up to brown the meat she was going to use in her famous nachos recipe.

"I know how to play, young man," Gail said. "And don't talk to your brother like that."

"Yeah, that's my job," Jocelyn said, readjusting her Red Sox hat.

"I'll call," Sid said, pushing the correct amount of chips into the center of the table.

"So, I have to burn one card and then turn three up?" Kenneth asked.

"That's right," Damon said.

Kenneth dealt "the flop" proudly. Gail examined her cards before checking and sending the next decision to Patrick. He thought for a moment and threw some chips in.

"I really don't get the appeal of this game," Tom said, showing frustration. He concentrated on the three cards on the table. "I might as well stay in. It's all based on luck anyway."

He threw his chips in and shrugged at Kristen. Having never played poker before, she was enjoying a glass of wine while determining whether it was for her or not. Sid knew Damon and Patrick were thankful for that. They were the real card players at the table and hated wasting time teaching the game, especially if it turned out that the newbie at the table won without having any idea what the hell he or she was doing.

Damon talked to himself a bit before throwing his cards back toward Kenneth. Sid could see his friend calculating the odds in his head even after his fold. Patrick folded as well.

Sid's cell phone squawked on the counter. He stood to go get it, but Patrick beat him there.

"Aw, Sid, it's Constance," he said, his several octaves higher than normal. "How long have you been apart from your love bug that she already misses you and needs to hear your voice?"

Patrick tossed the phone toward Sid, but Jocelyn snatched it out of the air.

"Sorry, she can wait," she said. "You're home with us, so you are all ours for the night."

Sid didn't know whether Jocelyn was jealous or not, but the fact that it could be a possibility made him a little happy.

"Play your cards," Sid said.

"Everyone dig in!" Gail said, putting the platter of nachos, cheese, and meat at one end of the table.

"Whew, listening to the kids bicker has made me hungry," Kenneth said, piling a big helping onto his plate.

Sid kept eye contact with Jocelyn, who just smiled seductively.

"I'm going all in!" She finally said.

Players threw in their cards before Sid could react.

"What are the odds that I have a better hand than you?" Jocelyn asked.

"Shut up, Damon," Sid said.

His friend's mouth had been open, ready to blurt his calculations. Damon closed it and chuckled.

"I'll call," Sid said, pushing his chip stack next to Jocelyn's.

"You are going down, Sanford," she said.

"Do I have to come over there and make you pipe down?"

"What would you do? Honestly, I'm your female best friend and we're surrounded by your family. You going to weep on my shoulder again? Because that's always fun."

"You suck."

"Well said. Remember, you'd be lost without me."

"Pft, I think I'd get by. I have Damon."

"Shut up, Damon," Jocelyn said.

He nodded, wisely withholding his comment.

"I'd miss you, I suppose, if you weren't around," Sid said, nonchalantly pulling a stray string off the felt.

"You'd be unable to function. You can barely function with me. Momma Sanford would have to quit her job to support you and your blubbering."

Sid laughed out loud, knowing that she was right, and she was indeed jealous of Constance.

"Why don't you get me another beer?" Tom asked Patrick, hitting him lightly on the shoulder.

"Because you have three open," Patrick said.

"Yeah, and you promised to drive home," Kristen said, swiftly collecting the three quarter-filled beers and bringing them to the counter. "I'd have been even more upset if I wasn't so used to it."

Jocelyn coughed into her fist dramatically and pointed her eyes toward the middle of table.

"So, I burn another card and only turn over one, right?" Kenneth asked, momentarily distracted by a fork full of nachos landing on his shirt.

Everyone said yes at the same time.

"Hey, wait, flip over your cards," Patrick said.

"What does that mean?" Gail asked, trying her best to get the stain out of her husband's shirt.

"Since they are the only two in the hand and they are both all in, they can flip their cards over while the rest of the cards are dealt," Damon said.

"You first," Jocelyn said.

"Nope."

"Let's do it together."

"I like the sound of that," Sid said.

"Pig," she said.

"Okay, on three, you flip," Tom said, his tolerance for the game waning.

"Deal!" The two shouted.

"One...

two...

three..."

153

Three weeks after the funeral, no one knew what to say.

Sid found the requisite flowers and sweet notes of condolences and encouragement on his desk after returning to work that morning. A few of his closer work friends had stopped by his cubicle, but had stood there awkwardly, wordlessly. Sid made a few cracks about the Giants losing the night before, which elicited a few tortured chuckles. He let most of them off the hook by lying about having to head to the printer or bathroom. Anyone who dropped by later that afternoon did so armed with an exit strategy.

The newsroom crackled with activity, but Sid couldn't feel it from his rear cube. It had been like this since his first day. There's nothing quite as useless at a newspaper than a cub sports reporter. It took him most of the day to sort through his emails and delete all of his inane voicemails. People didn't know what to say on an answering machine either. He leaned back in his chair toward the end of the day, hoping the last hour would provide him with an assignment to get him back in the world. However, he had a feeling his workflow was going to be a lot lighter, and the stories a lot puffier, during the next couple of weeks. Sid watched the rain outside the window behind him, wondering if this was any better than sitting in a dark room imagining his best friend's pink casket.

Sid swiveled his chair around so he could face his desk. He brought his coffee mug to his lips and drank deeply. He had been living off caffeine and peanut butter crackers because his stomach couldn't handle much else. All he did was replay how he had walked away from her. It would have been so simple to turn around. Eye contact or one more remark could have made the difference. Instead, he had been planning his night of debauchery as soon as the elevator doors closed. His life had ended before sitting down at the Mexican restaurant and he hadn't even known it. Sid longed for a cigarette, but he told Damon he quit this morning. He was determined to last a day to prove he could take something seriously.

Sid felt the newsroom's energy ramp up a few notches. Clumps of people stood around television screens. He envisioned managing editors constantly clicking their browser's "refresh" icon. He watched several reporters sprint back to their ringing phones.

Betsy Burke, the paper's short, deeply tanned gossip columnist, sat on the desk in the cube across from Sid's and slumped her shoulders.

"I've been elected to tell you," Burke said.

"I'm guessing it's not a porn star being hauled away after an overdose?"

"Boy, I wish."

"They get him?" Sid asked.

"They don't know who they arrested yet."

"But they think it could be him?"

Burke nodded weakly.

"Okay," Sid said. "Let's go watch."

In a Brooklyn precinct, the killer stared blankly at the gray wall in front of him.

He folded his shackled hands calmly on the wooden table. He had spent the better part of an hour trying to angle the handcuffs the right way so he could ingest the cold coffee they had begrudgingly brought him earlier. He hadn't been allowed to shower, so his gray hair and beard were matted and unkempt. His underwear rode up his ass, and his orange-colored prison jumpsuit made his underarms sweat profusely. Otherwise, he felt content. He wasn't feeling anything for the first time in weeks.

He had cut into dozens of faces, but hers was the only one that returned.

He coughed hard. He hadn't slept indoors since leaving the blonde's hotel room. Some nights, it had been the streets; others, a shelter. He had walked into the sections of Harlem he remembered as violent, hoping to be dispatched quickly, but he had only found clean streets and entitled inhabitants. He had woken up in Brooklyn during a rainstorm. He had wished he could just slip into the Hudson with his hand over his mouth, but felt the need to seek atonement. The prescient captain almost didn't believe him. He had sat next to the man's desk as he made a few calls confirming details. He had been roughly thrown into a cell moments later.

His feelings didn't fade completely. The memory of pulling his bloody hand out of her tangled blond hair caused his stomach ulcer to pulsate. Her sweet-tasting skin and desperate moans filtered into his thoughts every so often, forcing him to catch his breath.

"Sid, he's coming," she had said. "He loves me. He's on his way. Sid's coming."

He smiled knowing Sid hadn't loved her enough. He had left her alone. The killer had felt jealous, which only enraged him further. He had cured the blonde's pain, but caused his own. His life would end in blood and darkness, just like it had started.

156

The heavy door of the holding cell opened.

A woman dropped a yellow notebook on the table. She tapped a pen up against the pad before letting it fall. Her ID badge read, "Travis."

"Pretty cut and dry, huh?" She asked, straddling the chair opposite her prisoner. "Anything you want to add before we send you along your way to fry?"

"You mean haunt the prison system? Your state doesn't have..."

"I'm sure some of the states you've done work in have the death penalty," Travis said. "Just start writing some details for us if you could."

He twirled the pen in his right hand. Travis lifted her eyebrows. He opened his mouth to say something, but closed it abruptly. He licked his lips, which unnerved the glorified administrative assistant sitting across from him.

"I'll outline all of my crimes for you," he said. "You'll get all the names, birthdays, anniversaries, addresses, waists sizes, sexual transmitted diseases, and moral depravities you'll need to fill as many syringes with poison as you'd like."

He watched Travis swallow hard.

"But?" She asked.

"I have someone who I'd like to visit me before leaving this facility."

"Not going to happen. This place is locked down. I'm your only contact."

"Funny how this country can suspend its laws when it wants. You'll do this for me because you want to move up the ranks Officer..."

"Detective."

"Impressive. I imagine your name mentioned a few times in the paper as the one to catch me wouldn't hurt your career."

Travis stood. Her lips remained defiantly straight, but her eyes signaled she was contemplating his deal. He was betting her time here hadn't been pleasant.

"Fine," she said. "I'm going to monitor it and if I hear anything I don't like, I'm going to personally pistol whip you."

"Whatever you think is best," he said.

She turned to leave.

"Detective?" He asked.

"Yes?"

He flicked his tongue over his lips again. Travis recoiled.

"Have a nice day."

In Manhattan, Sid felt nothing.

His cell phone vibrated uncontrollably on his desk, and the work phone he had long ago silenced lit up every few minutes. He would diligently return calls later, but he wasn't sure which emotional response was appropriate for the situation. Was he supposed to cry, smile, or scream?

Sid wiggled his mouse and his screensaver snapped off. Every news website now had the story. Sid scrolled over details about the man's life, his appearance, and his alleged motives. It all sounded good enough to sell ad space, but no report contained enough truth to be considered news. Experts sounded off, each one had a different explanation for this monster. All Sid knew for sure was that his nightmare had a name.

Harrison.

"Do you have a minute?" A voice reeking of unfiltered Camels and a lifetime of shouting at disobedient journos.

Sid nodded at his editor Roger Ray, who was leaning up against his cube.

"There's nothing about your situation that don't smell like shit, kid," Ray said. "I thought you should know the publisher just got a call from the bastard offering us an exclusive interview."

"America at her best, isn't it Mr. Ray?" Sid said. "Some poor bastard is going to get stuck with that gig thinking it'll make his career."

Ray coughed. The short, wiry newsman put his head down and kicked at the edge of Sid's desk.

"Get the fuck out," Sid said.

"I didn't say anything."

"No, but you're going to."

"It's not an assignment..."

"You're damn right it's not."

"It's your decision."

"Easy. No."

"Let me just say..."

"No, allow me to tell you the myriad reasons why this isn't going to happen. One, he raped and cut up my best friend. Two, I would in no way be objective because he murdered the love of my life. Three, go fuck yourself."

Ray let Sid rant. This scene was an old one and typically ended with reporters getting fired.

"I wouldn't ask you..."

"So don't."

"Like I said, there's nothing about this that don't smell like shit. I told the publisher to fuck off, but..."

"But what? He wants to sell a few more papers before he fires us all because the sales department can't find their own pussies long enough to land some advertisers?"

"The prick asked for you by name, son."

Twelve hours later, Sid sat down in front of thick glass.

He waited uncomfortably for Jocelyn's killer to arrive. Detective Travis sat on a stool next to him.

"You okay?" She asked.

"Should be pretty obvious, right?"

"Sorry."

"Not your fault."

"He'll be out in a minute."

Sid opened his reporter's notebook and threw it down angrily. It was instinct more than anything. He had vowed not to record a single word of this conversation. No one would benefit from whatever was said here.

Sid watched a door open on the other side of the glass. A pile of muscles wrapped in a police uniform hustled a manacled Harrison into the room. Sid tried to hide his surprise at his age when the man's leathery, unshaven face finally appeared across from him. The two reached for the black phones simultaneously.

"Not what you were expecting? Hello, Mr. Sanford."

Sid remained silent.

"You know, it's rude not to respond to a greeting," Harrison said.

"I don't give a damn."

"Much like you didn't give a damn for your blond friend."

"Why am I here?"

"How disciplined you are. Not taking the bait. You must be a fine reporter. So few of those left I'm afraid."

"You could have written a thesis on journalism from your cell. What do you want with me?"

"We'll get to that."

"I think now would be a good time," Travis said grabbing the phone from Sid.

Harrison didn't say anything until Sid took it back and motioned for him to continue.

"Would it surprise you that I have a story for you?"

"I'm not Truman Capote. I don't give a shit."

"Well, you must. You're sitting here."

"Not for long. I'm doing this so my publisher..."

"Gets off your back? We both know I could fling my feces at you like an ape and the color of it would make headlines above the fold."

161

"That's a good idea, let's go with that."

"My father was murdered when I was a boy."

"Is that supposed to mean something to me?"

"Your friend was…"

"What?"

"She…ahem…was beautiful."

"And?"

"I haven't felt anything in a long time. I felt something during…"

"The time it took you to cut her face off?"

"It's why I turned myself in."

"Serial killers have a decent retirement plan?"

"I wanted to know why you fought with her that night."

The sweat on Sid's back chilled.

"That's not up for discussion," he said.

"Did you love her?"

"Yes."

"Funny way of showing it, leaving her alone with New York's monsters. I shudder to think what would have happened to her if someone other than myself followed her."

"Fuck you."

"There's that temper again."

Travis made a move to end the interview, but Sid waved her off.

"You must not have loved anyone," Sid said.

"Only my mother. She died."

"Pardon me if I don't offer condolences."

"I vowed revenge on those that murdered my mother and father. I was saved in order to cancel the hurt and suffering of others."

"So you became Batman with a license to kill?"

"I much prefer the Dexter analogy. I killed people who deserved to die."

"In what universe is it possible that you thought Jocelyn deserved to die?"

"The one in which you broke her heart, Mr. Sanford."

"That would hurt a lot more if it wasn't coming from you. Had to take a little piece for yourself, huh? Not exactly kosher for a man who claims he's in the business of simply settling debts."

"You're right. That wasn't part of my mission. I apologize."

"I think I can speak for her family when I say you can take that apology and shove it up your ass."

"Do you think they need my help as well?"

The killer flicked his tongue out of the corner of his mouth. Sid glanced at Detective Travis, who insensitively slashed the air in front of her throat with her index finger. Sid nodded and hung up the phone. Harrison moved as if he was going to knock on the window, but was violently held back by the guard standing behind him. The commotion dragged Sid's eyes back to the man in chains motioning to the phone. Sid nodded at the guard and picked it up.

"Thank you for speaking with me, Mr. Sanford. It's always polite to leave a conversation on a positive note."

"Again, I don't give a damn."

"Enjoy your life. I certainly hope you know the way home."

PART TWO

Daniel Ford

FOB

Sid stepped into the desert surrounding the cramped forward operating base just as the sun surged over the distant mountaintop. He scratched his patchy, three-day-old beard. He inhaled deeply, the already warming air singeing his raw nostrils. The sand didn't crunch so much as slither away from the hot breath of desert wind.

He eyed the line of beige Humvees parked by sandbags piled waist-high. He strode over and climbed into the makeshift garage. Sid propped himself against the tall front tire of the closest vehicle. He stretched out his legs and crossed them, feeling the full weight of his still stiff boots on his ankle. He shifted his position just enough so he could awkwardly pull his notebook out of his back pocket. He stuck his pen behind his ear, sure the words that had been eluding him since the troubled descent through the mountain range would come before the afternoon sun boiled his internal organs. For now, Sid propped his head up against the hard, black rubber and tried to remember how he'd landed in this dusty valley.

Roger Ray's slamming door muffled the newsroom's buzz. So many conversations from which Sid had long ago felt disengaged continued in shouted whispers once Ray started howling in earnest.

"I'd be weakening my damn city desk in the middle of a mayoral election," the aging editor said. "On top of everything else, I'd be giving you, a little pissant, a promotion ahead of, frankly, a long line of more goddamn qualified reporters."

"Someone else can cover the Bronx borough president's philandering and embezzling," Sid said over Ray's incoherent grunting and molar grinding.

"Plus, I'd catch all kinds of holy fucking hell from the board..." Ray said. "Wait, what did you say?"

Sid patiently reached into his messenger bag and retrieved a blue folder that looked like an overstuffed jelly donut. He tossed it on Ray's desk and watched as he casually flipped it open. Ray rolled his eyes as he read the top sheet, but that hadn't stopped him from skimming the tax forms, illicit photos, and tawdry phone records bulging underneath.

"Sources?" Ray grunted.

"Waiting for a phone call from whomever you decide to assign the story."

Ray held Sid's gaze, hoping his young reporter would wear his self-satisfied grin just long enough for him to slap it off his face with a hefty Sunday newspaper.

"This doesn't change anything," Ray said, slamming his hand on the pile of front-page fodder. "I could just as easily order you to write this."

"I have a draft someone can polish if that helps," Sid said. "You don't even have to use my name. Actually, I'd prefer you didn't, I don't want to get banned from Harlem and its chicken and waffles."

"Listen, son..."

"I believe you owe me one," Sid said, his jaw stiffening.

Ray waited a beat before nodding weakly. He got up, sat down on the edge of his desk, and put a hand on Sid's shoulder.

"A desert warzone isn't an appropriate place to overcome personal demons," Ray said.

"That's not what this is about," Sid said. "I've just moved beyond writing about tainted politicians and transit complaints."

"You better hope so. You survive our security training and I'll think about it. That's the best I can do."

Sid took the deal and flew out to the Middle East three weeks later.

A sharp pain in his shin brought Sid back into the present. He cursed his luck, certain he'd been stung by a scorpion. However, the pain dulled quickly, but not before another kick to his boots forced him into a crouch. His eyes burned red as he opened them fully. He put his hand against the sun and made out a camouflaged hulk wielding a wrench standing in front of him.

"Scared the fucking piss out of me," the soldier spat.

A tobacco-infused glob of spit now sparkled in the sand between the two men like a brushstroke of oil puddled in a Queens parking garage.

169

"Sorry," Sid muttered.

"You're not supposed to be here. I could have put a bullet in your fucking head. Probably give me a damn medal considering you're a reporter."

"I get it," Sid said. He brushed the sand off his pants as he stood. "I'm leaving."

"Don't be a pussy," the soldier said, extending his hand. "I'm Mason."

"Sid."

"Oh, I know your name. We get daily briefings on how to talk to you."

"Is that why no one has done it yet?"

"Fuck, easy killer," Mason said. "PR is not our strong suit."

"Funny considering that's part of your mission."

"Enjoying the heat while you're preaching at me?" Mason asked, slapping a wrench into his palm.

"Had to get out of the AC," Sid said. "Too small a space and too many closed windows."

"You want to open those bulletproof windows for the enemy, be my guest, but make damn sure me and my friends are all in the latrine when you do. And try not to make too much of a mess for us to sop up later."

"Yeah, well, never been a fan of central air. Messes with my sinuses."

"You been in a sand storm yet?"

"No."

"Might change a few of your preconceived notions about our little air-conditioned shit box."

"I didn't mean to offend anyone."

"Well, could you not offend anyone a few paces to your right. I've got to park my ass under the vehicle you've been using as a hammock."

"Right," Sid said. "Yeah."

He moved out of the way and heard Mason slide under the front bumper. Sid rubbed the back of his head.

"Something wrong?" Mason asked from beneath the vehicle.

"Can I help you with anything?" Sid asked.

"You know much about auto repair?"

"Not really, no."

"Then I'm good."

"Well, how about I just keep you company then?"

"Like to work alone."

"This is the longest conversation I've had in days," Sid said. "Give me something."

"I didn't shoot you, what more do you want?"

"Son of a bitch," Sid mumbled.

The clangs and grunts stopped. Mason wagged his boots back and forth.

"Coffee," he said.

"Do you want anything—?"

"Black."

"You got it."

Sid headed back to the FOB. He found another hulking figure in fatigues leaning up against the counter, waiting for the coffee pot to finish gurgling.

"Lieutenant Núñez," Sid said, keeping a respectful distance.

The officer growled something through his dark mustache that sounded like, "motherfucker." Sid contemplated reaching for his notebook and peppering Núñez with questions before the man had even poured his morning coffee, but thought better of it.

"Given any thought to my, um, repeated requests?" Sid asked instead.

The officer's severe, but sleepy, brown eyes motioned toward the coffee pot.

"Got it," Sid said, grabbing two Styrofoam cups from the stack.

"Thirsty?" Núñez asked.

"Getting one for your mechanic."

"Are you referring to Sergeant Ward?"

"This would be a lot easier if you didn't break my balls every time we had a conversation."

"But it wouldn't be as fun," Núñez said. He filled his mug and turned to walk out the door. "Don't bother my men without my permission or I won't talk to you at all."

The officer knocked into Sid's shoulder as he left.

"Sir?" Sid called out.

"You're not ready to leave the wire," Núñez said, pausing in the hallway. "Some of my men aren't ready. Request denied."

"Thanks for your time, Lieutenant…" Sid muttered.

He knew picking fights with commanding officers wouldn't get him anywhere, but he hadn't been raised to keep his mouth shut (or respect authority for that matter). However, Núñez had just confirmed Sid's suspicions about the base's preparedness. What Sid couldn't piece together is whether that mattered in this country or not.

Sid returned to the Humvee and found Mason's boots pointing out the opposite end. Sid pounded his fist up against the bumper.

"Jesus H. Fuck!" Mason yelled out.

Sid heard tools thump against the sand.

"Delivery," he said. "I'm allowed to give you coffee, right?"

"Hell yes," Mason said.

After climbing out from the car's underbelly, Mason grabbed the cup and downed the coffee in one swallow. He tossed the cup back at Sid who caught it while preventing his own coffee from sloshing out.

"That must have felt good," Sid said.

"Nothing feels good here. Needed a jolt."

"Happy to help. Does this mean I can ask you a few questions?"

"Hope you're not looking to fill column inches with me," Mason said. "I'm a pretty boring story."

"Yeah, I figured that out pretty quick," Sid said. "But I'll take what I can get right now."

"What are you writing about?"

"Don't know yet."

"See, you want us to engage, yet you have no fucking clue what your plan is."

"I'm here, that is the plan. A lot of people have questions about what's going on over here."

"Tell you what, a lot of guys over here have a question or two on what's happening."

"Maybe we can learn from each other."

"When can I say I'm off the record?"

"Whenever you want."

"And you can't use what I say?"

"That's how it works."

"Then I'm off the record."

"Fine by me."

Sid leaned up against the door, burning his elbow on the hot metal handle. He pulled it away, more pissed about the squad's antipathy than by the glowing red blotch on his arm. Mason wiped his forehead with an oily rag and then got back to work.

Mason clamped his thick hand down on Sid's shaking leg.

"Really? Still with the fucking nerves?" Mason asked. "The mission is over, fucking relax."

Sid adjusted his helmet and nodded.

"Lieutenant, Bob Woodward here is still pissing himself," Mason yelled above the roar of the Humvee. "Any suggestions on how he can calm his delicate senses?"

In the passenger seat, Núñez turned his head slightly and growled something that sounded like "fucker."

"Well, I wouldn't do that to your mother," Mason said. "Just sit tight, we're almost home."

Sid had hounded Núñez for nearly a month to authorize his first patrol. The squad now fancied itself a crack staff, impervious to the anxiety and turmoil endemic to other platoons across the desert. Outside of the occasional *pop-pop-pop* in the distance, however, none of the men crowded in the FOB had been in a firefight or had to halt a long caravan in order to investigate and detonate an IED. How would they react in the face of something more treacherous than cleaning out latrines or standing at attention for Reveille?

It turned out that Sid's hands refused to stop shaking the moment he parked his ass in the Humvee. They shook all through the meeting with the hard-eyed, sun-scorched elders of the nearby village. Núñez listened patiently to the staccato Arabic flying off the leader's rotten teeth like acid. He absorbed the overwhelmed translator's stuttering and backtracking while nodding and trying to maintain eye contact with his counterpart. Sid watched as younger, more anxious men prowled along the back of the tent, shouting and pointing every so often. They had been stripped of their arms before entering, but their danger still permeated the cramped space.

"What are they pissed about?" Sid had asked Mason.

"No water. Limited food. Enemy offering it all at discount prices," Mason had said. "It means we're fucked. Now shut up and keep close to me or anyone else with a gun."

Sid's concentration was broken by Mason leaping out of his seat and climbing on top of a snoozing soldier in the rear of the Humvee.

"I said move your hand, Bee," Mason shouted, slapping his subordinate on the cheeks. "Wake the fuck up, this ain't fucking nap time."

"Sorry, Sergeant," Bee said.

"Up all night playing 'Call of Duty' again?" Mason asked.

"Nuh-uh, Sergeant," Bee said.

"Christ, just what Uncle Fucking Sam had in mind when he signed your sorry ass up," Mason said, retaking his seat. "Has more goddamn kills online than he does in real life. Put that in your article, Sanford."

"Why do they call you Bee?" Sid said, ignoring Mason's jabs to his bicep. "Hard to figure considering your nameplate reads Zdunczyk."

Bee glanced at Mason, who nodded his approval.

"Real name's Frank," Bee said.

"I'm aware," Sid said. "Why Bee?"

"Aw, tell him," Mason said, throwing in another scoop of tobacco below his bottom lip.

"My first day in the mess I wanted to make conversation," Bee said. "So I started talking about this article I read about bee hives being like a communist society. Then I started in on the similarities and differences between hives and military bases. Kind of explains it all."

"You're so fucking lucky 'Queen Bee' didn't stick," Mason said. "Whole squad was fucking howling so bad Núñez smoked the shit out of us. So worth it."

176

Sid reached the pocket of his flak jacket and pulled out his recorder. He waited for Mason's affirmative before turning it on.

"Why'd you sign up?" Sid asked.

"No one needs to hear that fucking story," Bee said, wearily looking at the slim device. "No offense, sir."

"This is your penance for conking out," Mason said. "Be thankful it's not fucking licking my boot whenever the fuck I tell you to."

"Yes, Sergeant," Bee said. "It all started when my father was murdered…"

"Murdered?" Sid asked, the quake in his hands now having less to do with nerves or the Humvee's shimmy.

"Yeah, couple of townies broke into our house looking for shit to pawn to buy meth or some shit," Bee said. "My dad went to investigate and they dropped him with one to the head before he could raise his pistol."

"Holy shit," Mason muttered, spitting tobacco juice into a cup. "Where were you?"

"Getting high in the woods with a bunch of fucks from school," Bee said. "We all passed out there. Cops ended up coming out to find me. We all scattered thinking they were going to bust us for weed. Ran home and right into the yellow caution tape like a goddamn marathon runner."

"They catch the bastards?" Sid asked. "I mean…did they apprehend the suspects?"

"Nah, this is the best part," Bee said. "They stepped over my dad and started ransacking the rest of the house. Probably looking for money or trying to cover their tracks. Make it look like there were more than two shit kickers. My mother had holed up in her closet and waited for them with a Remington 870 shotgun she bought on layaway from Walmart. Blew both motherfuckers away when they opened the door."

"My kind of woman," Mason said. "Shit, sorry about your Pops, but this is making my shit hard."

"So how'd that lead to you enlisting?" Sid asked, once again ignoring Mason.

"Despite being relieved, my mother was pissed as hell I wasn't home when it all went down," Bee said. "She told me that since she took care of my father's killers, the least I could do was go shoot some towelheads in the desert. Sorry, is that too crass for a newspaper?"

"I'll clean it up, don't worry," Sid said. "You regret it?"

"Only regret I have is not killing those pricks myself. And not having a chance to kill anyone here. Fucking glad-handing political bullshit isn't my thing."

Sid nodded and pressed the pause button.

"Thank you for trusting me with your story," he said, extending his hand. "I'm sorry to hear about your father."

"Oh, I don't trust you for shit," Bee said, shaking Sid's hand. "But Mason does and I report to him. I'm just as liable to shoot you next time you come near me."

"Understood," Sid said. "Just make sure Mason's behind me when you do it. Takes care of both our problems."

"You fucks know I'm still fucking here, right?" Mason asked.

The Humvee's breaks squealed like a downtown bus as the hulking transport swerved abruptly. Sid tumbled into

Mason's lap just as the cup of dip flew out of the Sergeant's hands and onto Sid's chest.

Núñez shouted something unintelligible from the front of the vehicle.

"Shit," Mason said. "Look alive, fellas."

Sid's nerves actually calmed as the camouflaged men around him checked their weapons and reached for additional ammo. He heard a distant whistling that aggressively faded into dense thuds nearby.

"Fuck, we're in the shit now, boys," Mason said.

The Humvee shook after a mortar landed a few yards away, spraying sand and debris across the small windows. The whistle intensified as the enemy's aim improved. Núñez's orders came out in a stream of profanity and pseudo-Spanish as he exited the front seat. Sid could feel the ripple of steel and sand as the Humvee continued to race across the desert. Mason shoved a finger into Sid's chest.

"What did I fucking tell you before?" He asked.

"Stay close," Sid said. "Preferably next to someone with a weapon."

"Good," Mason said. "Don't fucking forget it."

And then the world went white.

A nurse nudged Sid's shoulder with a Styrofoam cup. He jerked, disturbing the sloppy cocoon he'd set up in Mason's hospital room. His *Washington Post* slid off his chest as he sat straight.

"No cream, no sugar, right?" She asked.

"Thanks," Sid said. "Any change?"

"He just made a pass at me," the nurse said.

Sid closed the laptop that had all but burned a hole in his crotch and peered over the edge of Mason's bed. The soldier's eyes were thin red slits, but a smirk lightened his bruised face.

"You finally going to tell me what happened to your girl?" Mason asked.

"You want me to get the nurse's number for you first?" Sid asked, moving to the chair closest to Mason's bed.

"Nah, she's an officer," Mason grunted. "She fucking scares me."

"Plus, I'm sure she's had to clean out your bedpan. Hard to overcome that first impression."

"You going to answer the fucking question or not?"

"Murdered," Sid said.

"Are you fucking shitting me?" Mason asked.

"No."

"Jesus, I wouldn't have made Bee spill his story."

"You didn't know," Sid said, trying hard not to think about coming to under Bee's torso-less corpse. "How are you feeling?"

"Not great, but I'm not going to complain about being alive. Heard you saved my ass."

"What was left of you," Sid said, trying not to glance at the sheet pulled up to Mason's chest.

"Thought I felt a few pounds lighter."

Mason squeezed his morphine drip. His reddened cheeks paled as the medicine took effect.

"Sorry, man," Sid said. "Not the ideal scenario, but it beats the alternative."

"I'll take it, I guess. Spinal injuries?"

"Not as far as they know."

"Cool. Assuming we got the motherfuckers."

"Núñez and crew took care of them."

"Why'd you stick around?"

"You told me to stay close. Just following orders."

Mason went silent for a few minutes. Sid retrieved his coffee cup and gulped the contents.

"So your girl gets waxed and you chase a war to get over it?" Mason asked.

"Not exactly," Sid said, sitting back down. "But sort of."

"You're just as fucked as the rest of us," Mason said, wiggling his remaining foot. "Is this what you're gonna write about?"

"Fuck, man, you lose a couple limbs and start asking more questions than I do.

"Must have fucking rubbed off. Well?"

"I'll send you a copy. Read for yourself."

"Shit," Mason said. "You worked me without me even knowing."

"Like you don't like the attention."

"Send it to my folks?"

"Sure. I'll grab your address from Núñez."

181

"On speaking terms now?"

"Intelligible grunting. Progress."

"He owes you now. We all do."

"You guys don't owe me shit. Just get your ass out of that bed. I'll buy you a beer stateside."

"Already headed back?"

Sid nodded.

"My broke ass will be right behind you. Don't worry, I'll get polished up for when you publish my heroics. Fuck, wait, speaking of polishing..."

Mason uncoiled his arm from the IV and groped himself under his hospital gown.

"Woo!" He shouted. "Thank fucking god."

"Now do you want me to get her number?" Sid asked.

"Can you at least leave the room for a few minutes?" Mason said. "We need to get reacquainted."

Sid mockingly saluted.

"Now that you're up, I'm going to get evicted," he said pointing a thumb toward his hovel. "Got to clean up and head out of Dodge."

"I'd say it's been a pleasure, but, fuck off," Mason said.

Sid filled the duffel bag he'd been living out of for the past month and shrugged it on his shoulders. He gave Mason a head nod as he walked toward the door.

"Hey, civvy," Mason called out.

"What's up?" Sid asked, half turning.

"Don't torture yourself for too long, okay?" Mason said. "I know it's a more complicated world out there than the one I live in, but bad shit happens for no fucking reason. But you're still stuck here, and so am I."

Sid remained silent. He pounded his fist up against the wall and weakly nodded.

"You hearin' what I'm saying, asshole?" Mason asked.

"Yeah," Sid croaked. "There are just times I think about that…beautiful life I could have had. And it kills me to know even if it had happened, I wouldn't have deserved it."

"You don't need me to explain why I think that's fucking bullshit," Mason said. "But it's your fucking life, you can be a miserable prick if you want."

"I know, I know," Sid said. "But you deserved an honest answer. That's the only one I have."

"They catch the guy?"

"They did."

"Then fuck 'em. Take time to get your crap straight, but don't be a pussy for the rest of your life."

"Can I quote you on that?" Sid asked.

"Fuck yeah, man," Mason said. "You should make that the goddamn headline. And send that nurse back in, I changed my mind."

"She's likely to kick your ass."

"I dig that. I'm defenseless too. She can be rough as hell and I can't stop her. Hell yeah!"

"Yeah, you're fine," Sid said. "Take care, Sergeant."

"Good luck, Sanford," Mason said.

Sid leaned against the airline counter.

"How can I help you, sir?" The male attendant asked.

"You called my name. You tell me."

"Sanford?"

"That's me."

"Seems as if you're being upgraded to first class."

"Really?"

"That's what the system says. Let me print you out a new boarding pass."

"Did my paper set this up?" Sid asked, finding it highly unlikely Roger Ray wasted his limited budget to give him a luxurious ride home.

"Um, I can check," the attendant said. "Does it matter?"

"I'm curious."

"Give me a few."

Sid drummed his fingers on the counter until the guy gave him the stink eye. He raised his hands in mock surrender and waited while the attendant clickety-clacked his fingers across the keyboard.

"Says a guy named Núñez put the request in," he finally said.

"Lieutenant Núñez?" Sid asked.

"Doesn't say. Just says Núñez. It's a personal Visa if that makes any difference. Not a military credit card."

Sid mumbled something that sounded like, "motherfucker." He took his new boarding pass and headed back to the waiting area. He propped his feet up on his duffel bag and rearranged his headphones. He leaned his head back and watched as the area filled with passengers A young Army solider wearing worn fatigues strutted in, carrying his boarding pass like the Holy Grail. Bruises and cuts marred the guy's sunburned face and his travel bag dropped dust and sand all over the linoleum floor. Sid felt his anxiety kick up a notch as the soldier sat on the edge of his seat and shook his leg uncontrollably.

"Son of a bitch," Sid said.

He pulled his boarding pass out of his jacket pocket and walked over.

"What's your name, Private?" Sid asked.

"Ryan Stevenson, sir."

"You don't have to sir me. Where are you seated?"

"The ass of the plane," Ryan said. "Fuckin' Army."

"That's what I thought. Here," Sid said holding out his ticket. "We're going to switch."

"Holy shit! You sure?"

"All yours. Just don't get too sauced. I'm a reporter. I'll have to write about it. Enjoy."

Sid retreated back to his seat without further comment. Ryan pulled out his phone and started texting everyone he knew. Sid felt the lump of his cell in his pocket and considered all the people he should be contacting to let them know he was safe and headed home. Instead, he opened up his laptop and started writing.

FOUND

In a Kansas elementary school, Damon held a shaking hand.

"You aren't going to leave me are you, son?" The old man asked.

"No, sir," Damon said.

"Good."

"Are you comfortable? Is there anything that I can get you?"

"I'm fine. Just stay where you are."

"Okay."

"What's your name?"

"Damon."

"Damon what?"

"Lord."

The old man laughed.

"Now that's ironic. Here you are with me during my last minute on Earth with your last name being Lord. I like that."

"You're going to be around longer than that. You have plenty of time left."

"See! The Lord Jesus Christ was an optimist. He always saw the upside. Are you religious?"

"Not especially."

"Well, nothing wrong with that. You have the freedom of choice and all that. I won't hold it against you."

"Thank you, sir."

"I might get testy if you keep calling me sir though. My name is Finn."

"It's been a pleasure meeting you, Finn."

"Would you mind pulling that blanket up a bit? It's cold in here something awful."

The room was quite warm. Damon's shirt clung to his back and his glasses were having trouble staying on his sweaty nose.

"Of course I don't mind," Damon said. "Is that better?"

Finn nodded.

"I don't blame the twister. I've worked on this land all my life. I've done some good. Have they found many others today?"

Damon shook his head.

"I figured," Finn said. "They will find more."

"You think so?"

"I really do."

187

"What makes you so sure?"

"I don't know. I just believe it."

"So much for you not being religious."

"I'm just an optimist."

Finn laughed weakly.

"I like you, Damon."

"I like you too, Finn."

"I'm going to sleep for a bit."

"Okay."

"You'll be here when I wake up?

"Yes."

"Thank you, son."

Finn died soon after from massive internal bleeding.

Later, Damon pushed open a back door.

He leaned up against the concrete wall and let the prairie breeze cool some of the perspiration off his face. He smelled cigarette smoke.

"Do you need one, man?" A voice asked.

Damon opened his eyes. A male paramedic held out a cigarette.

"I don't smoke," Damon said.

"Come find me when you're ready. You'll want one."

The man left, and Damon studied the devastation. He wasn't as shocked by it anymore. The human destruction had given his mind something else to focus on. The damage was total, an entire town leveled. The houses that had been spared were quickly consumed by relief workers, equipment, and the injured or dying. Those citizens lucky enough to have escaped injury were either put to work or evacuated to nearby towns.

After Jocelyn's death, Damon had abruptly left New York. Damon couldn't watch his friend unravel. He had moved to New Hampshire, became a volunteer fire fighter, and worked as an EMT. He had even married the most beautiful woman in the county (or so his father-in-law told him). They had quickly kindled something out of nothing and their courtship was still pretty young when Damon put a ring on her finger and married her in a small ceremony by a lake. They had a brief honeymoon in the mountains.

She hadn't been pleased when he told her he was leaving.

"Not everything is your fight," she said.

"People need help. I can be of use."

"I'm sure they have plenty of help. You can be of use here."

"I'm going."

"I need you."

"I won't be gone long," Damon said.

"You'll be gone long enough. You don't even want to work out our problems do you? It's easier to help others than to help your marriage. You're not the man I married. Maybe you never were."

"I don't believe that."

"I didn't ask you to believe it. That's what I feel."

"I'll come back to you."

"I don't even know if I want you to," she said.

Now, Damon pressed his thumb between his middle and ring finger. His wedding band felt cool despite the heat. He thought about her lips. He almost smiled.

His cell phone rang.

"Yes," Damon said. "I can do that. I am on my way. No problem."

He pushed the thoughts out of his head and started walking.

Much later that night, Damon collapsed on a cot.

He shut his eyes tightly and folded his hands together on his broad chest. He kicked off his boots.

"Relax your toes," he whispered.

Damon peeled his glasses off his face and dropped them into a small duffel bag that carried all of his possessions. There wasn't much; a notebook, a toothbrush, a comb, matches, his Swiss Army knife, extra clothes, a picture of his wife, and, now, his glasses.

"Relax your legs," he whispered. "Relax your arms."

Relief workers had taken over two classrooms. There were never more than two or three people resting at one time, so the group shared a handful of cots. More often than not, volunteers would just rough it on the floor, unwilling to let their bodies get too comfortable before going back to their grim tasks. Damon tried to learn all their names, but it was impossible. All he knew was that they were good folks trying to set things right the best they could.

"Relax your fingers. Relax your mind."

The heat didn't go away. A small breeze moved the hot air from one place to another. Damon's nostrils picked up a smell that stung. He couldn't shut his mind down. The rest of his body caught its restlessness. He stared at the ceiling. He yawned uncontrollably and thought about smoking and where the hell Sid was hiding.

Since the moment Damon helped him get on his feet, all Sid had done was fall back down. He never took Damon's advice or accepted his help willingly. Sid couldn't take criticism without it turning it into a personal attack. He'd spin everything to go on the offensive. Damon was constantly being driven crazy for want of a close friend.

He shook his head and wiped his face with his hands. He sat up quickly, reached into his bag, retrieved his glasses, and put them back on his face. He walked over to the desk at the end of the classroom and opened the laptop they were all sharing. There was a weak wireless Internet connection that usually lasted long enough for him to check his email. He never had many.

Damon quickly deleted all of the spam emails. He only had one more message in his inbox.

"I hope all is well," Patrick wrote. "I wouldn't have emailed you if it weren't important. I know you are probably in some other country helping people a hell of a lot worse off than my family and I. If that's the case, don't read any further. Keep up the good work. If you happen to be free or in need of someone to help, I could surely use it. Sid hasn't come home since Harrison's capture and refuses to speak to anyone. My mother has threatened to do whatever it takes to get him to respond. My father has stonewalled any attempt at us getting through to Sid. He believes Sid will come around on his own and that none of us would be any help to him even if we could talk to him. While I believe there is merit in that argument, I'm not sure if there will be anything to come back to if he ever decides he wants his family's help. It would embarrass me to beg, but I'll do it. If I don't hear from you, I'll keep trying until you slap a restraining order on me. Your friend needs you, Damon. He doesn't deserve you, but he needs you. I think you might need him too. Look forward to hearing from you."

Damon again pressed his thumb in between his middle and ring finger. He felt his wedding band and twisted it up to his knuckle. He pushed it back down and made a fist. He moved the cursor over the reply button. His eyes came to rest on his meager belongings under the cot. He took his glasses off and rubbed his eyes quickly. He put them back on and started typing.

"On my way," Damon wrote.

In New York City, Sid sat down to write.

"The father had lost everything," he wrote. "He had seen the woman he woke up to every morning and the young girl he pinned all his future hopes and dreams on brutally taken away from him at the hands of violent thieves. He had seen every second of their ends. There were no goodbyes because their mouths were taped shut. His life could have ended there. No one would have blamed him. He could have crawled into the first bottle offered to him. No one would have thought less of him. He could have been found fast asleep forever, gripping a bottle of pills. It would have been understood. However, this man whose whole life had been dedicated to helping others—first as a member of the Peace Corps in Africa and Southeast Asia, and then as a world class surgeon—kept waking up to the dawn his loved ones could no longer see and offered hope to others."

The noise of fingers hitting a keyboard stopped. It had thundered and echoed in the small, sparse apartment. The fingers balled themselves into a fist and then stretched out again. One hand reached out and fingered the rim of the sweating glass next to the laptop. The ice cubes had long since melted into the alcohol, taking away its bite. The hand moved away. The glow of the laptop's screen amplified against the pure white walls.

Sid flexed each finger one at a time. Each one had its own crack, its own groan of pain, exhaustion, and pleasure. He coughed hard. His eyes moved to the discarded cigar in the ashtray. His mind was foggy. He yawned. He grabbed the glass and brought it over to the small sink. He dumped everything out. He quickly rinsed it and put it in the drying rack. He opened the refrigerator and grabbed the last bottle of water. He stood with the fridge door open and chugged. The plastic bottle cringed and crackled as he sucked the last drops out of it. It noisily returned to its original shape as Sid pulled it away from his mouth. He breathed a sigh of satisfaction and tossed the bottle into the garbage can.

Sid didn't return to the laptop, but walked slowly to the small bathroom. He flipped the light switch and looked in the mirror. He had shaved this morning, but there was now faint stubble on his cheeks. His eyes didn't look too bloodshot and his hair was trimmed. He had to keep up his appearances. It was expected of him. It was expected of everyone.

Sid splashed cold water on his face and gasped. He toweled his face, and then took the musty towel with him as he walked back into the living room. It didn't take him many steps to reach his bedroom. The small twin mattress rested on nothing but the scuffed hardwood floor. He opened a small closet door and dropped the towel into the half-full hamper. He didn't do laundry if he could help it. He would buy a new outfit when he really needed one. He just needed a clean shirt.

Sid pulled his t-shirt over his head and dropped that into the hamper. He closed the door and headed back into the living room. His eyes moved up and down his laptop's screen. The left side of his mouth moved into half a grimace. He knew he wasn't finished, but it could wait. He closed the screen and plunged the room into darkness.

Sid heard a rumble. He moved to the window and raised the blinds just as the lightening ripped across the dark sky. He heard the rain, just a handful of drops at first. The hiss of heavy rain soon battered his air conditioner. He closed the blinds again, adding more darkness. He laid down on his bed face first. He had no intention of going to sleep, but his body felt tired.

"No one understands the darkness of a white room," Sid told the ceiling. "How could they?"

"So you're the one here to save Sid Sanford, huh?"

Damon jumped. He had been absorbed in staring at the bottom of his coffee cup for the past forty-five minutes, slowly losing hope that anyone remembered he was in here. He adjusted his glasses and did his best to smooth his rumpled shirt. He grimaced when he saw that his boots had left a line of dirt on the carpet.

"Sorry, son, didn't mean to startle you. Force of habit. I like to get my writers' attention." A man with silver hair extended his hand. "I'm Roger Ray, Sid's editor."

"Good to meet you, sir. I'm Damon Lord."

"Our Lord and savior. You mind if I have a seat and talk with you a bit?"

"Not at all."

"Roger's fine."

Damon's gaze returned to the bottom of his cup. He hadn't anticipated this and like always found himself anxious and tongue-tied.

"You're Sid's college roommate, correct? The one who gets paid to volunteer and ambulance chase across the country?"

"That's right. That sounds like something Sid would say."

"That's because those are his exact words. He mentioned you might be stopping by at some point. I apologize for the wait and the inquisition. We've all become pretty protective of Sid around here the last couple of years. He hasn't gotten or allowed many visitors."

"I understand."

"Did you know her well?"

Damon nodded.

"I don't need to tell you Sid hasn't been the same since. He's doing tremendous work in our features department, but he's a void of a human being. We've all tried to help bring him out of it, but if you know him as well as I think you do, you know there's no helping Sid if he doesn't want to help himself. What did you have in mind?"

195

"To be honest, I'm not sure. His family is everything to him and he hasn't seen them or talked to them in two years. They are worried and I think are at the point of giving up. I'm here for them really. I was hoping to have a conversation with him and go from there. What would you do if you were me?"

"If I had the answer to that, I'd have done it myself. We've gotten a lot of yahoos coming in here asking for him, so we like to screen whoever walks in. You passed."

"Thanks."

"I'm going to tell Sid he's got an interview with human resources." Ray gave Damon a final handshake. "But don't worry, if he runs out of here, I'll have someone clothesline him and glue him to a chair."

Damon remained standing after the older man left the room. He grabbed a small towel out of his duffle bag and wiped his brow. The air conditioning was on full blast, but he was still sweating. He rubbed his sore eyes, doing his best to shake off the red-eye flight. He paced around the room, dragging more dirt across the carpet. He sat back down when the door creaked open.

Sid stared at a piece of paper. He wore a blue-checkered shirt tucked into a form-fitting pair of blue jeans. His sleeves were rolled up and he had a pen perched behind his right ear. The tips of his fingers left black smudges on the white paper.

"I figured it was you," Sid said, "I only hear from HR when I don't hand in my expenses in on time."

"Good to see you," Damon said.

"I read your group was in Kansas cleaning up the aftermath of that tornado."

"It was."

"How was that?"

"A mess."

"So you left that one to fix this one. Is that it?"

"Uh..."

"Who strong-armed you into it?"

"They haven't seen you for two years. That's a long time for any family. They didn't know what else to do. No one does."

"It's not like I've been hiding." Sid crumpled up the piece of paper and heaving into a trashcan. "I have a semi-regular newspaper column, an online blog I update three times a week, and I've done more than a few television appearances. I didn't fall off the face of the earth."

"You haven't answered any of their calls, letters, or emails. What are the odds you would have stonewalled them if they had come down here?"

"They were free to come visit anytime. None of them did."

"Hard to believe considering how inviting you've been."

"What else you got?"

"She was important to us too"

"Constance is constantly blowing up my cell phone, email, my Twitter account," Sid said. "I think she's been harassing my door man as well. She questions my lack of ambition."

"Is she right?"

Sid shrugged.

"Listen, you're an adult," Damon said. "Your family doesn't deserve to be treated like this."

"Are you sticking around the city?" Sid asked.

"I don't know…"

"Why don't we drop your stuff off at my apartment? I have an interview in a little bit. You should come."

"Really? I don't have to. I can bum around your apartment. Or grab another coffee. Or make coffee if you have a coffee pot. Or…"

"Yeah, maybe you've had enough coffee." Sid got up out of his chair and motioned Damon to the door. "You might come in handy. I'm interviewing a wife who lost a husband and a two-year-old in a car crash last year. She's hosting a dinner to raise money for a children's hospital. She could use your empathy I'm sure."

Waiting in the living room, Sid checked his notes impatiently.

"Are you here to talk to my Mommy about the dinner we're hosting for my Daddy and baby brother?" The woman's daughter asked. "I wrote a bunch of things for it. Can I show you and your friend?"

Before Sid could answer, she scampered down the hallway. Sid made quick eye contact with a solemn and serious Damon. Sid patted him on the shoulder.

"I'm having a hell of a time with these cookies." The mother said from the kitchen. "Why don't you two just come in here?"

Flour, sugar, and M & M's were everywhere, leaving a sticky residue every surface. Cookie sheets with burnt remnants of what could have been tasty treats lay defeated on the kitchen table.

"I'm not much of a baker as you can plainly see," she said. "Even though the event is catered, my mother always told me it's good to have something homemade to offer."

"Sounds a lot like mine," Sid said. "This is my colleague Damon. I'm showing him the ropes today."

The little girl walked into the room with a pile of notebooks, scrap paper, and poster boards.

"Honey, why don't you wait until Mommy has all this cleaned up," the mother said. "Let me talk to these nice reporters for a bit."

"She's terrific," Sid said.

"Forever the optimist. If more people dealt with things the way she did, this world would be better off."

"How did the idea for the dinner come about?" Sid asked.

"That hospital did everything it could to keep my son alive. My husband didn't have a chance, but our son was a fighter straight out of the womb. There was hope there and those wonderful people exhausted every ounce of it to try to save him. They wouldn't accept anything I tried to give them then. I thought feeding a bunch of people to raise money just seemed like a good idea to give back. Maybe the money will help buy more hope for someone else."

Sid stopped writing. He admired the woman's strength, but he also felt angry and deflated.

"Everyone's been really supportive," she said. "Friends, family, and strangers have offered so much to make this a success. My husband was a good person, way better than

I'll ever be. Our son had his eyes and his laugh, but my attitude. He would have tortured us for sure. Thank God our daughter got all of her father's good stuff and only my eyes."

Sid glanced into the living room. The daughter was writing furiously on a fresh piece of paper. She noticed Sid looking at her, stopped, smiled, and waved enthusiastically. Sid could only manage a weak wiggle of his fingers in return.

"You guys should attend," the mother said. "Always room for more."

"Thanks, but we won't take up anymore of your time," Sid said.

"Thank you ma'am," Damon said. "Don't worry, there's always hope."

He put his hand over the mother's for a moment and her forced smile was replaced by real emotion filling her eyes. Sid grabbed Damon gently by the arm and started toward the door.

"Thanks for coming to talk to my Mommy!" The little girl said.

"No problem, kiddo." Sid said. "Keep writing."

The two walked out.

"You had to get in that last part, huh?" Sid asked.

"Occupational hazard," Damon said.

Later that night, Sid opened a bottle of bourbon.

"Do you want a drink?" Sid asked.

"Maybe," Damon said.

"Maybe?'

"Is this one drink, or one drink that leads to ten drinks?"

"Which do you want it to be?"

"One drink."

"Then that's what it is."

Sid poured out two glasses and handed one to Damon.

"Can I get water or ice?"

"No."

"No?"

"You heard me. I'm not letting you defile this."

"How many drinks have *you* had tonight?"

"That information is not relevant to this conversation."

"How was the dinner?"

"Great, they raised a ton of money. Everybody cried."

"How many drinks did you have?"

"Again, that is not relevant..."

"Sid, tell me you didn't sleep with the mother."

Sid set his glass down.

"How many drinks have you had tonight?" Sid asked. "Even I have my limits."

"I know she's contacted you a few times. Tell me you didn't sleep with her."

"That information is even less relevant than how many drinks I've had."

"I beg to differ."

201

"You weren't the only one begging for something this evening."

"You have got to be kidding me!" Damon stood up. "I don't know what's more fucked up, you actually screwing her or joking about it."

"Ha!" Sid reached for the bottle on the table behind his head. "I knew I could get you to curse. That's $10."

"Shit."

"$20."

Damon sat down.

"You remember the last time we had bourbon together?" Sid asked.

"Sly Fox Inn," Damon said. "You fell into roughly seven of the biggest puddles I've ever seen on the way home. I then got a text from you the next morning asking why you had woken up nude, bruised, and alone."

"I thought you had taken advantage of me. Turns out, you only let me fall up the stairs twice. Why I was naked remains a mystery."

Sid finally undid his tie.

"How do I do it?" He asked.

"How do you do what?"

"Go home."

"Buy a train ticket."

"They are going to hate me."

"They'll hate you a lot less if you talk to them. They need you as much as you need them."

"I don't know if I'm ready to face them. I don't know if I'm ready to talk about her."

"I need to leave tomorrow morning," Damon said. "I'm going to have to tell them something."

"Tell them I'm working on it."

A week later, Sid's drunken eyes stared icily out his foggy window.

He ran his finger through his greasy, matted hair. He snorted as he saw a white hair fall into his bourbon. He belched to the empty ceiling and then downed the remaining drops of alcohol. Sid knocked the nearly empty bottle over putting his glass on the table. He watched helplessly as a stain seeped into his carpet.

He staggered into the kitchen and felt along the wall for the light switch. He only found the tack holes that pimpled the lazily painted white walls. He spat as he gave up. Blind, he moved toward the liquor, already tasting the next bottle of the night. He crouched down in front of the cabinet and leaned forward to open it. His face slammed into the ancient wood, and he fell dead into darkness.

It felt like Jocelyn kissed him awake.

It wasn't really her, for she was all but gone. His apartment was still dark. He didn't have the energy to find that damn light switch. The cool kitchen floor held him there.

He yelled into the darkness, angry at the shadowy images it possessed. Hours went by on the floor. He felt his stomach rumble underneath his thin t-shirt. He ignored it.

The cell phone rang. Sid waited and then listened to the voicemail his mother left.

"Please, come back home baby. Let us help you. I love you, my dark-haired prince. Bye."

Sid felt his cell phone vibrate again. He answered impulsively.

"Hello?" He asked.

"Sid, it's me."

"Who is this?"

"Constance."

"Been a while."

"I stopped trying, but we really have to meet."

"Okay."

"Morning Star Cafe in Manhattan? Are you busy now?"

"No."

"Meet you there."

Sid sat in an empty booth far from the windows. He mumbled "coffee" to the waitress.

Constance walked in when the coffee arrived. She sat down wordlessly. The waitress quickly took her order. He sipped his coffee.

"You look like shit," Constance said.

"I've been busy."

"Let me get right to it. I'm getting married."

"Okay."

"Please, say something else."

"Okay."

"That isn't something else."

Sid reached numbly for his wallet. He fished out for the bills he needed.

"Don't leave," Constance said. "Please, I just wanted you to know. Don't walk out on me."

"Constance, I wish you the best of luck. You're going to need it."

He reached into his pocket. He didn't know why he had brought it. He had kept it locked up for ages.

"Goodbye," Sid said.

The ring clanged against his empty coffee cup, and he was out the door before she even realized what it was.

In his dream, something slipped out of his hand.

He couldn't see it, but he knew he didn't want to let it go. The harder he pushed to grasp it, the farther away it became.

"Let it go," his mother said.

"No!"

"It's not worth this pain."

"Yes, it is!"

"You can do better."

"I don't want to!"

"You're better than this."

He felt his body crumble.

205

"Baby, it's over."

His mother stepped away.

A train ran over his head.

"Momma!" Sid screamed.

He had fallen asleep on a bed of bottles.

His alarm clock read 2:30 a.m. He picked up his cell phone, and cycled through his contacts.

"I'm coming home," Sid told his mother's voicemail.

BUILDING

The roots in Sid's hands wouldn't budge.

Sid pulled again, but the earth held tight. He brushed off his gloves and got a better grip. He bent his knees and blinked away the bead of sweat that had become trapped in his eyelashes. He loosened his arms slightly, preparing for a mighty tug. He mentally counted down from three and pulled sharply. The main root slipped out of Sid's grasp and he fell backward into the pile of sticks that had accumulated behind him.

Sid stayed still for a moment and listened to the sound of the sticks slowly cracking underneath him. The sky was cloudless. He could see and feel the sun's heat shimmering everywhere. His long-sleeved shirt and dark khakis were soaked through.

"You okay?" Patrick asked.

"Sure," Sid said.

Patrick grabbed the roots with one hand and forcibly yanked them out of the ground. He tossed the clump of earth at Sid who caught it with both hands before it made impact with his gut.

"Come on, city slicker," Patrick said. "Let's take a breather and go pick on Tom."

Sid took his brother's outstretched hand and stood up. He kicked the dirt from under his green-stained work boots and followed his younger brother across the half-mowed lawn. The two found Tom positioning a ladder against the house. The older brother stepped back for a moment, shook his head, and moved the ladder a couple of inches to his right. Tom put his foot on the first rung, but jumped off immediately and examined the ladder's location. He took off his bucket hat and scratched the back of his head. He picked up the ladder and moved it a foot to his left. He moved back again, this time walking into Patrick, which startled him.

"What's up?" Tom asked. "You guys tired already?"

"Well, I've mowed more than half the lawn and Sid has most of the undergrowth taken care of," Patrick said. "It looks like you've accomplished nothing."

"I made sure the paint was mixed thoroughly."

"You're afraid to go up the ladder, aren't you?" Sid asked.

"No," Tom said. "I'm making sure the ladder is as level with the ground as possible. Now, shut your mouths and make sure I don't break my fucking neck."

Tom stood tentatively on the first rung holding his paint can. He tiptoed and hung the can on a hook above his head.

"Don't worry, if you see the ladder shaking, it's just my legs," Tom said.

"I can already see your skirt shaking," Patrick said.

"Fuck you," Tom said. "Just hold the ladder and withhold the commentary."

"Fine, but I may get bored and shake the ladder just to keep you on your toes."

"You're an ass."

"I've never denied that."

Sid walked away. A memory pulled him toward their neighbor's red fence. A number of posts were rotted and others had been replaced by unpainted, pale wood. Sid placed his hand on the point of one of the posts and felt the wood dig into his palm.

"I can hit the ball farther than you!" Jocelyn said. "I was wondering if you wanted to be my best friend."

Sid put his head down and gripped the fence with both hands.

"You okay?" Patrick asked.

Sid rubbed his hands together, feeling the deep impressions the post had left.

"You're not going to run away, are you?" Tom asked.

"No," Sid said. "We've got work to do. Let's get this done so Pop doesn't have to worry about it."

"I miss her too, man," Patrick said. "I'm always here to talk. You don't have to hold anything back with me. No pressure though, whenever you feel ready."

"Thanks," Sid said.

Patrick slapped Sid on the back and starting walking toward Tom and the ladder.

Sid surveyed the red fence one more time and followed.

"Do you want to keep score?" Kenneth asked.

"Huh?" Sid asked.

He had been watching the grounds crew manicure the field before the first pitch.

"I got you a program if you wanted to keep score," Kenneth said.

"Sure, Pop," Sid said. "I haven't done that in years."

"You know, I almost like going to a minor league baseball game better than going to a major league game."

"Why's that?"

"You just have more of a fun, family-oriented atmosphere. You have kids running around everywhere, crazy mascots and promotions, hungry players who really want to do well to move up, and it's more goddamn affordable. It's a sunny day. I have a cheap cold beer and my son. What more do I need?"

"They hire you as their public relations director when I wasn't looking?" Sid asked. "Speaking of sun, did you put sunscreen on that dome of yours?"

"I can't help it if I'm eloquent," Kenneth said. "And your mother lathered me up earlier. I should be all set until the sixth inning."

"So, what gives a major league game the edge?"

"Other than our home, I would rather be in the stands at Yankee Stadium than any other place on earth. Once you see Mickey Mantle play centerfield on a clear summer day, there really is no topping it."

Sid opened the program and flipped through the pages. He stopped once he found the score sheet. His eyes scanned over the blank spaces reserved for the starting lineups and game action. There was nothing he didn't know about keeping score at a baseball game. Once his father had taught him, he quickly gobbled up all the little intricacies.

In high school, he had been offered a chance to become an official scorer for a park and recreation league. He had accepted the opportunity immediately. There were some legitimate players in the league who didn't want the stress of playing for the American Legion team, but it was mostly a motley crew of players whose careers weren't going much past Sid's. Needless to say, it made for some interesting, and long, games.

Sid had seen every play imaginable and had written down number combinations that he hadn't thought possible. He remembered going over the sheets at night with Jocelyn, trying to piece together enough information to crunch stats. They would recreate the game inning by inning. She would have a million questions and have a million theories about why certain plays happened. She would get so frustrated when she couldn't decipher Sid's handwriting. She would berate him constantly and lecture him that this stuff was important and required more focus. It was hard to believe she was more passionate and old school about the game than Sid, but it was true.

"What are you thinking about?" Kenneth asked.

"Huh?" Sid asked.

"You're smiling."

"No reason," Sid said.

"Okay."

Classic aging rock 'n' roll music pounded out of the sound system. The home team huddled together. They shouted something and charged onto the field. All of the kids went crazy. They whistled and hoisted their foam fingers and plastic bats into the air. The players rushed out to their positions and dropped their gloves to the dirt or grass. The announcer told the crowd to rise for the National Anthem. Everyone stood up at the same time. Sid removed the dusty Yankee hat from his head and placed it over his heart.

On a hot summer day, the Sanford backyard is mowed short and white plastic bases are spaced out evenly. The back deck is alive with bright red, white, and blue streamers. Chairs are aligned in a row in the right field area. The patches of dirt that represent the mound and the home plate area are raked clean. There is a plastic Wiffle ball waiting on the plastic plate that was serving as the pitching rubber. Music loudly streams out of an old karaoke machine. Lawn chairs serve as dugouts for both teams. Dozens of colored bats are waiting patiently in a bright blue bin in each dugout.

A bunch of kids from the neighborhood prepare for the game in the porch. Well, everyone but Jocelyn. She had been ready for hours and is currently switching the cassette tape every time a song ends. Neighborhood parents arrive and she leads them to their seats. She makes sure they had enough ice in their coolers filled with beer and sandwiches and then yells for the players to get into position.

Jocelyn switches cassette tapes again, this time putting in a special one. She had worked with Sid the previous night to make this perfect. She pushes play and quickly dashes through the screen door and gets into her place in line.

"Ladies and gentlemen, welcome to Sanford Stadium…" Jocelyn's recorded voice says.

The parents cheer.

"And now, here are today's starting lineups…"

One by one, the players line up along the first and third base lines.

"Play ball!" Kenneth says.

"Wait!" Jocelyn says. "We need to play the National Anthem first!"

She rapidly makes another tape switch and hurries back to her spot. The opening of the Anthem blares triumphantly.

Sid winks at her from the opposite baseline. She blushes and smiles.

"What's up?" Kenneth asked. "You are wearing the biggest grin I've ever seen."

"I am not," Sid said.

"Keep telling yourself that."

"Did you catch that last play?"

"Yes."

"Was the second baseman or the shortstop the cutoff man?"

"I'm not telling you."

213

"Why not?"

"Not until you tell me what you're thinking about."

"Really, Pop? Are we teenage girls?"

"In this instance, yes."

"Great."

"So?"

"I'm just putting it down as the shortstop taking the cutoff."

"You're really not going to tell me?"

"No."

"Fine."

"You want me to go get you another beer?"

"That would be nice of you, son. Thanks."

Sid handed the scorebook to his father. He worked his way through the people sitting next to them and headed for the concession stand. He paid for the two beers and carefully made his way back toward his seat. He paused as he exited the tunnel. He hated moving toward his seat when the pitcher was in the middle of his delivery. A group of kids milled around the team's mascot next to him. A lower murmur of conversation permeated the stadium. A cool breeze rifled through the place every so often, but did little to take away from the warmth of the abundant sunshine.

Crack!

The batter had swung early at an inside pitch and broke his bat. The barrel landed past the pitcher's mound, leaving him with only a jagged handle. Sid couldn't tell exactly where the ball was hit. Every head around him looked up in a state of confusion and excitement. It didn't take him long to figure out the ball was headed his way. His baseball reflexes took over. Sid managed to find a spot to set down his beer and lift his hand to block the sun all in the same motion. He could see a tiny dot in the sky. He had a perfect beat on it. He felt himself getting jostled by the kids who had long abandoned the mascot. He didn't take his eyes off the ball, battling the sun every inch of the way. It started making its decent. Sid was going to catch it. Five more feet...two more feet...a couple more inches...

Damn!

The ball smacked off Sid's palm and rolled away.

He dove after it, but wasn't alone. There was now a scrum of teenagers, prepubescent boys and girls, and middle-aged men with rusty dreams tearing at each other to claim the prize. Sid was not going to let anyone of them beat him. He had had it in his hand. The ball was his by right and would remain his by force.

He spared no one his flying elbows. He knew he could spend $5 in the team's gift shop and head home with a perfectly white, unsoiled ball, but there was no honor in that. Certainly not when he was trying to impress Jocelyn. At least he thought he loved her. Either way, coming away empty handed was not something Sid was about to accept.

Victory!

Sid had to rip it out of the hands of a kid ten years younger, but it was worth it. He hightailed it away from the mob before he could hear any tears being shed. He retrieved the two sodas he had left on a ledge near the foul ball's ground zero, and headed calmly back to his seats.

"Did I see you drop that foul ball?" Jocelyn asked.

"I recovered it," Sid said.

"I don't know if it counts. I think our wager is still on the books."

Sid held up his hand in protest.

"I don't think so. A deal is a deal. I got you a foul ball. You need to pay up."

"Technically, I don't have it yet. You haven't given it to me."

Sid flipped the ball to her casually and Jocelyn scooped it out of the air.

"So?" He asked.

"So, what?"

"You are going to make me beg aren't you?"

"Am I that cruel?"

"Yes."

"Well, we never specified when this was going to happen."

"Valid point."

Sid turned his attention back to the baseball game. He didn't notice Jocelyn finger the ball's red stitching and smile.

The home team had lost it all in the last two innings. There had been a lot of walks, errors, and dispirited play, not to mention a slew of unreliable relievers. Still, they had a chance in the ninth inning to at least tie the score. Two strikeouts had ended any dream of a dramatic comeback.

Sid was about to ask Jocelyn something about the last at-bat, but her lips prevented him from uttering another word. She grabbed the hair at the back of his neck and forced him closer and deeper into her embrace. She felt warm all over. Her tongue ran across his lower lip and he felt himself fading into some permanent state of transcendent emotion.

Jocelyn backed away from him suddenly. They were both out of breath. They both smiled at each other. Sid didn't have to reach out to her in order to bring her back. She leapt up into his arms and kissed him even harder. His arms hung on to her with everything he had. She was weightless, save for the love and spirit radiating from her entire being.

"I love you," he said.

"I love you too," she said.

"Did I just see you give up a foul ball?" Kenneth asked.

"I did it for the kids," Sid said.

He handed his father a beer. He took a sip of his, half of which he had lost in the scuffle.

He retrieved the scorebook and quickly got caught up on everything he missed.

"Thanks for the beer."

Sid nodded.

"You okay?"

"I was thinking about Jocelyn before," Sid said. "About all the times we spent around baseball."

"Good memories?"

Sid nodded again.

"That's good. It's always the good ones that end up sticking with you. You've got to let time take care of all the bad ones first."

"Hard to argue with that."

"Damn straight. I'm your father, I know everything."

Sid laughed.

Ready, set, go. Then, scoop, step, throw.

It's an age-old baseball maxim Sid learned at a young age. You stay loose before a play, imaging that the next ball is being hit your way. As the pitcher stops before his delivery, you stop kicking the dirt, get into a defensive position, and focus your complete attention on the next pitch. If the ball is hit to you, and you happen to be an outfielder, you bend your knees, keep your glove to the ground, scoop the ball up, take a step toward where you're throwing the ball, and then release. Nothing to it, it's easy; especially if you've been doing it your whole life.

Ready, set, go. Then, scoop, step, throw.

The mechanics change slightly when you are having a catch. You still have to step and throw, but the mindset is different. The ball comes into your glove and you have time to think about what you're going to do. You can hold the ball in your hand a minute. You can position the seams exactly the way you want them to fit in your hand. You can take your time as you raise the ball over your head and go into your throwing motion. Not every throw has to be right on the money, but you can make your mechanics right every time. Baseball, like everything else, isn't an exact science, having a catch even less so. But the steps are still the same; it's the result that can vary.

Sid was never able to master the steps like his brothers. He knew where he had to go with the ball, but could never figure out exactly where his release point was. His mind was too wrapped up in everything that he was doing. Patrick slung the ball to him on the money time after time, but Sid would eventually get lazy and out of rhythm and the ball would sail over his younger brother's head. Since their street was on an incline, Sid had been quickly banned from throwing downhill. It hadn't taken long for Patrick or Tom to get tired of sprinting after balls before they rolled into the sewer at the bottom.

Sid pounded his fist into his glove. His mind, body, and soul were totally absorbed in the moment he was living in. Sid stretched out his glove hand and the ball rammed into the leather with a crisp thwack! His bare right hand plucked the white sphere out of the pocket. He gripped the seams, took a small step in front of him, and delivered a strike to Patrick's chest.

"Nice," Patrick said. "You're due for a shitty one though."

"Car," Sid said.

The brothers moved to the curb to get out of the way. Patrick gave a friendly wave. He got one in return from a grizzled, long-time neighbor behind the wheel of his hulking crimson Ford Bronco pickup.

"Finally, someone waves back," Patrick said. "You'd figure with all the new people in this neighborhood, they would want to be friendly to get to know people, but no, of course not."

Sid's cell phone vibrated on the back of their father's car. He walked over to it and saw "Constance" crawling across the screen. He scratched his chin for a moment and then answered.

"Do you get news up there in Podunk?" Constance asked.

"What happened?" Sid asked.

"Crane collapsed on a building in Midtown Manhattan. East Side."

"Anyone hurt?"

"Yes, but don't have numbers yet. Waiting for an update. Ambulances have made multiple trips. They're worried about the fire spreading."

"There's a fire?"

"Why don't you get to a computer and see for yourself."

Sid powerwalked into the house, not completely comfortable taking orders from Constance again. He did what he was told, however, and found the story online.

"Well?" Constance asked.

The shaky Web video he clicked on wasn't a big help. All Sid could see was black smoke curling around a green street sign.

"What time did this happen?" Sid asked.

"What did you say?" Constance replied, sirens drowning her out.

"My Internet isn't working very well, what have you seen?" Sid shouted.

"When I first got here, there were a few people standing on the corner like statues. They were covered in dust. I tried to ask a few questions, but they didn't seem to register anything. All the emotion had been sucked out of them."

Sid stopped listening as Constance continued. All he could think about was that his city was on fire and another friend was close to flame.

"Are you okay?" Sid asked, finally blinking.

"Yeah. Why?"

"Just be safe. Keep me posted."

"Are you coming back? This is kind of your beat."

"I don't know. I'll call you back," Sid said, closing the phone.

Later that night, Sid walked into his parent's room. He found his mother in her rocking chair surrounded by tissues. Gail had stolen his laptop and was now watching a news report about the accident. She jumped when she finally noticed Sid was watching her.

"Sorry, I didn't mean to scare you," he said, sitting on the edge of her bed.

"It's okay," Gail said. "I'm just playing solitaire."

"No you're not," Sid said, unable to force down a smile. "But that's okay."

"I'm assuming you know all about this," she said.

Sid nodded.

"You're going back, aren't you?" Gail asked.

"I hadn't thought about it yet."

"You're a horrible liar."

"How do you know I'm lying?"

"You couldn't stay away if your life depended on it. You have too much time and heart invested in that city. People are hurt and worried, and you're their voice. Plus, Constance."

"She's getting married," Sid said.

"And?"

"She can take care of herself."

"When has that ever made any difference to you?"

Sid shrugged.

"I know you're still hurting. You've come so far since you've been back. Your father told me that when you were having a catch with your brother, it was like nothing had ever happened, and everything had been wiped away. You're stronger than you give yourself credit for."

"Thanks. You want me to stay?"

Gail reached out and grabbed Sid's neck.

"Baby boy, there is no one on this earth who wants you to stay put more than me. But you do what you do for a reason. Someone has given you a talent that you need to use now. As much as we need you, those people need you to tell their story. We didn't raise you to hide while you could be helping someone."

"I love you, Momma," Sid sobbed.

"I love you too," she said. "We still need you in this family. I don't ask for much, just please return to us."

Sid nodded, not sure if he would.

THE AIRMAN

"So did you ever have the talk with Patrick?" Tom asked.

The rehearsal dinner hadn't filled Sid and Tom with a sufficient amount of Guinness, so the two brothers had barhopped around town for a couple hours. This particular dive had overpromised on live music and cheap beer.

"Which talk?" Sid asked.

"You know, the marriage talk every groom needs to hear so he freaks out and comes out drinking with his brothers the night before his wedding."

"See him sitting on the stool next to him?"

"No."

"There's your answer."

Six months ago, Patrick had graduated basic training at Lackland Air Force Base. He wasn't afraid that the nation was perpetually at war or that he'd be flying men and material overseas frequently as a C-5 crew chief. He

223

felt a sense of duty that no one, including his tearful mother, could talk him out of. Sid had taken up long distance running while Patrick was in basic in the spirit of shared sacrifice, so when the brothers embraced in 100-degree heat in Texas, they were both deeply tanned and rail-thin. It had been the proudest moment of Sid's life and he could only marvel at his younger brother's later stories about runways in Kyrgyzstan and Iraq.

Patrick had called Sid around midnight four months ago. He had met someone, of course. Patrick had sent Sid a picture a couple of weeks later, which confirmed in Sid's mind that his brother was a goner.

The romance had been kept under wraps for a few weeks, but it hadn't taken long for word to reach all corners of the family. Patrick had impulsively bought a ring and proposed, which raised more than a few eyebrows, but no one could deny the two were destined to be together.

"I think I need another drink," Sid said, the mix of good and bad memories brewing uneasily in his stomach.

"Me too," Tom said.

"Can you order us another round while I go to the bathroom?

"Again?"

"I'm old."

"Ancient."

"Shut up."

"The only time I've seen you piss more is that night we went to the Neil Young concert in New York."

"In my defense, we were drinking from beer steins that were as tall as you."

Sid ordered more beers, and then watched the delicious dark liquid cascade down his pint glass in reverent amazement.

"Mmmm, dark and stormy beer sure to destroy my digestive tract," Tom said upon his return. "Seriously though, this has to be the last one. We can't have hangovers tomorrow."

"You said that three bars ago," Sid said. "To Patrick."

Sid and Tom had clinked pint glasses as the lights dimmed.

"I think we're going to get that live music up in this hizzy," Tom had said.

"Please never say that again."

The singer appeared to be a local, however, someone not scared of performing in front of a small, inattentive audience.

"Catch her name?" Tom asked.

"Olivia something."

"I'm, I'm so in love with you, whatever you want to do, is alright with me," she sang. "Cause you make me feel, so brand new, and I want to spend my life with you..."

Sid tuned in fully once Olivia started singing his favorite Al Green tune. She had long amber hair that curled as it reached her shoulders that matched her soulfully earnest hazel eyes. Her skin was soft white and seemed full of life with all the lights on her. Her curves sashayed sensually to the beat of the song.

"Holy shit," Sid said.

"You should talk to her," Tom said.

225

"Yeah, okay, sure."

"Seriously, go for it."

"I'm not that drunk."

"Even better, she'll appreciate the confidence."

"No chance."

"Wuss."

"Yep."

"Come on, you're the last single Sanford left. You're not doing this just for you. Make us proud little brother."

"How many drinks have you had?"

"Many."

"Okay."

"I believe in you."

"Thanks, but I'm good."

"I'll talk to her for you. I'm a great wing man."

"Fuck, dude, sit your ass down."

"Nope, her sets over and here she comes. It's either you talk to her like a man, or I make you look like a baby."

"Fine, wait here."

Sid walked a few steps away and tapped her on the shoulder.

"Excuse me," Sid said. "Your voice is unbelievable."

"You think so?" Olivia asked, clearly flustered by the attention now that she was off stage.

"I do," Sid said.

"You're very sweet."

"We're at the tail end of the night. You want to grab a coffee with me?"

"Sweet and forward."

"Cute, too."

"Unfortunately, I'm married," Olivia said. "I need to get home to my little girl as well. But thank you for making my night.

"Ah, well, can't blame me for trying," Sid said, eager to accept failure. "Enjoy your night."

Tom's eyebrows raised as Sid made his way back to his seat. Sid shook his head. Tom signaled the bartender for two more beers.

"I'm not done with this one," Sid said.

"Nah, you can't drink that," Tom said. "Too unlucky. A fresh one will help with the next one."

"Next one?" Sid asked, surveying the male-dominated bar.

"Good point," Tom said. "Well, chug that one so that by the time you get to the second one, you'll have forgotten all about crashing and burning. What was her deal?"

"Married."

"Ouch."

"Yeah, didn't feel great. Has a kid too."

"Okay, my bad," Tom said.

"That is for damn sure," Sid said, finishing his beer in two gulps. The bartender grabbed his empty glass and set a full one down on the dampening cardboard coaster. Sid eyed it suspiciously, knowing it wasn't the end. Ordering another had gotten to be habit, one that disregarded the dull, dispirited orchestra tuning up for tomorrow morning.

"You okay?" Tom asked.

"Yeah, why?"

"You know stories like this endear you to people, right?"

"Sure," Sid said. "I don't mind people having a laugh at my expense."

"You mean that?"

"Yes."

"Cool."

"Let me ask you something," Sid said. "You think she'd be proud of me?"

"Who?"

"Who do you think?"

"Yes, I do."

"Why?"

"Because I am. I'm proud at how you've put your life back together," Tom said. "I know it wasn't easy."

"That's the alcohol talking."

"I'm serious. A lesser person might have stayed away forever. You came back."

"Thanks. I'm getting there. It's a process."

"Finish that beer," Tom said. "We can have a bourbon for the road."

"I don't think..."

"Of course it's not a good idea. But humor your older brother for once."

Sid nodded. A glass of Blanton's appeared in short order. It went down so smooth, it made ordering another that much easier.

The next morning, hot black coffee burned Sid's dry throat.

"Shit," he said, spilling some on his sweat-stained shirt.

He put the cup down on the nightstand next to him and did his best to wipe down some of the mess. He breathed the warm air sluggishly circulating in his childhood room and reached for his crumpled papers. He started muttering, reading the words on the page out loud.

Sid moved his eyes away and tried to recite his speech from memory, but his alcohol-scarred and under-caffeinated mind was useless. He sat at the edge of the bed and took another pull of coffee, this time spilling black liquid on his bare legs. He smirked warily and glanced around the room that hadn't been his since he left for college. The only thing left that was truly his was a desk he put together with his father as a high school sophomore. The bookcase that once held histories, literature, and coffee table books on topics only interesting to Sid now held Bob Dylan biographies, airplane manuals, and guitar songbooks. A large navy blue Air Force flag took up an entire wall, while posters of Elvis and James Dean covered the others. Patrick had relegated the rest of Sid's leftover belongings to two trunks in the basement.

Sid picked up the red Power Ranger off Patrick's dresser. He remembered the two of them running wildly

229

around this room with various figurines in their hands. Memories of late night discussions about women and "Star Wars" followed. Sid returned the action figure and thought of how he'd been Patrick's hero in those days. He noticed the dress blue uniform hanging in Patrick's closet, the one the youngest Sanford would wear while marrying his soulmate, and knew the roles had changed.

Sid's cell phone vibrated.

"Hello?" He asked.

"Hey," Patrick said.

"Where are you?" Sid asked.

"Living room."

"Then why are you calling me?"

"I knew you were writing or jerking off, so I didn't want to bother you."

"If that's the case, why didn't you text me?"

"Because I actually wanted to bother you."

"You're right outside the door now, aren't you?"

"Yeah."

"Get in here."

Patrick walked in wearing a gray Air Force t-shirt and a pair of fatigues.

"What's up?" Sid asked.

"Last minute bachelor-type stuff. Hookers, blowies, handies."

"Sounds better than last night."

"You're being too hard on yourself," Patrick said. "Rejection does a best man good the day before a wedding."

"I think the bourbon to finish off the night did more damage. Tom told you already, huh?"

"Yup," Patrick said. "If you guys were planning on getting shit-faced, the least you could have done was invite me."

"Your commanding officer ordered us otherwise."

"Ah, that's right, she did. Married already."

"Can I get back to fictionalizing folksy anecdotes about you, or do you need something?"

"Would you mind doing me a favor?"

"What?"

"If I gave you some cash, could you take a trip to Walmart to grab me a pack of white undershirts?"

"Seriously?"

"Give me a break. I've been living between two places. I forgot mine at base."

"Can't you just borrow one of mine?" Sid asked.

"Bro, I outweigh you by fifty pounds of muscle, most of it located across my chest, and I'm at least six inches taller than you."

"How is this helping your cause?"

"It's not. I just like pointing out all those things."

"Fine. Need anything else?" Sid asked.

"Black socks if you could…"

"Explain to me again why you can't go yourself."

"Pop's making me eggs."

"Makes perfect sense. Give me the cash."

"Thanks!"

Sid tied his shoes and walked out of the room. He found Kenneth in the kitchen stirring scrambled eggs in a pan on the stove.

"Any coffee left?" Sid asked.

"Little bit, but it's cold," Kenneth said. "I can make more."

"That's okay, I can heat it up. Need it to go."

"Little bastard has you running errands, huh?"

"He can repair an engine on the world's largest aircraft, but can't keep track of his own laundry."

"Sounds about right to me. Let me give you money for it."

"He took care of that."

"Just take a few bucks out of my wallet. Get yourself a Dunkin' on the way back."

"Is this your way of telling me you ran out of coffee and want me to replenish your stock?"

"Yep."

"I'd ask if you needed anything else, but my list is full."

"There is one more thing."

"What's that?"

"You want to tell me why you came home at three this morning?"

"I do not."

232

"Scared the crap out of me."

"Think about how I feel. You were in your underwear while staggering and farting across the living room."

"We can discuss later when you have a few beers in you," Kenneth said.

"Good idea," Sid said. "I'm on a mission."

Later that day, Sid stood next to Patrick, watching guests file into their seats.

Rain clouds had threatened to move the ceremony indoors at one point earlier in the afternoon, but had since disbanded. The white folding chairs, set up in tombstone precision, awaited aunts, uncles, cousins, and friends. The rest of Patrick's groomsmen helped older relatives navigate the grass still slick with rainwater.

Sid noticed a stray piece of string on his younger brother's uniform. He swiped at it with his finger, but it was stubbornly attached. He used more force the second time, knocking a confused Patrick out of his rigid stance.

"Sorry," Sid said.

"No problem," Patrick said. "I almost passed out."

"You know, I would have laughed before picking you up, right?"

"I'd expect nothing less."

"Good."

"Did you really get home at three in the morning?"

"Who told you that?"

"Pop. Tom failed to mention it in his text."

233

"He's an aggressive wingman."

"That can't be true."

"He was over-served, scrambled his senses."

"So, what happened? With the married singer?"

"Kind of felt good to hit on someone again," Sid said. "Even if it didn't go well."

"Give you credit for..."

"Don't say trying. It sounds like I got cut from the high school baseball team."

"Sid, you did get cut from the high school baseball team."

"All the more reason to just let it lie," Sid said. "Proves I've still got the ability to, I don't know, desire someone enough to talk to them. Who knows how I would have felt if she said yes. Anyway, I don't think this is the right time. You're about to get married."

"Come on, humor me. Talking about your love life is keeping me from throwing up all over the place."

"You ready for this?" Sid asked.

"Yes sir."

"You're taking on a lot."

"Are you trying to talk me out of this right now? I think it's a little late to have this conversation."

"I'm actually trying to make you throw up. It would make for a good story. Like when your zipper broke during your graduation from basic training."

"Ugh. My training instructor ran me up and down and there was nothing I could do. I hope I gave you all a show when I marched by."

"We were proud. Disgusted and concerned as well, but proud."

The two brothers straightened up a bit as they heard preparations being made for the main event to start. The justice of the peace appeared and guests who weren't seated rushed to find a good spot. The string quartet situated in a gazebo closer to the reception hall started playing.

"I'm right here, man," Sid said. "Don't worry, once you see May, you'll forget you were ever nervous."

"Thanks, brother. Glad you're standing up here with me."

"Just returning the favor," Sid said, patting his brother on the back. "There's one more thing I need to tell you."

"What's that?

"I farted."

Patrick laughed out loud as May's parents made their way down the aisle.

"Shut up, you idiot," Patrick said.

Sid watched May walking with her father down the aisle. She was already crying, but beaming at Patrick. In that moment, Sid remembered something an old friend had told him one night while looking up at the stars and dealing with a pair of breakups.

"Life is made up of moments that remind us how much good every one of us has inside, and those moments should

235

be treasured and remembered forever," Jocelyn said. "And, sometimes it's okay for men to cry."

Later at the reception, Sid gripped a microphone.

"Good evening," he said. "I'm the middle child, so this is a big moment for me."

During the murmur of laughter, Sid winked at Tom who had warned him not to try being funny.

"I'd like to share with you a quote from a letter I found while writing this speech," Sid said. "'I don't know how much pleasure it affords you to go over these days of the past, but to me they will ever be remembered as days of felicity. And how happy the thought that years increase the affection and esteem we have for each other to love and be loved. May it ever be so, and may I ever be a husband worthy of your warmest affections. May I make you happy and in so doing be made happy in return.'

"Harvey Black, a surgeon in charge of the field hospital for the 2nd Corps of the Army of Northern Virginia during the Civil War, used these words to express his love to his wife Mary from the battlefield in 1863. Despite being written almost 150 years ago, they still beautifully express the sentiments that we came together to celebrate; fidelity, happiness, and love."

Sid paused for a moment, folded his notes, and then put them back in his pocket.

"When Patrick was sent on missions to Afghanistan the past few months, May expressed to me her worry that the Air Force would conveniently schedule a return trip that would force her man to miss their wedding. I reassured her that he'd be there no matter what. You see, the Sanfords have a legacy of going AWOL to get married. That's just what my grandfather did before he was shipped off to World War II. He was going to be there for the woman he loved by any means necessary, and that's a trait he's passed down to his grandsons.

"Needless to say, I've never been more excited to tell someone 'I told you so.' And I'm sure Patrick's relieved that he didn't have to break any laws to be here."

Sid paused for more laughter.

"My brothers and I were lucky enough to be born into a family defined by good men. Our father, our grandfathers, and uncles on both sides of our family, are all men who value honor, trust, and dedication to their families above all else. Patrick, never forget these good men that came before you and the place that you hold in that legacy, especially since you put on that uniform. No matter how hard life might get, these men, those that are with us and those that aren't, support you. As an added bonus, the Sanford family has also been blessed with strong women. I'm sure most, if not all, of you in this room have met my mother."

Relatives responded with hooting and hollering.

"You mean that as a compliment, right?" Gail asked.

"Yes, ma'am," Sid said.

"Good boy, keep going."

"As my mother will tell you, without women like the Sanford men would be lost in the tall grass. May, it's been an absolute joy getting to you know, and I'm proud that you'll be joining these amazing women. I know that you'll keep Patrick on the right path all of his life. He's my best friend. I've gotten him this far; you've got him the rest of the way."

Sid's voice cracked, but he continued.

"Regardless of all the family support you'll have throughout your marriage, it's up to you two to protect and grow your love. Everyone in this room will tell you that it's not going to be easy all the time. Life isn't supposed to be. Every kiss, every hug, every good moment is made that much sweeter by persevering through every fight, every hurt feeling, and every moment of doubt. You two are a team. You will get through everything together. Trust in each other, respect each other, and love each other."

Sid raised his glass of bourbon.

"So let's drink to a good man and a good woman. I love you both, and I wish you the best of luck."

Patrick and May hugged him before he could take a sip.

Much later, Tom handed Sid a glass.

Sid nodded his head in appreciation and loosened his bowtie.

"What I wouldn't give for a couple of cigars right now," he said.

Tom glanced through the reception hall's windows and reached into the inside pocket of his jacket. He pulled out two Ashton cigars and a lighter.

"Who are you and what have you done with my older brother?" Sid asked. "Your wife is going to notice you smell like a used litter box when we go back in there."

Tom sighed as he lit his younger brother's cigar and then his own.

"Why is a glass of bourbon and one of these so delicious?" Sid asked.

"I got you a gin and tonic," Tom said. "But you're right in principle."

"Indeed," Sid said, looking down at his drink.

He plopped down into one of the chairs on the deck area and propped his feet up on the railing. Tom quickly followed suit.

"I have some intel for you," Tom said.

"Are we planning a heist?"

"This is more fun. I have it on good authority one of May's single bridesmaids wants to dance with you. She thinks you're cute."

"Oh really? How'd you find this out?"

"I did some investigating."

"You asked all of them if they were single, right?"

"Hey, I don't reveal my methods. Take it or leave it."

"I'll take it," Sid said.

"Really?"

"I'm buzzed, on the verge of drunk," Sid said. "No problem."

"That's the spirit!" Tom yelled, spilling most of his drink and dropping his cigar.

"What's her name?" Sid asked.

"Sarah. She should be on the dance floor."

"Is she the one with the curly brown hair?"

"Yep."

"Well done, sir," Sid said. "Wish me luck."

Sid waded through his family and friends on the dance floor. Patrick gave him a huge bear hug that lifted him off his feet. Sid whispered something in the newly married Airman's ear. Patrick gave him a hearty pat on the back and shoved him toward the edge of the party.

Sid held out his elbow for Sarah to take. She accepted it shyly, but eagerly walked with Sid back out onto the dance floor. One song ended and another began. The familiar voice of Al Green filled the air as they danced.

OLD WAR STORIES

Sid moved June's hair away.

He carefully untied the top of her apron. Her skin shuttered as he gently kissed the back of her neck. He held onto her hips and swayed. She giggled nervously and wriggled away. She quickly tied her apron back around her neck and put the tray of chicken into the oven.

Sid didn't give up. He wrapped his arms around her and she pushed her ass up against him anxiously. June started breathing heavily, but she gripped the edge of the counter and calmed herself down. Sid felt her body slacken. He walked away disappointed.

He stared out the cabin's bay window and listened as June chopped tomatoes. It had started to snow again. Bulky snowflakes fell slowly to the ground, making the wooded area look like someone had dumped a box of confectioner's sugar all over it. Sid smelled the chicken baking in the kitchen and felt the room heat up a few degrees. June approached him from behind. She rubbed his shoulders.

241

The trip had been her idea. She still believed their relationship was worth saving and that this getaway was the way to do it. Sid had fought her, knowing it was ridiculous to burn vacation days on a long weekend for a terminal union. June had gone as far as enlisting Damon to her cause. Following his divorce, Damon had signed up for the Peace Corps and was headed to Zimbabwe to work with diamond miners. He had offered his New Hampshire cabin free of charge, which hadn't made Sid all that happy. This wasn't how he handled pain. He had grown tired of June's needy and controlling nature. He understood it, but that didn't mean he had to stick around. He had done enough. He didn't want to feel guilty anymore for coming home smelling like the floor of a dive bar.

"I can hear your tummy rumbling," June said after dinner.

"What did you say?" Sid asked.

"I knew you weren't paying attention. Your stomach is noisy. Does that mean you didn't like the dinner I made you?"

"Not at all. It just feels good to be full."

"Do you think I'm still pretty?"

"Yes."

"Really?"

"I think you're pretty."

"Why do you love me?"

"Why do you ask?"

"It's an honest question."

"You know the answer. Nothing has changed."

"You sure?"

Sid paused, wanting to reassure all of her insecurities for a moment. However, he couldn't do that without acknowledging his own. The two remained quiet until settling into bed a few hours later.

June kissed his earlobe.

It had been forever since the last time she had instigated anything sexual. Sid had told her they could take as much time as she needed before making love again, but the urge had disappeared completely. Sid slipped his hand under her shirt and ran his finger along her long spine. She squirmed approvingly. Sid lifted her shirt over her head and then June pulled the quilt over the both of them. Sid tickled her stomach and untied the strings at the top of her sweatpants. June squirmed again as his hand under her underwear and inched his way down.

"Sid," June said.

He didn't stop. She felt smooth and clean.

"Hang on a second," she said. "I mean it, stop! Don't touch me!"

Sid jumped. June appeared shell-shocked.

"I'm sorry," Sid said.

"It's okay."

Sid dressed and grabbed his winter jacket out of the closet. He didn't look back after wordlessly walking out. June cried as she heard the front door slam.

The bar was a neon stain against the white New Hampshire backdrop. Sid had seen it out of the corner of his eye after hours of driving. He had stopped several times after almost skidding into the woods on both sides of the road, but he couldn't stop because his body screamed for alcohol.

Sid finished his fourth beer. The woman he had hit on talked about leaving a bad boyfriend. The jukebox played one Johnny Cash song after another. Every now and then, a cue ball connected with another pool ball. The lights were low, cigarettes smoldered in the ashtrays all. The spirits of past townie patrons gave the place a stale odor not entirely unpleasant. Sid did his best to avoid the long mirror behind the bar.

"Bad enough I'm losing it," Sid told his beer. "I shouldn't have to watch it happen"

"You should come to the bathroom with me," the woman next to him said.

"Nah," Sid said. "I'm good."

"One minute youse all ovah me, and now youse gonna be an asshole."

"Find some Rs and I'll get interested," Sid said.

She kicked his seat as she walked out of the bar. Sid burped and tasted dinner from hours ago. He closed his eyes and took a deep breath. He got off the barstool drunkenly and took his jacket off the coat rack.

An hour later, outside a different bar, a woman fumbled with Sid's belt.

Sid struggled with her bra. He gave up and leaned back against the seat, trying not to vomit or cry. She finally got his belt off and undid his zipper.

"That feels good, June," Sid said.

244

"Beth."

"What?"

"My name is Beth."

"Do you know my name?"

"No."

"Then stop talking."

She kissed him while unzipping his fly. She tasted like pretzels and zinfandel.

"Am I not doing it for you?" Beth asked.

He had gone flaccid.

"I have a girlfriend," Sid said.

"Fucking bastard," she said. "Fuck yourself."

Beth spit in his face before leaving the car mumbling more profanities. The cold wind stung him immediately after she opened the car door. Sid zipped up and dug his keys out of his jacket pocket. He went to turn the ignition, but stopped when he noticed the bar's neon lights were still on. He rubbed his eyes and decided to keep drinking.

Later, Sid's skin blistered under the water of the cabin's shower. Sid steadied himself against the wall and vomited. He slumped, watching the alcohol and half-digested chicken circle the shower drain, and wept.

In bed, June wondered why she hadn't gotten used to this. She had lost track of how many hours she had wasted waiting for him to return. She was thankful he did his best to clean off whatever smells that were stuck to his body. She burrowed under her quilt and jumped when she heard the running water shut off abruptly. There was a time

245

when she would roll over and pretend to be asleep. Sometimes, Sid would be too drunk to notice much of anything, so she stayed as still as possible until he passed out.

Sid walked out of the bathroom wearing only a towel. Beads of water clung to his pink skin. His soaked hair was pushed forward messily, almost covering his bloodshot eyes. June watched silently as he stood in the middle of the room confused. She wanted to get out of bed and help him, but she knew it would just start another fight. She didn't want him to leave again so she stayed under her quilt.

Sid collapsed on the bed after removing his towel. June felt his hair dampen the pillows. She inhaled deeply. He smelt like him again. His breathing quickly became heavier. She got as close to him as she could and shared her quilt. He grunted quietly, but didn't move.

June put her hand on his chest. She felt something warm inside her. Maybe it was the fact that he was clean and naked or maybe she needed to feel something other than the inside of her pain. Maybe she was ready now.

June wanted him. It took her a minute to get used to the feeling. It had been so long since the last time she felt it. She wanted his love and attention, but for whatever reason, not his body because it now scared her.

"Please make love to me," June said. "I want you."

"No," Sid said.

"I promise I'll be good."

"No."

"Please, hun, I'm ready."

"No."

"I love you. Please."

Sid didn't answer.

"Then I want you to get the fuck out of this bed," June said.

Sid pushed away the quilt. He didn't say anything to her as he put a fresh pair of clothes on.

"Are you ever going to stop walking out?" June asked. "Are you ever going to realize I need you and that you should fight for me instead of shoving me away? When are you going to realize what's two feet in front of your damn face?"

Sid ignored her and walked out into the living room. This time, June followed.

"Stop damn it!" She said.

He did as he was told.

"Fuck you, June," Sid said. "It's too late."

"You son of a bitch! I carried your fucking baby! The very least you can do is fucking love me!"

"Pack your bags. This trip is over."

In Queens a year later, Sid got up from his bar stool to stretch his legs and bumped into an old man waiting for a drink. The man teetered momentarily before falling to the ground.

"Shit!" Sid said. "Sorry about that, sir, are you okay?"

The old man accepted Sid's hand and pulled himself up slowly.

"I'm fine," he said. "Buy me a club soda and we can call it even."

"You don't want a beer?"

"Don't enjoy alcohol. My wife's doing la spesa next door. I'm just killing time."

"What's la spesa?"

"Grocery shopping in Italian."

"I'm French."

"I don't know any French."

"Me either."

"Make friends?" Constance asked, returning from the bathroom.

"Yep, this is…"

"Tony," the old man said. "Forget the club soda, I'll just take this beautiful woman."

"I'm Constance," she said. "And why am I being sold into slavery?"

"I knocked him down," Sid said.

"I left you out here for three minutes and you start a fight with a poor old man."

"By poor, you mean handsome, right?" Tony asked. "Because I was just telling…"

"Sid," Constance said.

"…Sid that I wake up every morning and thank the Lord for my good looks and superior intelligence," Tony said. "You know what I ask for next?"

"What?"

"If he has any time to help out my friend Sid."

"Ha!" Sid said. "What's he say?"

"Lost cause?" Constance asked.

"Close. 'I'm only a god, Tony, give me a break.'"

The old man laughed cheerfully.

"While Sid was shoving you to the ground, did he happen to tell you that we're celebrating our wedding anniversary?"

"He didn't mention it," Tony said. "How many years?"

"Too many," Sid said.

"Not nearly enough," Constance said at the same time.

Tony held up his finger and answered his ringing cell phone.

"Yeah," he said. "Okay, so get two pounds. I'm sure we have room in one of the three freezers we have downstairs. What am I doing? Hitting on married women half my age. I'm on my way over."

Sid elbowed Constance, who kissed Tony warmly on the cheek. He winked at her as he left.

"So now you've lied to the bartender and a random stranger that we're married," Sid said. "Tell me, did we have a nice ceremony with family and friends or did we elope at city hall?"

"Big ceremony, of course," Constance said. "We invited all the people who thought it would never happen."

"There isn't a reception hall in New York State that large."

"Shut up and buy me another beer," Constance said. "So, you really got her pregnant, huh?"

"I did."

"You went from scared to ask anyone out to getting someone preggers. That's fast even by your standards."

"Don't say preggers. She wasn't some barely legal teenager I roofied and you don't work for E! News. It was a nice relationship while it lasted."

"She miscarry?"

"Let's drop it. What else do you want to know?"

"Did you ever cheat on me?"

"No."

"Really?"

"Really" Sid said. "Did I mention you look sexy in that dress?"

"Many times."

"I'm just saying, it's been a while since we've seen each other. You upped your game. Also, I'm shocked you're wearing a dress."

"Shut up." Constance said, sipping her beer. "How badly do you want to kiss me?"

"The usual amount."

"Which is?"

"Quite a bit."

"Me too," Constance said. "You really didn't cheat on me?"

"We didn't date long enough for me to acquire a side piece," Sid said. "Even if I had wanted to, I was too busy fighting off half the men on campus."

"I wasn't that desirable. There weren't that many."

"They could have started a fraternity. Some of the women I dated asked if you had beer-flavored nipples."

"I think you've made your point."

"You cheat on me?"

"I dumped you for someone else. My conscience is clean."

"No wonder your articles lack empathy."

"Hey! I'm tough and newsy, not a robot," Constance said. "When did you start drinking regular Budweiser?"

"I wrote a short story whose main character drank it," Sid said. "It stuck."

"A little psychotic, but acceptable I suppose."

"Thanks for your approval."

"You're welcome. Tell me what happened with June."

"Not going to let it go, are you?"

"Never."

"But then we talk about you?"

"That's only fair."

Sid drank half his beer and set it back down on its coaster nervously.

"I really loved her," he said.

"Really?"

"Yeah."

251

"How'd you knock her up?"

"Tequila and kitchen floor sex in the middle of the day."

"Nice."

"That part was fun."

"I bet. Then what happened?"

"She told me she was pregnant..."

"How'd she tell you?"

"Surprised me by decorating our Christmas tree with blue and pink ornaments."

"That's sweet."

"It was until it wasn't. A few weeks later I found her in the shower standing in a quarter inch of blood. Probably wasn't that much actually, but it was enough to cause me to vomit in the sink before helping her. Turns out, she has this rare uterine condition that causes her walls to weaken during pregnancy. Egg had nothing to hang on to at the end. So, no Baby Sid."

"This was around when you got laid off?"

"Yep."

"I wish I knew what to say, but I don't," Constance said. "Do you miss her?"

"It ended badly, so I'm not sure," Sid said. "She's better off without me though."

"You tell your parents?"

Sid nodded and scrapped the label off his beer with his thumbnail.

"Sorry. I really am."

"Thanks," Sid said. "Bad ones leave scars, good ones leave canyons. It is what it is."

"Maybe you're a good one."

"Not likely."

"You regret loving me?"

"No."

"Did you hate me for breaking up with you and forcing you to be my friend?"

"You didn't force me. And I hated you then, but we were young. I didn't know anything."

"How about when I told you I was marrying Derek."

"I honestly don't remember feeling much," Sid said. "I was dealing with a lot, so it was just another arrow in my chest. You go numb after a while."

"Well, I'm here now unattached. You've got nothing to worry about."

"So what happened?"

"He hit me."

A year ago, Derek's fist pounded Constance's cheekbone. She felt a tooth crack as he pulled his arm back to strike her again. She had been standing up to that point, but the blow had knocked her to the floor.

"I fucking told you I wasn't in the mood, bitch!" Derek screamed. "Jesus, all I wanted to do was watch the fucking game without you acting like a fucking slut. When I want to fuck you, I'll fucking tell you."

Constance curled into a ball, but the next punch never came.

"I'm going to the bar," he said. "You better be in goddamn bed when I fucking get back."

Constance heard him slap cologne on his neck. Then, he whistled while taking a piss. She knew he was going to cheat on her tonight. She had mentioned the foreign numbers on their phone bill once, but hadn't been able to walk for a week.

"See ya," Derek said slamming the door.

"Please, don't come back," Constance whimpered.

Not surprisingly, Derek's dark side revealed itself gradually. Derek started sleeping days at a time after getting fired for drinking at his factory job. He would start falling asleep in the middle of conversations. Constance found bottles all over their apartment. She didn't remember exactly when the beatings started. Derek would slap her and then apologize immediately. She accepted every one because she loved him and believed she could help him get better. However, the slaps turned into shoves and those became violent slams into walls and doors. She had been tripped, pushed, cut, demeaned, yelled at, bruised, and concussed. Constance couldn't remember a time that her skin wasn't bruised. She had been prone to bruises all her life so each one was easy to explain to the outside world. She let Derek explain her visits to the hospital. He had become a skilled liar. Constance was scared that he would find her alone one day, kill her, and then disappear.

Her stomach churned. She crawled into the humid bathroom after mixing vodka and painkillers. Bile bubbled up her throat. She balanced the best she could on her shaky knees and bent over the toilet bowl. She felt water and vomit splash back against her face. Eventually, the vomiting stopped, but not the dry heaves. When Constance's body finally quieted, she coughed hard and flushed the toilet. She didn't move right away, not completely convinced that it was over.

Constance stood and washed her face. A skeleton with yellowed, bloodshot eyes appeared in the mirror. The bags under her eyes were so bad that she knew she wouldn't be able to cake on enough makeup to hide them. She slumped up against the bathroom door and took her cell phone out of her pocket. Her fingers pushed the phone's tiny buttons lethargically.

"I'm not here right now, but leave a message and I'll get back to you," Sid said on his voicemail. "Thanks!"

"Fuck!" Constance screamed.

She threw her phone into the shower where it shattered against the tiled wall. She resolved to end her life.

She needed more pills.

She opened the medicine cabinet and found another bottle of painkillers. Constance shut the bathroom light off and walked back into the bedroom. She crawled under the covers, poked her head out, and then opened the bottle. She cocked her head back and swallowed a handful of red pills. Constance put her head on the pillow and waited for unconsciousness.

Around midnight, she woke.

Derek hadn't come home, which meant he wasn't coming home at all. Constance's stomach rumbled, but she wasn't sure whether she was hungry or had to throw up. Either way, she wasn't getting out of bed. She couldn't feel most of her body anyway. She reached for her cell phone. One of the jagged pieces of what used to be her phone drew blood. She cursed and tossed the ruined phone into the trash.

Constance prepared her body for movement. She swung her legs out from under the covers and landed her bare feet on the cold wood floor. She rested her elbows on her knees for a moment before standing. She knew she had more pills, but couldn't remember where she had hid the bottle. She tore apart her nightstand drawer with no luck. She emptied out her pocketbook, but there was nothing there either. Constance stumbled over to her desk. She went through each disappointedly. She carefully poked through Derek's nightstand, but came up dry.

She went to the closet and knocked down all her clothes trying to retrieve her old backpack. It had to have pills in it. She had lived off Advil during college. She ripped opened each pocket violently. There were old papers and blue test booklets, but no pills.

"Damn it!" Constance screamed.

She turned the backpack upside down and shook it. After it had completely emptied, she flung it across the room. Constance started to cry while sifting through the mess. She pawed through the piles without any luck. She saw double and couldn't wipe away the tears fast enough to see through them. She lost her balance and fell to her knees. She put her hand on the floor to prevent her from falling over completely.

Something stuck to the palm of her hand. The gold band was slim and the diamond was starting come loose from the molding. She picked up the ring and brought it closer to her face.

"Good luck, Constance." Sid said the last time they saw each other. "You're going to need it."

She read the word, "Hope," inscribed on the inside of the band.

Constance felt her lungs inflate. She ran her fingers through her brown hair. The clouds in her mind dissipated as she eyed the front door. She walked out and started running down the street.

In the present, Sid kissed Constance passionately.

He had been rubbing her back since they arrived at his apartment. He couldn't help himself. He wanted to take away some of her pain. Sid didn't know if his lips were still capable of doing that, but he went for it anyway.

He pulled away from her. Constance's eyes had returned to the soft blue he had fallen for. Sid studied her face, looking for signs telling him that it was okay. He wanted to kiss her again.

Constance beat him to it.

She moved forward and kissed him full on the lips. Sid's eyes snapped shut as she pushed her tongue into his mouth. He gently grabbed the back of her neck and pulled her in closer.

Constance moved one of her hands to his face and wrapped the other arm around him tightly. Sid stopped kissing her. He used his nose to push past her hair and ran his tongue over her neck. He used his muscle memory to remember all the spots that used to get her going. It was like nothing had changed. Constance moaned, causing him to suck on her neck even stronger. She started to unbutton his jeans.

"Hey there," she said grabbing him.

Sid grunted as she stroked him harder and faster.

"We have to take off more clothes," he said.

Constance let go of him for a moment and stripped off her shirt. She forced Sid's shirt over his head and pushed him playfully down on his bed. She helped him out of his jeans and boxer shorts. She licked her bottom lip before she took Sid in her mouth. She made eye contact as her head bobbed. Sid did his best not to explode, but it was hard with her tongue around him. He had to take control.

Sid waited for Constance to take a breath to act. He grabbed her under her arms and led her back up his body. He went right for her neck again, unclipping her bra at the same time. She swatted the bra away with one hand and moved Sid's face to her chest with the other.

"Are we being stupid?" Constance asked.

"The only stupid thing we did was waiting this long," Sid said.

He didn't wait for a response and flipped her over on her back. Sid smiled as he pulled off her pants and thong.

"You think we're just desperate?" Constance asked.

"Nope."

"You think I'm trashy?"

"Nope."

"Did you really not cheat on me when we were dating?"

Sid stopped kissing Constance's stomach and leaned his weight on one of his elbows.

"Do you really want to do this?" Sid asked.

"Shut up and get back to work. I want you inside of me."

Constance moaned as Sid slide insider her, and screamed every time he thrusted.

"Holy shit, I forgot how good you feel," Sid said.

She propped herself up on her elbows so she could get a better view. Sid's face was forced into one of her breasts and he swallowed one of her nipples. She giggled. Constance wriggled her body out from under him. She hopped off the bed and waited for him to lie down. She slowly positioned herself on top of him. She grabbed his wrists, held him down hard, and worked herself down on him. Both of them gasped.

Constance let go of Sid's wrists and allowed him to caress her body. Sid grabbed her hips and helped her to slide up and down faster. At the same time, he lifted himself off the bed and penetrated her deeper.

Sid reached for her hair and pulled it gently. She got even wetter allowing him to slide in and out easily. Sid grabbed her ass with both hands and felt himself about to let go.

"I'm coming!" Constance screamed.

"Fuck, me too!" Sid screamed.

Sid felt her relax as he pulled out. He fell hard onto the mattress and felt all his emotions go right to his head as soon as it hit the pillow. Constance snuggled against and kissed his cheek.

"I'll never let anyone hurt you again," Sid said.

"Promise?"

"Promise."

The two fell asleep.

Years earlier, Sid headed home to Connecticut.

Constance waited patiently with him in Grand Central Station. They didn't want to be separated, not even for a weekend.

"I don't want to miss you" Constance said. "I want you here all to myself."

"It'll go fast. Promise."

Sid's track was announced and he muscled his heavy duffle bag over his shoulder. He helped Constance to her feet, but she didn't let him walk away just yet. She flattened him against the wall and pushed her tongue into his mouth.

"Marry me, Constance," Sid said.

"Got a ring on you?"

"No."

"Not much of a proposal, is it?"

"Be right back."

Sid returned a few moment later holding a small plastic ball.

"You're kidding," Constance said.

She opened the ball and pulled out a small ring.

"This is from a vending machine?" She asked.

Sid nodded proudly.

"You're comfortable with a twenty-five cent proposal?"

"You'll get a real one. You say yes and it's a done deal."

Constance laughed and rubbed Sid's shaved head.

"Let's get you on that train," she said.

Sid walked on the train and realized he wasn't going to get a seat. He stood awkwardly by the door. Constance blew him a kiss and then decided that wasn't good enough. She raced over to him and kissed him hard on the lips. Constance stepped back off the train as the conductor made the final call. The bell rang signally the train was about to pull out of the station.

"I love you," Sid said.

"Yes!" Constance yelled. "My answer is yes!"

The doors closed.

Sid's eyes opened slowly.

His whole body was sore. He rolled over, but only found empty space. Sid panicked until he saw a lean figure struggling to put on clothes in the darkness.

"Tell me you were going to at least say goodbye," Sid said.

"I'm going to get us some food," Constance said. "I'm actually hungry for once and I know you can always eat."

"Hey, did we have sex again last night, or was I dreaming?"

"No, that was real life. It was good too. I'm glad you had to ask."

"Wait up, I'll walk you out."

261

"Well this is a new side of you."

"I'm turning over new leaves every day."

Sid held her hand as they walked down the hallway. He unlatched all the locks stepped back. She paused before opening the door.

"I'm going to give you back something" Constance said. "You're going to need it in the very near future."

Constance pressed the small engagement ring into Sid's palm.

RELEASE POINT

"Sid, did you hear that?" Constance asked, throwing the blankets off her sleeping husband.

She got out of bed and put on her robe. Sid didn't reply. Constance pulled her husband's old aluminum bat from behind their bedroom door and aggressively poked him with it.

"It's the dog," Sid said. "Come back to bed, babe."

Constance nervously opened the door and listened closely. She heard nothing, but she wasn't convinced.

"I'd feel better if you'd go check it out," she said.

"Okay, okay," he said. "But if I step in dog shit like I did last time, you're sleeping on the couch."

Sid put on a t-shirt and pair of mesh shorts and headed for the door.

"You're sure it wasn't maybe Bobby coming home?" He asked, taking the bat from his wife. "I know he said he was hanging out with some friends tonight and was going to be late."

"He came in about a half hour ago. I know he's okay. Just trust my womanly intuition for once and get your ass down there."

"I live to serve you."

Sid managed to get down the stairs without seriously injuring himself.

The living room was quiet and nothing appeared out of the ordinary. He was about to head into the kitchen when he heard a grunt come from the couch over by the bay window.

"Huck, get off the damn couch," he said. "You're lucky it was me, otherwise you'd be glue."

The black Lab lazily leapt off the couch and stumbled toward his master.

Sid removed the gate that kept the dog cut off from the rest of the house. He opened the porch door and let Huck head to the backyard on his own. Sid sniffed the air and heard his dog whimper. He turned the backlight on and found a trail of vomit leading from the screen door.

Huck retreated back into the house.

"Damn dog," Sid muttered.

Sid warily turned on the kitchen lights to grab some paper towels and Huck remained glued to his side looking less guilty than usual. The dog lifted his snout and led Sid to Bobby's room.

Sid quietly opened the door and peered into his son's dark room. The smell intensified and Sid saw Bobby leaning over the side of his bed.

"Bobby, are you okay?" He asked.

Sid didn't turn on the light just yet and there was a part of him that hoped he wouldn't have to. The fifteen-year-old responded by spitting off the side of the bed. Sid grimaced.

"Everything okay down there?" Constance asked.

Sid headed back to the hallway.

"Yep," he said.

"You sure?"

"I'm sure. Just going to let Huck out one more time."

"What's that smell?"

"I don't smell anything. I'll be up in a bit.

Sid retreated back to Bobby's room, knowing he didn't have much time before Constance would storm downstairs to demand better answers.

"Let's get you to the bathroom," Sid said.

"Ahhhhh!" Bobby screamed happily.

Constance echoed his screech upon arriving at the scene.

"What the hell's wrong with our son?" Constance asked. "Do we need to take him to the hospital?"

"Nope, he's drunk," Sid said.

"Are you fucking kidding me?"

"'Fraid not. We can talk about it later, we need to get him to the toilet."

Sid gagged, but managed to get Bobby mobile. He winced seeing Bobby leave a crime scene cut out surrounded by vomit on the bed.

"What the fuck did he do to himself?" Constance asked. "Don't just stand there, jackass, get him moving."

"Not helping!" Sid screamed.

The two of them lifted Bobby to the bathroom, dropping him in front of the beige toilet. Sid walked back into the bedroom to collect the soiled sheets. He grimly saw his son's sneakers sinking in a pool of dark bile.

"I think I'm going to be sick!" Bobby shouted.

"How does he have any left?" Constance asked, bringing in a roll of paper towels. "You put the seat up for him, right?"

"Shit," Sid said.

"I don't fucking believe how useless you are right now."

Both parents returned to the bathroom just in time to watch their son vomit sudsy alcohol all over the lavender toilet seat cover. Sid went to lift up the seat while Bobby caught his breath.

"Don't do it now!" Constance said.

Her warning fell on deaf ears. Sid lifted the seat, flooding the bathroom floor. Bobby's pants soaked through instantly. Constance grabbed a towel from the storage closet and thrust it into Sid's hands. He started mopping up everything. Bobby put his hands on the edge of the bowl, ready to heave again. He did his best to aim for the middle, but missed badly and instead threw up all over his father's leg. Sid swallowed hard.

"I swear to God, if you get sick on me, I'm leaving the house for good," Constance said.

Once Bobby had emptied his stomach completely, Sid and Constance dumped him in the shower and turned the cold water on. Bobby promptly passed out. They washed him as best they could, toweled him off, and threw him back on his bed, which was devoid of any kind of linens. They stood there for a handful of moments and listened to their son snore.

"He's all yours," Constance said. "You Sanford men fucking deserve each other."

"Run, pussy," Sid said to himself the next morning.

Sid passed a neighbor or two walking their dogs and offered a smile as he continued his rapid pace. He could hear his feet thumping up against the concrete, but refused to acknowledge the pain that brought.

"You're not too old," he said. "Keep moving."

Sid had been running for close to an hour now. He had given up trying to stay asleep on the couch. He had watched Sportscenter a half a dozen times and had finally decided to run off the ache in his muscles and joints. Sid's shirt was soaked through and his socks had fallen down to his ankles. He had abandoned his iPod for this run because he didn't need any extra motivation.

"Five more minutes, you little bitch," he thought. "Run up that hill one more time and you can be done."

He chugged up the hill slowly. Sid sucked in air greedily. He stopped once the pavement leveled off. He put his hands on his hips and walked slowly around the block. His knee throbbed. Sid coughed hard and spat. His muscles trembled, a mix of fatigue and worry. Sid finally stood up and looked up to the brightening sky.

His father would have known what to do.

The family had lost Kenneth the previous spring. Constance's parents had passed a few years before and had left her and Sid their Astoria home. Constance invited Kenneth and Gail to move into the downstairs apartment, which they happily accepted. Kenneth hadn't been a New York resident since the age of three, so he had been eager to explore the city his parents had originated from. However, a month after arriving, he contracted a bad cold that turned into pneumonia. Sid knew his mother had dealt with just about everything when it came to her husband's health, but even she couldn't mask her anxiety. His coughing had worsened and the emergency room became more frequent. During the last ambulance ride, Kenneth's lungs and heart had just stopped fighting and he was gone.

The spring wasn't the same without him. He was buried when he should have been watching his grandsons running around the base paths. Kenneth should have been making his annoyed grunt when Tom's son Jack or Bobby popped up or struck out looking, not being cried over by the family he loved more than anything else in the world. He would have hated the fact he had inconvenienced everyone and that they weren't off doing something else in the beautiful spring weather. Sid felt the loss of his hero every day, feeling helpless because he hadn't been able to do anything at the end for the man who had picked him up so many times throughout his life.

Sid tried to switch to another gear. He knew his mother would be back from her visit to the casino. He needed to fill her in on last night's festivities before she caught a glimpse, or whiff, of her grandson.

"Run, dammit!" He screamed.

Gail was already in the kitchen baking something when Sid walked in the door. She had various bowls spread out on the counter and she had her apron securely tied around her. Sid gave her a kiss on the cheek as she was taking a sip of her giant diet soda.

"Get away from me, you're all sweaty," she said. "Were you out running in this heat? I thought I raised you to be smarter!"

"Heh, been no evidence of it so far," Sid said. "Win any money?"

"I lost twenty bucks at the slot machine and then shopped the rest of the time."

"Buy anything for yourself?"

"Of course not."

Sid smiled and pulled a bottle of water out of the fridge. He took a long chug, spilling water all over himself and the floor.

"Don't you dare mess up your wife's kitchen," Gail said. "I'm surprised Bobby isn't up yet, he's usually such an early riser. Hey, can you grab me the metal pot from the bottom cabinet? Do it quietly, I don't want to wake anyone up."

Sid took out the tall pot his mother needed. An idea crept into his head and grabbed a big metal spoon from the counter and walked toward his son's room.

"You might want to cover your ears," Sid told his mother. "This is going to be loud."

269

Sid turned the light on rattled the spoon inside the pot violently. Bobby leapt out of his coma. He put his hands to his ears, but Sid kept banging away. He stopped just long enough for Bobby to say something.

"Dad, leave me alone," he said. "Oh man, my head is killing me."

"Yeah, that happens when you drink and come home and scare your parents to death," Sid said. "But you don't talk unless I tell you that you can. Go shower up and get your baseball stuff. Meet me out front."

Sid made sure his son actually got out of bed before returning to the kitchen, where he found Gail and Constance standing with their arms across their chests.

"Sorry," Sid said. "He needed a rude wake up call."

"And me?" Constance asked.

"Collateral damage."

"As always."

"Hey."

"I changed my mind," Constance said. "You can have him back."

"Don't look at me," Gail said. "I told you to run. No returns!"

At Cunningham Park, Bobby stepped slowly off the faded white baseline.

He crouched down and rocked on the balls of his feet. He started at the imaginary pitcher standing on the empty pitcher's mound and waited. His muscles cramped, but he remained quiet.

270

"Go!" Sid yelled.

Bobby sluggishly tore off toward second base. He reached the bag and nearly collapsed with exhaustion. He did his best not to puke, but he knew it was inevitable. He spit into the puddle he had just created at the beginning of the outfield grass and jogged back to first base. Sid happily chewed on an apple. Bobby had lost count how many sprints he had done and he was sure he wasn't even close to finished.

"Okay," Sid said. "I need you to sprint a homer and then we can start batting practice."

"Dad, you know your arm can't..."

"First of all, I didn't say you could talk. Second of all, my arm is fine. Just don't tell your mother."

Bobby powerwalked to home plate and waited. Sid shouted "go!" and his son sprinted drunkenly around the bases. Sid walked to the mound and hurled some balls toward the aluminum backstop. His arm tightened immediately. His grimace turned into a smirk, remembering how as a teenager he'd throw batting practice to Jocelyn at neighborhood parks. His ability to throw strikes would wane rather quickly, causing Jocelyn to fling the bat away in disgust. "Let me show you how to throw like a girl," she'd say, firing perfect fastballs over the plate again and again. Sid coughed into his hand, forcing the memory down with all the others he kept guarded. He continued to worry about his son.

Sid had never really had to discipline his son before. Bobby was a good kid who cared about good grades and doing the right thing all the time. He volunteered at a senior center close to the house after school some days and

271

didn't need to be asked twice to do his chores. Last night was totally out of character.

Sid watched his son reach home plate and start dry heaving. Bobby managed to walk himself over to behind the backstop before throwing up. Sid waited patiently until his son was finished.

"Grab your bat," Sid said. "Now."

Bobby did so and settled into the batter's box. He got into his stance and took a quick practice hack. Before he could get back, Sid had rifled a ball behind him.

"Sorry, that one got away from me," he said.

"Yeah, that's not going to be the last one either," Bobby mumbled.

"What's that?" Sid asked.

Bobby just shrugged his shoulders and signaled to his father that he was ready. He tried to wipe away as many cobwebs as he could, but he knew this was going to be a painful experience. He watched his father fire the ball down the middle. Bobby swung and missed badly. He also missed the next five pitches and then hit a few weak groundballs. Bobby hung his head when Sid reached the bottom of the ball bucket.

"What if you were in a state tournament game?" Sid asked. "What if your team was counting on you to come through and you couldn't because you were out partying all night the night before. I can't even imagine what your defense would be like and you're lucky your old man doesn't have the energy to keep going. My guess would be that you couldn't track down a well-hit ball to the outfield if your life depended on it. So, let's skip all that. You can talk now, but all I want to hear about is what happened last night."

"Well, Jack knew about this party these kids were having in the woods and invited me," Bobby said. "I'm always turning him down because I'm always busy, so I figured this time I'd say yes. I wasn't going to get drunk, but I liked the way I was feeling. It felt good to hang out with Jack and all his friends and be a part of something cool. This kid who wasn't drinking drove us home. I thought I was fine. I realized when I laid down and the room started spinning I was in trouble. You know the rest."

"Did this scare you at all?" Sid asked.

"Yeah. I used to ask myself before why kids would do this to themselves and after last night I still don't have an answer. I felt awful because you and Mom had to deal with it. I'm sorry. I really am. Are you going to get Jack in trouble?"

"I've talked to your Uncle Tom already. If he decides to punish Jack, that's his decision. Was he as bad as you were?"

Bobby nodded.

"Then Jack is pretty fucked," Sid said. "You know why your mother and I are so upset, right?"

"Yeah."

"So tell me."

Bobby shrugged.

"I mean you're too young to be drinking" Sid said. "Jack is older than you and he's too young to be drinking. More importantly though, there is a history of alcoholism on both sides of your family. That's not a good road to start

273

going down because there is rarely a way back. You have so much potential and I don't want to see you fuck it up. You're our star and you don't need to do anything to yourself that's going to burn you out. We love you and only want to see the best for you. You understand that?"

Bobby nodded and wiped his tears that were falling down his cheeks. Sid gave him an encouraging pat on the shoulder.

"Pick up all the balls and we can go back home," Sid said. "Your old man didn't do half bad on the mound today, huh?

"Hey, Dad, does Mémère know?" Bobby asked.

"I'm sure your mother filled her in."

"Then I guess I'm pretty fucked too."

"Take your whoopin' like a man, son," Sid said. "And watch your mouth."

"Well, I got that to look forward to."

"Hey, you play, you pay, partner."

"You know, Pépère would have said the same thing."

Later that night, Sid repositioned the pillow behind his back. He closed the hot laptop that was burning a hole in his sweatpants and tossed it in his wife's empty spot. He rubbed his sore shoulder and yawned. Constance still wasn't home after being called in for a last minute meeting. Sid had been re-writing the same sentence in his next novel for twenty minutes and it hadn't gotten any better.

Sid's second cup of coffee wasn't helping his nerves and the Yankees had lost the game in the first inning. He glanced back up at the television only to see another

274

Orioles homerun leave the yard. Sid's ears perked up when he heard the front door open. Constance yelled at the dog on her way into the house. Sid waited patiently for her to make her entrance in their bedroom.

"Oh my God!" She said waving her hands manically. "That man is insane. He went over every little thing thousands of times. I swear to God, it's a miracle we put out a magazine every month. But Bobby called and apologized. How's your arm?"

"I still can't find my release point, but the old cannon is fine."

"Liar."

"Yeah, it's on fire. And not because of the tub of Icy/Hot I dumped on my shoulder."

"Did you talk to Tom?"

"I did. Jack's also in rough shape too. A lot of yard work is going to get done between the two of them."

"Good."

She pulled on a pair of Sid's mesh shorts that were a couple sizes too big for her. She rolled them up on her waist and hopped into bed next to her husband.

"You remember when we brought him home?" Sid asked. "We were terrified. We had this little life that relied on us for everything. It was so easy when all he wanted was a bottle or his diaper changed."

"Pft! It wasn't any easier," Constance said. "You had to guess what he wanted when he cried, and, thanks to your genes, he did that often. At least when he started talking we could figure out what the hell he wanted."

"Quite the display of parenting on our part last night."

"Hey, we're going to drop the fucking ball sometimes. At least he didn't choke on his own vomit."

"I told myself when he was born that I wouldn't let him make any of the mistakes I made. I know he's smart, but a part of me that was worried I didn't do enough to warn him about nights like that."

Constance stopped brushing her hair and elbowed her husband lovingly.

"You're a silly man," she said. "I'm going to ignore all that and ask you to nuke one of those hamburgers you saved for little ol' me?"

"Ketchup? Mustard?"

"Yes."

"You're lucky I love you."

Constance kissed him before he left the bed.

"Yes, I am," she said.

Six months later, Gail followed her husband into death.

She had gotten sick and her doctors couldn't figure out what was wrong or how to fix it. All they knew was that she was fading rapidly. Everyone in the Sanford family was frustrated and devastated at the same time. However, Gail had lived a long life and the last thing she wanted was to fight against something so expected and deserved as a good death. She had worked hard to create a generation that was already surpassing the successes of those who came before them, and now her work was done.

Her remaining time was anything but wasted. She told stories about her farm girl days in upstate Maine to any family member who would listen. Her body had failed her, but her mind remained as sharp as it had ever been. She told everyone about the time her father had slaughtered a pig for Easter and had left its head on the carving table in the barn. Gail had wandered in on her tricycle and had come face to face with the head. She ran out screaming and didn't set foot in the barn without her father ever again.

She told Bobby about the time she had been the only girl brave enough to climb a steep hill during a snowy winter. All the boys had told her she was too chicken to do it and that she would end up running home crying. She had ignored all of them and didn't stop moving until she had reached the top of the hill. Gail had been so nervous and so scared, but all her sisters cheered loudly as she stuck her tongue out at her older brothers on the way down.

No had one had been prepared for the stories to stop one morning in May. The family she loved so much surrounded her and watched as their matriarch closed her eyes for the last time.

She had been holding Bobby and Jack's hands and it had broken Sid's heart to watch her grip slacken. Gail had made Tom, Sid, and Patrick promise to cremate her. They had argued, but like always, her mind was made up and that was that. She had requested a tall, skinny urn so she could experience both once in her life and that she wanted to go home. The boys agreed without asking any more questions.

In the present, Sid drank cold coffee at his kitchen table.

Constance had left him a mug before packing food in the car. She had even left out the sports section of the newspaper for him to read. He allowed a small smile to crease his face. She had also put a bowl of fruit in his spot, but he wasn't hungry.

"You should really eat something, love," Constance said, sitting down next to her husband. "You're going to need your strength for the drive."

"I like all the subtle hints," Sid said. "I'll grab a donut or something when we get gas."

"You need good food, not junk. I packed a lot of veggies and healthy snacks."

"What are we rabbits?"

"You're my rabbits, and I'd like to keep you men around long enough to see some grandkids."

"Don't worry, I'll stick to coffee."

"Well, at least I tried," Constance said. "Go on and get your son. I'll make you guys some egg sandwiches."

"I love you."

"I love you too. Git."

Sid found Bobby on the front stoop.

"You forget anything?" He asked.

"I'm ready," Bobby asked.

"Pack any good comic books?"

"I'm too old for comic books."

"Don't tell your Uncle Damon that."

"I sell the ones he gets me for Christmas on eBay."

"Wouldn't tell him that either. How much you get for them?"

"You know that iPad I bought a while ago?"

"Give your old man a cut next time, will you?"

"Sure, Dad."

"Your Mémère loved you very much, kiddo."

"I miss her. I don't like the fact that she's going to be so far away."

Sid nodded, thinking about the ten-hour odyssey to upstate Maine ahead of them.

"I know, partner," Sid said. "But she spent every day giving herself up for everyone else around her. She gave us so much love and protection without asking for anything in return. Don't you think we owe her something?"

"I guess so."

"And it's going to be a fun ride up with your uncles and Jack. We'll do our best to keep Uncle Tom from being his usual boring self so we don't drive off the road. That's if we decide to pick them up in Connecticut."

Bobby cracked a smile. Sid ruffled his son's hair and squeezed him tight. He heard his wife come out the front door.

"My men!" Constance said.

"We should get on the road," Sid said.

"You make sure to call me every so often so that I know you Sanford men aren't getting into trouble," Constance said. "And drive slowly! I know all of you inherited Grandpa Sanford's lead foot, but try to keep it under control."

Bobby gave his mother a kiss as his father walked toward the car. Constance pulled him into a quick hug.

"Please take care of your Dad," she said. "He's going to need you."

"I will Mom. I'm going to need him too.

Hours later, Sid heard Patrick chewing.

"Are you still eating?" He asked.

Patrick didn't answer right away because his mouth was too full. He gave his brother a sloppy smile. There were crumbs all over his shirt.

"It turned out there was one more glazed donut in that box," Patrick said. "My will power can stand up to a lot of things, but a lonely glazed donut is not one of them."

Sid rearranged himself in the driver's seat the best he could and yawned. Sid had been driving the whole time and they had only made one pit stop. He had been trying to keep himself awake by singing along to the music on the radio. Everyone else had fallen to sleep once they left Connecticut and hopped on the Massachusetts Turnpike.

"How long have you been awake?" Sid asked.

"Long enough to hear you butcher songs that will forever be ruined for me. I thought you did a lovely job with 'Born to Run' though. I didn't know someone could screw up lyrics that badly."

"Shut up."

"Hey, whatever works, brother. I figured it would be the least I could do to help keep you company up here. Well, that and I wanted to make sure we were headed in the right direction."

"I'm never going to live that down, am I? I went east on a trip through New York State thirty years ago. Big deal."

"Dude, you drove two hours in the wrong direction."

"It was scenic."

"And unnecessary. I had never seen Pop so pissed off."

"Yeah, yeah," Sid said. "How's my beautiful niece?"

"She's all kinds of pissed I wouldn't let her come with us. I'm lucky the other two are at school. I owe her big time."

"Yep."

Silence returned momentarily.

"Momma used to make fun of Pop for saying 'every reason I have for living is in this room,'" Patrick said. "But she was the same way."

"Yeah."

"May said she had a question about something and picked up the phone before realizing she couldn't do that anymore. Momma probably pissed herself up there after that one."

"I think Constance must have shouted a million different curses the other day trying to make one of her cake recipes. She spent all day in the kitchen crying and swearing. How she got any baking done is beyond me."

"Speaking of profanity, you remember that Christmas with the tangled lights?"

"First time I heard 'fuck,' I think. She screamed for us to get in the car and I never moved faster in my life. That ride to CVS was tenser than a couple headed to buy a pack of Plan B."

281

"How many times do you think she said 'son of a bitch' in her lifetime?"

"You could fill the National Archives with transcripts of all the ones directed at me alone."

"Scariest sound in the world was her yelling 'boys!' at the top of the stairs. She had a crazy look in her eyes that night that I will never, ever be able to forget."

"I don't know, our wives have honed that look pretty well over the years."

"Well aware."

"Imagine if she was a drinker? None of us would have made it out of that house alive."

"She was tough, all right. Three boys and Pop, she had to be. I'd take her over any of my commanding officers any day."

Sid nodded and started singing along to a Bob Dylan song.

"That's my cue to go back to sleep," Patrick said. "Keep up the good driving, bro."

Hours later, Tom nudged Sid, who had fallen asleep in the passenger seat.

Sid drowsily swatted his brother's elbow away and pressed his face back up against the window. Tom persisted.

"What," Sid said.

"Take a look in the backseat. Patrick's head is taking up the whole rearview mirror."

"And most Russian spy satellites. This isn't news."

"I require sustenance."

"How is that possible? You've got three empty bags of Pirate's Booty on your lap."

"I need solid food."

Sid reached in front of him, pulled out a Cliff Bar from his backpack, and flung it at his older brother.

"Nice shot, dick, it's under the seat. Open one up for me, will you?"

Sid sat up and rubbed his eyes. Tom banged his hands on the steering wheel to the beat of the Tom Petty song on the radio. Sid sensed his older brother was more chatty than hungry, so he officially put his nap on hold.

"Do you remember all those weekends we used to go shopping with her?" Tom asked. "All three of us would be forced to go clothes shopping or grocery shopping. After spending hours wherever we were, she'd reward us with McDonald's. We used to go to the same one and sit in the same seats every time. It's a good thing we were all active, because it seemed we pigged out there every single weekend. We would have been fat little kids without baseball, that's for sure."

"Yeah, it seemed like it. How about the huge meals she'd make on Sundays? We used to chow down and then pile on her bed to watch a movie or television show."

Raindrops dotted the windshield. The sky had been getting grayer and grayer as the car made progress north. The precipitation intensified and soon the windshield wipers were going as fast as they could go.

"What is it with shitty weather every time the two of us are in the car together?" Tom said.

Sid shrugged.

"It was only every trip with Pop driving you to school in New Hampshire, every weekend Yankees home game for a three-year stretch, and two Bruce Springsteen concerts at Gillette Stadium."

"All I remember about one of those Bruce shows is drinking two expired beers I found in my trunk because my back was in so much pain."

"At least you didn't whine through his whole set list..."

"Hey, it's not my fault he played for three plus hours," Tom said. "Anyway, this rain is nothing compared to the blizzard the night Bobby was born."

"I've never heard anyone curse as violently as you did your car when it died in that snow bank. Would have helped if you listened to me well before you buried us in that snow bank. It's fine, though, you were only going seventy on an icy road."

"I wasn't worried because I discovered your secret stash of candy bars. I should have stolen them all and walked. But then I would have missed your screaming like a teenager at a rave when Momma knocked on your window."

"Didn't recognize her or if she was there to help or murder us. I squealed accordingly."

"I didn't think she had it in her to drive through that mess," Sid said. "Don't think she drove for a while after that though."

"She even picked up Pop and Constance's parents who were stranded as well. He talked about how proud he was for months."

"I don't know if you noticed, I drove for a couple hundred miles earlier, so I'm going to pass out," Sid said.

"What?" Tom yelled turning the radio's volume all the way up.

The Sanford men in the backseat murmured and kicked Tom and Sid's seats.

The next morning, the rural air smelled sweet and clean.

Gail's sons and grandsons gathered in front of the crimson house she grew up in. Her father Arthur's potato farm remained abandoned across the street. The crew had spent the night at their cousin Eric's house, which had previously been Tante Valeda's home and was only a handful of gravel away.

"Do we have anything to toast with?" Bobby asked, holding the white urn.

"I almost forgot!" Patrick said, racing back into the house. "I'll be right back."

Sid found his mother's window, the one with the white crescent moons carved into the white shutters, on the second floor of the house. He wondered what thought she might have had looking out of that window as a kid. Did she ever imagine she'd end up states away married to a former New Yorker? What kind of life was she planning and did it include having the boys that were standing outside in her former front yard? Sid kicked a few pebbles of gravel, upset with himself that he hadn't asked any of those questions when he had the chance.

"What the hell?" Tom asked, eyeing the six-pack of Diet Pepsi Patrick returned with.

"We couldn't toast her with alcohol, she never drank. This'll do."

"Where do you want to do this?" Sid asked.

"Mémère told me stories about schools shutting down so the kids could pick potatoes," Jack said eyeing the potato field. "She hated the hard work, but she liked hanging out with her brothers and sisters all day."

"What do you think?" Patrick asked.

Sid and Tom nodded approvingly. The men walked across Route 1 and stood in the mud of their ancestors.

"You're the writer, Sid," Tom said. "You should say something."

"I'm all out," he said. "It's the next generation's turn."

Jack nudged Bobby who cleared his throat and twisted the soda bottle's cap.

"What I'll miss most is Mémère yelling her heart out at my baseball games," Bobby said. "It didn't matter if I struck out or got a hit, she always screamed encouragement. She would sit in the stands and eat sunflower seeds, but she wasted so much time splitting the shells open with her hands and then eating the seed. She never left a game early and she always had a hug and a snack waiting for me. I miss her and I'm bummed that I'll never be able to tell her that I loved her just as much as she loved me."

Sid raised his bottle toward his nephew Jack.

"I was lucky when I was the only grandson," Jack said. "I got all the whoopie pies, all the toys, and all the love. I thought when all my other cousins came along, it would never be the same and she wouldn't love me as much. Mémère never let that happened. She explained to me that

286

she had enough love for everyone. She said that was what a being a family was all about. In fact, she never stopped teaching me lessons. She taught me about love, life, hard work, honesty, toughness, and what it means to be a good person. I love you Mémère. I'm glad I could help bring you home."

Bobby passed the urn to Tom, who said goodbye. He passed it to Patrick, who did the same.

"I tried to reach the stars, Momma," Sid whispered, opening the jar. "Hope I didn't let you down."

He slowly tipped the urn, letting the Maine dirt swallow the ashes.

LAST DAY

The television screen splashed light and shadow across the bare, white walls.

The camera moved away from the action on the baseball diamond and panned the stands of the sold-out Yankee Stadium. Middle-aged men and ten-year-old boys alike cheered and screamed, and the opposing team's dugout grimaced incredulously. The scene shifted back to the pitcher's mound. The Yankees' closer adjusted his pinstriped jersey and rearranged the dirt beneath his feet. The camera followed him as he checked the runners on first and second. The Red Sox third baseman stepped out of the batter's box and called timeout. The crowd hissed and jeered.

Sid lowered the volume. He had dozed off again and the hostile crowd had snapped back into reality. His eyes widened.

"What the fuck," he said out loud. "I fall asleep for an inning and they let those bastards right back in."

He'd been here before. Hell, he felt like he'd been trapped watching this moment for seventy-five years. That's how long he'd been a Yankees fan, and that's how many years the team managed to make every game this interesting. For once, he wished he could enjoy a quiet American League Championship Series and not have to hear "Game 7" and "Boston Red Sox" in the same sentence.

His wrinkled hand rubbed his knee. He stretched out his right leg. He repeated the action more slowly with his left leg. He flexed his wrist and heard what sounded like twenty bones cracking all at once. Sid closed his eyes and smiled contently. He couldn't complain. His doctor had made it clear there was more wrong with him than a couple of achy joints.

"There are no outs folks and the bases are loaded for the Red Sox," the announcer said. "This is not good for Yankees fans."

"No shit," Sid said.

Most people rolled their eyes at the devotion Sid still gave to baseball. He knew stats from eras no one talked about, collected obscure baseball cards, and religiously watched every inning of every regular season and post-season game the Yankees played. Damon would try to rip him away from the television long enough to have dinner out or to go on one of his silly retreats, but typically was unsuccessful. Sid never budged between the months of April and October. Why would he? This is just what he did. He watched. The game was all he had left.

Tom and Kristen had moved to Florida and now spent the majority of their time buying water and canned goods in bulk and pounding slabs of wood across their windows. Sid was fairly certain the worry would get to those two long before a hurricane did. Patrick had relocated to the West

289

Coast an eternity ago and ran a foundation for disabled veterans. May started her own line of strawberry jam while helping her husband keep his head on straight. Patrick would call Sid often and agonize over all the work he had put upon himself.

Unlike Sid, Tom and Patrick didn't move around too well, which meant the three rarely got together in the flesh. Sid liked to kid that it served them right for inheriting all the baseball talent. However, he missed his brothers, which led to gargantuan phone bills and sore ears.

Bobby had been trying to move his father out to California for at least a decade. Sid would get phone calls, emails, and letters saying he would be able to buy his son's books in Los Angeles just as easily as he did in New York City. Bobby even promised to mail multiple copies at a time. Sid always refused. He liked watching his son's novels conquer the best-seller charts right where he was. Bobby had inherited every drop of his mother's stubbornness and never showed any sign of giving up. He had even gone so far as to enlist his agent to his cause. It didn't hurt that Bobby's agent just happened to be Sid's godson Jack. Sid didn't think that was fair, but it was what it was.

Sid also didn't feel right leaving Constance alone in that cemetery. He still thought she was right there beside him. It was hard to think of her at times, but he always went to bed believing she had somehow forgiven him for all his sins. His picture of her might have faded a bit and her kisses might have long since dried out, but for better or worse, his memories of her were as crystal clear as his eyesight.

"And the Yankees will come to bat in the bottom of the ninth inning down by a run," the announcer said. "Don't go anywhere folks."

"No problem," Sid said.

The game still connected to him to both ghosts and living flesh. He'd spent a lifetime watching others excel at a child's game he loved like a member of the family. At times, Sid was convinced the Sanford family was strung tightly together with bright red lacing and densely packed yarn. Baseball had never been just a game to them. Sid fully credited his relationship with his brothers to their marathon Wiffle ball games in the backyard. They had kept stats, wore base paths into the grass Kenneth half-heartedly tried to maintain, and had seasons end with tears of sore losing and Momma Sanford's stern voice.

Baseball hadn't been a game then, and it wasn't just a game to the Little Leaguers that Sid had coached eons ago. He had been humbled to find out that a bunch of prepubescent kids had more talent that he could ever dream of. But he was grateful to have found a few players that were just like him. They loved the game and played their hearts out, but knew that their time playing it would be as short-lived as his was.

Sid remembered how devastated Patrick was when the younger Sanford had finally put away his cleats for good. Sid had forced his brother to continue to at least throw the ball around in the backyard. He tried not to admit it too often, but watching Patrick play had been one of the best things in his life. The catches served as a reminder to both that they had once played the game for real.

The announcer went hoarse. Some no-named rookie had just hit a bomb into the upper deck in left field. The

Yankees were in the World Series again. Everything was right in the world.

"The Yankees will be flying out to the West Coast shortly, I assume," one of the announcers blurted out when the camera cut to them in the booth. "Those Dodgers are itching for a fight and will be ready for them."

"Hmm," Sid muttered.

Patrick would be awake. He was just as bad as Sid when it came to the Yankees.

"What do you think about that, huh?" Patrick asked, picking up on the first ring. "That guy's set for life. He could retire now and live off that moment until he's old like us. What's up, brother?"

"Do you still have that connection with the Dodgers?" Sid asked.

"Yeah, why?"

"Any chance you could get tickets to the Series?"

"I can try, why?"

"How would you like to see your older brother for a couple days?"

"So two tickets it is then?"

"Yep."

"Am I going to have to make all your travel plans because you're a helpless old man?"

"Yep."

"Well, start packing now. That way by the time you're done, the Series might still be going on."

"Funny. Hey, get three tickets, okay?"

"You think he'll come? Does he even like baseball?"

"He doesn't have a choice. Call me with the details, bud."

"Sounds good."

Sid hung up. He glanced at Constance's picture next to him on the tray table. He fell asleep and dreamt.

Her body is soft.

He tasted the little hairs standing erect on her skin. He felt her body quiver—a mix of nervousness and acceptance. Her eyes are shut tight, her mouth opened slightly to moan, her cheeks flushed.

He kissed her nose.

She giggled.

She wrapped her arms around him. He felt her hot breath on his ear.

"Make love to me," she said.

He can't move despite hearing the words he's been waiting for more than a month.

"Well, I'll get the...umm...yeah."

He leapt out of the slim hotel sheets, and rummaged through his backpack. He found the treasured box of Trojans. He fumbled opening the bright blue package. He rolled the sticky condom onto his rigid penis.

He settled back under the covers.

"Are you sure you want to do this?" He asked.

She innocently nodded her head.

293

He moved on top of her. She squirmed.

"That's my leg, Sid!"

"Oops."

"That's it."

He worked his way in slowly. She cried in pain. He felt tears on his neck. He stopped.

"We don't have to do this," he said. "I hate hurting you."

"Don't be ridiculous," she said. "It feels good too."

He resumed. She felt so warm. He finished suddenly.

"I love you so much," he said. "I love you so much."

She showered him with salty kisses, her lips tender from tears and passion. He felt the tug of sleep.

On the Upper East Side the next morning, Damon took groceries from the conveyor belt and put them into a tall brown paper bag. He grabbed the bag with both hands and placed it gently into the shopping cart next to him. He told the young mother to have a great day and stepped away from his workstation to let an acne-plagued teenager take over for him.

"Thanks for helping me bag today!" The cashier said.

Damon politely nodded. He shuffled over to the customer service desk to sign out. He bought a candy bar and a soda, which he knew was going to tear apart his system. But he's been here since six in the morning and he wasn't going to make it home without eating something. He felt embarrassed holding up foot traffic as he slowly walked out of the store and into the crisp Sunday afternoon air. He breathed in deep and started coughing. Damon reached into his pocket and pulled out his inhaler. He took a gulp from it and felt better instantly.

Damon got on the bus. He'd given up his license years ago. He could barely manage to get up to go to the bathroom late at night, never mind operate a moving vehicle. He didn't want to be one of those old guys that stubbornly clung to false pride long enough to get somebody killed. No, Damon dealt with being old like he dealt with everything else in his life, stubbornly rational. Sid liked to kid him that if he could have created a spreadsheet for his old age, he would have.

Damon took a seat in the back and rubbed his sore, well, everything. He knew he'd have to give up this job sooner rather than later. His body continued its rebellion against him and he wasn't putting up much of a resistance. Damon took a rainbow of pills every morning and there wasn't a moment during the day when something in or on his body didn't scream. He guessed the good news was that the double knee replacement had thinned him out quite a bit. Of course, the down side was that he had plenty of extra skin to wrinkle.

He coughed hard again and leaned back. He tried to remember the days when he had the stamina to hop from country to country and do good hard jobs like building houses or lugging large barrels of supplies to families in need. Now, after six hours of bagging groceries for yuppie families of four, he could barely stay awake. Damon tried to his best to keep busy in other ways. He played chess with Sid at the park, enjoyed the occasional bingo game, and explored neighborhood tag sales. His mind always came back to the dark idea that kept him awake at night.

"Death," he heard himself mutter.

He focused on a group of young children laughing a few feet in front of him. He felt certain they were laughing at him. Hell, he'd be laughing at him. What was funnier than watching an old man fall apart in the back of the bus? The kids started to giggle and point. They were laughing at him! He could feel his nerves tense up and his shirt dampened with sweat. He hung his head to avoid looking right at them. Damon's face reddened. He still had his apron on. He must have forgotten to take it off before leaving the store. He looked back at the kids and made a face. They exploded into laughter and hid behind their seats.

Damon's phone rang the moment he stepped into his apartment.

"Where the hell have you been all day?" Sid said. "I called a hundred times this morning."

"I had work. Some of us do that to pay bills and things."

"Speaking of, did you pay off that walker yet?"

"What do you want?"

"I need you to come over tomorrow."

"I always come over."

"I need you here earlier. Bobby's coming too. He doesn't know that yet, but he is."

"Why, what's going? Are you okay?"

"Yup, just be here. Please go take your pills, bud. That should take the rest of the afternoon."

Sid hung up.

Damon put the phone back on the hook and rushed to the bathroom.

In upstate New York, Bobby smacked the delete key.

He did it again. Then, he did it again. He didn't stop until all he was left with was a white screen and a flashing black cursor. He rubbed his eyes, knowing he was nowhere. He kept typing the same crappy sentences. The ideas were there, but for whatever reason they were telling him to fuck off for the moment. They would come. They always did.

The bathroom door of the hotel room opened. A blond-haired woman came out wrapped in a soft white towel. She walked over to Bobby and planted a wet kiss on his cheek. He watched her as she walked over to the bed and collapsed on it. Her wet hair fanned out across the unmade bed. There were a lot of things Bobby could ignore for his writing, but his girlfriend just out of the shower wasn't one of them.

"I'm exhausted!" Stephanie said.

"Am I that good?"

"Not really, I just didn't sleep well."

"You've got a comeback for everything, don't you?"

"I get my wit from my father. Blame him."

"He's a lot bigger than me, so I think I'll just take it out on you," he said.

"This could go on all day," she said. "Get in this bed."

Bobby had met Stephanie at a book signing a few years back. She had thought he was cute and bought a book just so she could talk to him. They hit it off and had been dating on and off ever since. Bobby was still convinced that she still hadn't read the book. Despite that, he loved her deeply. He never thought it would happen to him, but like his father always told him, love happens to everyone whether they want it or not. He was scared of committing and spent a lot of his time on the road, but he just couldn't help loving her unconditionally, wildly. Her spirit and hardwired goodness ignited every fiber of his heart. Bobby would eventually accept an editor position or professorship and settle down. He had hidden a ring with his father so he'd be prepared when that day came.

"You're vibrating," Stephanie said.

"That's a new trick," Bobby said.

"You're such a guy."

Bobby checked the caller ID. He couldn't ignore this call.

"Hey, Dad, what's up?" He asked.

"Hey, partner," Sid said. "I need you to do me a favor."

"Sure."

"I need you to come see me tomorrow. I got this crazy idea I want to talk to you about."

"You didn't burn through my inheritance already, did you?"

"What inheritance?"

"Touché. Seriously, what's up?"

"You don't need to know at the moment."

"Come on, I'm not trucking all that way for what I'm sure is a harebrained scheme."

"You're too much like your mother," Sid said. "Took a small army of trained ninjas to surprise her. How's the book coming?"

"It'll be a lot better if I stay here and write it."

"Yeah, but I'm your father."

"Fine," Bobby said. "I actually have a meeting with my agent in a few weeks. Can it wait until then?"

"Nope," Sid said. "Tomorrow. I'd get on the road."

"You okay, Dad?"

"Don't worry, I'm not dragging you to my deathbed."

"Well, that's a relief. Can I bring a date?"

"That's my boy."

Bobby heard his father hang up.

"How is he?" Stephanie asked.

"Senile," Bobby said. "Up for a road trip?"

In Queens, Sid resumed his catnap.

He wore a torn shirt and dusty khakis.

He closed the town car's trunk. He felt at home instantly. Yet another war seemed a lifetime away already.

He had covered the deaths of those not so much younger than he. The fall wind was strong enough to part his hair, but he still felt the hot desert sun sting his leathery neck.

He had forgotten what she felt like, what she tasted like. She opened the door timidly.

"Hi, beautiful," he said.

He smelled her perfume, an innocent, sweet fragrance.

"I love you, Sid Sanford," she said.

He said it back and moved. He lifted her into his arms and carried her into the bedroom.

"Don't you leave me again. I'll die if you do. Swear it. Promise?"

"Promise."

"Make love to me. Make me smile again."

She curled up against his chest after they finished and fell asleep. He did the same.

"That's an interesting move," Sid said.

"Shut up," Damon said.

Damon's fingertip stayed on his queen. He moved the piece back to its previous position. He mumbled and studied the whole board once more.

"What's that you say?" Sid cupped his hand to his ear. "My hearing isn't so good."

"There's nothing wrong with your hearing."

Damon made up his mind. He picked up the same piece and moved it to where he wanted to put it in the first place. He waited a moment before removing his finger.

Sid coughed. He surveyed the board quickly and then captured Damon's queen with his bishop.

"Checkmate," Sid said. "Told you that was an interesting move."

"Shit," Damon said.

Bobby and Stephanie knocked and walked through the front door. The couple was loaded down with plastic grocery bags.

"What did I tell you?" Sid asked.

"I know, I know," Bobby said. "I figured you could use some fresh fruits and vegetables. It was no trouble."

"Damon had the same idea," Sid said. "Do you guys think I'm incapable of taking care of myself?"

"Yes," Damon said.

Sid ignored him and kissed Stephanie's hand. She giggled and enveloped him in a hug.

"I'm going to put some of this stuff away so you three can catch up," Stephanie said.

"I'm going to hit the bathroom," Damon said. "Bobby, I know I'm getting old because your father is starting to beat me at chess pretty regularly."

"He's cheating somehow," Bobby said.

"That's what I said."

Sid motioned Bobby to a chair.

"I talked to Uncle Patrick last night and I'm going out to Los Angeles to see him," Sid said. "He's getting World Series tickets. Damon is coming with me."

"Finally! That's great, Dad. You know, you should just stay..."

"We can save that argument for later. Right now, we have more serious things to talk about?"

"Oh?"

Sid took a small box out of his pocket.

"Now is a good time," Sid said.

Bobby turned purple and wiped sweat from his eyebrows.

301

"I don't know..."

"You're going to do it right now."

"Are you crazy? I don't think so. I don't even know if she'll..."

"Of course she'll say yes. She's been waiting for you to shit or get off the pot for some time now," Sid said. "Don't be afraid. I'm right here if you need me."

"Really setting the mood here, Dad," Bobby said.

"Hey, Stephanie, darling, can you come in here for a minute," Sid said.

"Dad!"

"You need me to draft you a few lines?" Sid asked.

"How'd you ask Mom?"

"We were in bed together," Sid said. "Nine months later, we had you."

"Jesus Christ," Bobby said. "You expect me to drop a knee in front of you while Damon's in the can?"

"I mean, you can wait until he gets out, but he typically takes a while," Sid said.

"I can't believe you're making me do this."

"I'm not going to be able to see anything else, son," Sid said.

Bobby's eyes filled with concern, but his father's eyes didn't lose an ounce of their sparkle. Sid shook his head and patted his son on the shoulder. Bobby took a deep breath and stood. He rearranged his shirt and brushed off imaginary lint.

Stephanie breezed through the door and pushed back a blond strand of hair that had escaped her ponytail.

"I have to ask you something," Bobby said.

"Sure thing," she said.

Bobby giggled nervously. The box felt heavy. He couldn't make eye contact with her. He turned his palm over, revealing the black box his father had been entrusted with for months. Sid heard her breath suck in the moment Bobby's knee hit the floor. She cried and put her hand to her chest. Sid watched his son take her left hand. Bobby kissed it before he said anything. He straightened up on his knee and finally looked up.

"Will you marry me?" Bobby asked.

The bathroom door opened. Sid groaned. Damon knocked over a lamp on his way into the room.

"Sorry," he said. "Is lunch ready?"

"Shut up, Damon," Sid said.

Neither one of them saw Stephanie nod.

Undone by too many bottles of celebratory red wine, Bobby and Damon fell asleep on the couch together, their feet propped up on Sid's newspaper graveyard that doubled as a coffee table. Sid sat at his kitchen table, nursing a mug of coffee and listening to his future daughter-in-law talk about her fiancé's upcoming book tour. He tuned in and out, remembering how much Constance hated being apart during his own tours. He had managed to keep his nose clean for years, but she never stopped worrying. Maybe it wasn't enough that he told her how much he loved her every five minutes. Maybe his past had wedged a permanent divide between them that narrowed but never closed. Maybe she died knowing she had settled for a man who didn't fully trust or love himself.

"So you're leaving us for good, huh?" Stephanie asked, bringing Sid out of his dark musings.

He put his mug down on the kitchen table and smiled awkwardly.

"I'm coming back," he said.

"We both know you're full of shit. Your eyes never lie to anyone."

The CD player stirred in the corner. George Harrison's voice filled the room.

"This was one of Bobby's mother's favorite songs," Sid said. "We used to dance not too far from where you're sitting. Might have been playing the last time we saw each other."

"How long have you been sick?" Stephanie asked, wiping a tear from her cheek.

Sid shrugged.

"You're not going to tell Bobby, so at least tell me so I can help him through whatever is about to happen," she said.

"I've got something that won't let me say goodbye to everyone," Sid said. "So feel lucky."

"You're not going to fight?"

"Nah, I've had enough of that. I've fought myself my whole life. It's peacetime. One more baseball game is all I need."

"Which one are you going get to spend eternity with?" Stephanie asked.

"Bobby told you everything, huh?" Sid asked, admiring the woman's sass. "What makes you think I can't have both in the afterlife?"

"The way I figure it, Bobby's mother had you for a lifetime; she might be ready for Jocelyn to take over."

Sid bit his lip. He hadn't heard her name spoken out loud in years.

"This conversation seems pretty silly considering I don't believe in heaven or hell," he said.

"A heathen to the end," Stephanie said.

"Why change?" Sid said. "Listen, I should get to bed. Early flight tomorrow."

"You haven't packed at all, have you?"

"Not a thing."

Stephanie sighed.

She stood and hugged Sid tightly before he could move. He was always awkward embracing her because she had a good four inches on him. He pulled away and wiped another tear that had escaped her eye. He shook his head and winked.

"Did you find what you've been looking for all these years?" Stephanie asked.

"I'm sorry?"

"I've heard all your stories and I just got the feeling you never quite got your hands on something. I don't know, maybe some sort of redemption."

"I don't know, maybe something like that. What do you think?"

Stephanie leaned in and kissed his cheek.

"You take care of that heart of yours for as long as you have it. It's a good one."

Her body was young, fresh.

He felt her shiver helplessly as he kissed her. She responded to him.

She purred. Her eyes were half-open.

Lust closed his mind. He lost himself to animal instinct. His fingers disappeared into her long, damp hair. He watched her lips curl mischievously.

"I want you inside of me," she said.

Her youth forced him to go faster and faster. He felt too old to keep up. She took over. He became a spectator.

"I can't believe you talked me into this," she said.

Her youth was gone, but her beauty remained.

"You have plenty of time to get there," he said.

"I'm always late because of you."

"You could have said no."

"I wanted my man."

She finished her work with him and slid off. Her smile filled up his whole life. He held her hand.

"Why don't you stay? It's pouring. Or let me drive you."

"I'll be back soon enough silly. I'm not done with you yet."

She made her way down the stairs and grabbed her keys.

He summoned what's was left of his youth and raced after her. He stopped her at the door.

"I love you," he said.

"I love you too," she said.

Sid woke in a panic.

"Are you sure you have the tickets?" He asked. "I don't want to get up there and seem like a couple of idiots because we've been relying on your crappy memory."

Damon reached into his jacket and showed Sid the boarding passes.

"Is there anything else?" Damon asked.

"Yes, what time is it?"

"It is 6:30 p.m."

"How long did they say the delay was?"

"They said fifteen minutes. Are we really going to go through this every two seconds?"

Sid shifted in his seat. Driving Damon insane was his way of killing time.

"If I had known you were going to be this grumpy, I wouldn't have brought you along. Can you take a pill for that too?"

The loudspeaker crackled and informed the terminal that the flight to Los Angeles was now boarding. Sid swatted Damon with his newspaper and stood.

"Move your saggy ass," Sid said. "The sooner we get on the plane, the sooner you can go to the bathroom again"

It took another fifteen minutes for the pair to finally get to their seats. Damon graciously gave Sid the aisle. A deeply tanned and attractive flight attendant hovered over them moments later.

"Is there anything I can get you gentlemen before we leave the gate?" She asked.

"Well, now that you mention it, I was really hoping you'd give me your phone number," Sid said. "It's easier to coordinate dinner plans that way. It would be fine if you just wanted to skip to the wedding too."

"I'm afraid I might be a little young for you, sir."

"That's nonsense. How old are you?"

"I'm twenty-seven."

Sid put his finger to his lip as if he were thinking hard about something.

"Yes, I see where you'd be concerned. We can start slow then. I'll take a pillow."

She laughed and handed him a pillow and blanket. Damon waved his hand indicating he was fine.

Sid glanced out the half-opened window. The sky was alive with vivid pink and pale blue colors. There was nothing but soft fluffy clouds that were outlined in bright red scarlet.

"You think the sunsets out west are any more beautiful than this?" Damon asked.

"I've seen plenty of sunsets," Sid said. "For fuck's sake, let me sleep."

He snapped his seat belt together and propped his pillow in just the right spot behind his head. Damon nudged him.

"You have to be kidding me..." Sid said.

"Sorry," Damon said. "It's either I go now or I go in my pants during takeoff. Which do you prefer?"

Sid waited impatiently while Damon took his time getting up.

"I changed my mind," Sid said. "I'll take the middle seat, you can take the aisle. The extra leg room isn't worth this little dance every two minutes."

As he watched Damon slowly maneuver his old bones up the aisle, he felt a familiar pain in his chest.

Sid closed his eyes and died.

Daniel Ford

ACKNOWLEDGEMENTS

First of all, a humble and grateful thank you to Stephen Hall and Megan Cassidy at 50/50 Press for giving Sid a home. Your appreciation and support mean the world to me.

Thanks to Lisa Carroll and Pamela Hayward who pulled me out of my shell kicking and screaming. Thanks to Jocelyn Wheaton for letting me borrow her name all those years ago, and to Brian Deguzis for providing the early inspiration for Damon Lord. Thanks to the St. John's crew, especially Derek Smith (and Bamms and Potus), Steve Taras, and Catherine Kearns (and the Cazzorla family). Thanks to past and present *JCK*-ers including Julie Sheridan, Rob Bates, Cristina Cianci, Rich Dalglish, Heather Kuka, Jeremy Fogel, and Bill Furman. Thanks to the Pegas: Paul Lenzi, Ross Foniri, Liz Mullane, Zoe Kazmierski, Tom Bachmann, Mike Gnann, and Mike Nelson.

Special thank you to designer Jonathan Lee for designing the cover and depicting Sid where he truly belongs: waitin' for a train.

Thanks to my podcast/website partner Sean Tuohy for his boundless enthusiasm and constant encouragement. Thanks to the rest of the *Writer's Bone* crew: Lindsey Wojcik, Rachel Tyner, Gary Almeter, Alexander Brown, Adam Vitcavage, Matt DiVenere, Hassel Velasco, Danny DeGennaro, and Rob Masiello. Special thanks to Dave Pezza and his red pen/samurai sword.

Thank you to all the authors that have guided me along the way including Stona Fitch, Brian Panowich, David Joy, Scott Cheshire, Steph Post, Erica Wright, Matthew Hefti, Peter Sherwood, Anne Leigh Parrish, Dimitry Elias Léger,

Daniel Paisner, Michael Farris Smith, Joshua Mohr, Min Jin Lee, Nicole Blades, James Tate Hill, Ross Ritchell, W.B. Belcher, Doug Richardson, Julia Claiborne Johnson, and Josh Cook. Special thanks to rock star literary agent Christopher Rhodes for telling me my query letter sucked and for helping me re-write it.

Thank you to my grandparents on the Ford, Blanchette, and Cassidy sides. Thank you to my aunts and uncles including Cathy, Dennis, Bernadette ("Peewee" for those confused), Skip, Ellen, Stephen, Jimmy, Clifford, Roland, Lucille, Pit, Bobby, Sherri, Kathy, and Craig. Thank you to all my cousins (and their significant others), especially Caryn Brannen, Judith Dietrich, and Kim Pascarelli. I'd have been lost without you all.

Thank you to the Schaefer and D'Angelo families for making my transition to Boston an easy one. Special thanks to Dick, Karen, Justin, Janet, Shirley, Tony (who has a starring role in the chapter titled "Old War Stories"), and the late Felicia.

Thank you to all of my nieces and nephews—Katie, Madeline, Elizabeth, Sarah, Joshua, Matthew, Kevin, Chase, and Carter. Special thank you to Jack Ford for providing a dark, cynical world with plenty of humor and optimism. Don't read this book until you're older.

Thank you to my brothers Tom and Patrick for giving me two shining examples of good men. I owe you both a 30-pack of cheap beer. And, of course, thanks to my sister-in-law Kristen (who runs the show).

To my mother and father: Nothing I can say or do will ever repay you for what you've given me or accurately convey how thankful I am that I'm your son. You're the best people I know and I hope I've made you proud.

And, finally, to my beautiful Stephanie. Your passion and tenacity inspire me on a daily basis. The best words, stories, and love are yet to come.

Daniel Ford

ABOUT THE AUTHOR

Daniel Ford is the author of *Sid Sanford Lives!* He is the co-founder/co-host of *Writer's Bone*, a literary website and podcast that champions aspiring authors and screenwriters.

Ford's journalism and fiction can also be found on JCKonline.com and his personal blog Hardball Heart. *Sid Sanford Lives!* is his debut novel. Ford lives with his fiancée Stephanie in Boston, Mass. He can often be found coaxing words out of a half-empty bourbon glass.

Follow Daniel on Twitter @danielfford
Facebook @SidSanfordLives

Threadwalkers
A New Young Adult Title
From 50/50 Press & Melody Ink!

After her father's death in a plane crash, 16-year-old Miranda Woodward's life begins to unravel. Her pet cat is replaced with another, her teachers don't have her on their roll call at school, and even her closest friends forget who she is. When her mother also vanishes, Miranda follows clues to meet a man known only as the Tailor, who reveals her father was part of an elite group of people known as Threadwalkers—those with the ability to see and even travel through "thin spots" in the fabric of space-time. Miranda must find a way to stop her past from being altered beyond repair before it's too late.